Please, please say you want to kiss me. Where the hell was all of this coming from?

"You okay?"

"I was laughing at my thoughts. I was thinking about how we know each other, well, *knew* one another... before."

"Before prom night?" It was Josh's turn to laugh. "We were the best of friends, weren't we?"

"Until we weren't."

"So you're still single."

"We already went over this."

"I want to make sure I wasn't dreaming." He stared at her, his expression neutral, but his eyes, his eyes made Annie want to close the distance and kiss him for the umpteenth time since she'd first seen him again in the police station. So she did.

* * *

We hope you enjoy the Silver Valley P.D. miniseries.

* * *

If you're on Twitter, tell us what you think of Harlequin Romantic Suspense! #harlequinromsuspense

Dear Reader,

Welcome back to Silver Valley with *Reunion Under Fire*! Our Russian Organized Crime miniseries continues with NYPD psychiatrist Annie Fiero and SVPD officer Joshua Avery. Upon return to Silver Valley, Annie quickly finds herself drawn into the life of a woman she suspects is being abused by her husband—and Annie's correct. The victim is married to an ROC operative, which pairs Annie with Josh to save this woman's life.

I found writing about domestic violence challenging, and I wanted to keep the emotions surrounding it real while bringing you a happier ending than many victims experience. Add in the ongoing human-trafficking subject matter, and this story had the potential to get too dark and heavy. But Annie's and Joshua's respect and eventual love for one another encouraged me to keep writing, and to uncover the latest scheme the ROC is hatching in their attempt to take over Silver Valley. My hope is that you find respite in Silver Valley as you join Annie and Joshua on their journey.

Please don't miss any of the Silver Valley P.D. stories. Sign up for my newsletter at gerikrotow.com/contact/ or Facebook.com/gerikrotow.

Happy reading!

Peace,

Geri

REUNION UNDER FIRE

Geri Krotow

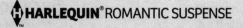

HARLEQUIN® ROMANTIC SUSPENSE

**Recycling programs
for this product may
not exist in your area.**

ISBN-13: 978-1-335-45651-9

Reunion Under Fire

Printed in U.S.A.

www.Harlequin.com

Former naval intelligence officer and US Naval Academy graduate **Geri Krotow** draws inspiration from the global situations she's experienced. Geri loves to hear from her readers. You can email her via her website and blog, gerikrotow.com.

Books by Geri Krotow

Harlequin Romantic Suspense

Silver Valley P.D.

Her Christmas Protector
Wedding Takedown
Her Secret Christmas Agent
Secret Agent Under Fire
The Fugitive's Secret Child
Reunion Under Fire

The Coltons of Shadow Creek

The Billionaire's Colton Threat

Harlequin Superromance

What Family Means
Sasha's Dad

Whidbey Island

Navy Rules
Navy Orders
Navy Rescue
Navy Christmas
Navy Justice

Visit the Author Profile page at Harlequin.com for more titles.

For Ellen—you are the strongest woman I know.
I couldn't be more proud.

Special thanks to: Amy Whitworth for insight
on volunteer matters; Dick Hammon for key
pointers about police procedure; and to
Alex Otteson and Family.

Chapter 1

Annie Fiero's vision blurred as she tried to make sense of her grandmother Ezzie's bookkeeping. She stretched in the comfy leather swivel chair and took a long sip of her tea. Annie didn't use spreadsheets in her job at the New York Police Department, but back in her hometown of Silver Valley, Pennsylvania, she was struggling. She was a police psychologist, not an accountant or small-business owner. Except, for the next three months, she was the manager of Silver Threads Yarn Shop. Since Grandma Ezzie had a minor stroke and had flown to Florida to be nurtured by Annie's parents, Annie's sabbatical had appeared as the perfect solution to Annie's mom. Annie had never been able to say no to her mother.

Annie looked around the historical room and couldn't stop a grin. Grandma Ezzie's yarn shop sat in what had once been the library of a grand Victorian home. Floor-to-ceiling shelves were positioned against the circular wall, the original sliding ladder intact. Afraid of destroying the antique wood, they used modern stepladders now for insurance purposes. Hanks of hand-dyed wool hung over the rungs, drawing the customer's eyes to the vast inventory. Instead of leather-bound books, the library shelves were chock-full of yarn. A rainbow of colors in various fibers surrounded Annie as she sat behind the service counter. It was a far cry from the noisy din of the NYPD offices and the trauma that had made her decision to return to Silver Valley an easy one.

"I'm so glad you've come home, finally! Your grandmother must be ecstatic." Ginny Vanderbruck, Grandma Ezzie's lifelong friend and one of the shop's most frequent flyers, glowed with small-town wonder. As if their town cornered the market on a happy life.

Annie looked up from the shop's business records to watch Ginny place three hanks of the expensive cashmere blend on the counter.

"My grandmother's happy I'm here to help, but it's only temporary." Annie didn't want anyone to think she'd stay away from New York City longer than she had to. She might be a Silver Valley native, but she was a city person through and through, happily so. Except she hadn't been feeling the love for city living lately, had she? And since Rick's death, along with his wife's, she'd been flat-out miserable.

An immediate cascade of horrible memories associated with the reason she was on sabbatical assaulted her. She gripped the service counter and fought the urge to run from the shop. Run, run, run. But it wouldn't bring her former client—one of her best friends and oldest work colleagues—back to life. Wouldn't erase the fact that she'd failed at what NYPD had trusted her to do: keep officers safe.

"Annie, are you okay?" Ginny's face creased with concern and reminded Annie why she'd been eager to take a longer break than normal from her job. She needed to be in a familiar place.

"I'm good, thanks. I guess I'm getting used to the idea of being back in Silver Valley for the next three months, is all."

Ginny waved a hand at her. "You made the right decision to come back and help out your grandmother. You know all of her customers are grateful you've kept the best yarn shop in the state open for us." Ginny's smile turned contemplative. "You do know that your old flame is still single, don't you?"

And just like that, Annie remembered why she'd stayed in the city. She ignored the pang that poked her heart at Ginny's assumption that she was single by proxy and not choice. "Ms. Vanderbruck, high school was a long time ago for me."

"You're still so young, dear. Do you have someone special in New York, though, is that it?" The way Ginny said "someone" made Annie wonder if the woman thought a passport was needed to travel to Manhattan.

"Oh, no. I'm enjoying my single life." Liar. *Big-time* liar. "Looks like you're having some luck finding the fiber you wanted. What have you decided on for your cardigan pattern?" Ginny had shown Annie a quite contemporary photo from a recent knitting magazine when she'd entered the shop. A tiny tug of excitement surprised Annie. She hadn't picked up knitting needles since she'd worked for Grandma Ezzie during college summers. When she'd avoided the high school "flame" Ginny pointedly mentioned.

"Do you like this shade?" Ginny brought her back from the edge of another awful flashback. Annie eyed the pile of purple fiber, trying not to mentally add the sale before it was a done deal. She was here to help, to keep things moving, not to beat any sales records.

"I do. It's lovely next to your skin."

"I really shouldn't spend the money this month."

"Grandma Ezzie always preaches that if you're going to hold yarn in your hands for an entire project, make it the best you can afford."

"You're right, of course. I'll take it. And I may be back to get enough for a second one if I like this pattern." Ginny pulled out her credit card.

"You've picked the exact same shade as your hair." Annie began to ring up the order, wondering for the millionth time how her mother had convinced her to use her sabbatical from NYPD in sleepy Silver Valley, no less: the hometown she'd fled and vowed to never return to, save for family visits, over twelve years ago.

It's for Grandma Ezzie.

"Isn't it fab?" Ginny ran her fingers through her short violet hair, the ends tipped with fuchsia. "Who says my teenage granddaughters should have all the fun?"

"Not I." Annie began to wind the hanks on the swift that stood next to the counter, quickly producing neat cakes of yarn. "I need to thank you for agreeing to run the knit and chat tonight. I'll be here, but this way you're giving me the freedom to ring up orders. I really don't have a handle on everything yet." As evidenced by her hot-and-cold emotions over her return to her hometown.

"No problem! And give me a break—like you said, you're a city girl now. There's nothing you can't handle." Ginny's sincerity slayed her.

"I'm hardly equipped to run a business. Different brain cells than working at NYPD." Annie's grandmother had bragged to all of her customers about her one granddaughter's "big city" job, so she wasn't telling Ginny anything she didn't already know.

"We're all glad you agreed to help Ezzie because this shop is important to a lot of us in Silver Valley. It gives us a reason to get out of the house. Speaking of which, I'm going to run out to the grocery store to pick up a birthday cake for Lydia, with whipped cream frosting and strawberry filling. She's seventy-five tomorrow." Annie knew that Lydia was one of the dozen or so women who religiously attended knit and chat sessions.

Annie couldn't help but notice the far cry running a yarn shop was from the life-and-death atmosphere of NYPD.

As they planned for the weekly Friday night gathering, a new customer came in. Petite, blonde and made up like a movie star, with perfect makeup, designer clothing that hung perfectly where her two-hundred-dollar jeans weren't hugging her tiny frame. A large, leather designer bag that complemented the heeled sandals finished the woman's ensemble. Annie couldn't help but take notice of her. It wasn't as if there weren't other women in Silver Valley who dressed with high fashion in mind, but it wasn't her outward appearance that pinged Annie's internal radar. It was how she held herself as she slowly walked to the counter. The blonde's eyes darted from Ginny to Annie and back again, her mannerisms a little jerky. Something had her wound tighter than a cheap skein of acrylic yarn.

Ginny caught her staring past her shoulder and turned around. "Oh, hi, Kit! Are you going to stay for knit and chat?"

The woman shook her head like a shy child. "No. Maybe. I thought about it. I don't know. I should go home earlier than I did last week. I'm almost done with my shawl."

Ginny waved her hand at her, much as she had done with Annie. "Oh, no, missy. You're having fun, and that's all there is to it." Ginny turned back to Annie, her eyes wide. "Kit's new to our group, and I told her we need fresh blood."

"Where is Ezzie?" Kit spoke with a slight accent, which Annie would bet was Russian. Annie had studied it in college and worked with a lot of Russian-speaking cops. Kit's pronunciation was distinctly Russian, maybe Ukrainian. The pale woman under the heavy makeup looked lost, as if she'd never been in the store before. Her obvious wariness combined with the way Ginny treated her flipped Annie's internal alarm bells, and her training shifted into full alert.

"Hi, Kit. I'm Annie, Ezzie's granddaughter. She's had a mild stroke and is taking a break from the shop for a bit." She stepped from around the counter and held out her hand.

Kit took it, but instead of the timid grip Annie expected, it was a strong, almost painful clench. As if Annie were her lifeline. Kit's motions were more like those of a frail octogenarian instead of a young woman Annie estimated was in her twenties.

"I need to talk to your grandmother. I'm sorry she's sick." Kit's eyes blazed. "Is she in the hospital? Will she come back soon?"

Annie looked into the woman's stunning ice-blue gaze and saw fear, trepidation and concern for Ezzie. Something else, too. Anxiety that didn't have a name, the result of living with a constant threat to your life. Annie had seen enough of it in victims and police officers. She knew how stress affected first responders over the years, and it was even worse for civilians. Kit displayed outward symptoms of a trauma survivor.

Keep her calm, show her she can trust you.

"Grandma Ezzie's fine, really. My parents insisted she go to their place in Florida for a few months while she does some rehab and relaxes. Since my grandfather died, she hasn't given herself a break from the business, and my parents knew she wouldn't do an honest rehab if she stayed here."

"I understand." Kit said it as if she'd been betrayed. Annie made a mental note to ask her grandmother about Kit. Annie was certain there was more to the woman than knitting a shawl.

"Can I help you pick out some yarn today? A pattern?"

"You can trust her, Kit. Annie's from New York City and…" Ginny trailed off at the "shut the heck up!" look Annie threw her. She instinctively didn't want Kit to know she was in law enforcement. Not yet. She wanted this woman to trust her first.

"New York?" Kit's brow wrinkled. While her eyes seemed wise and old, her skin was positively translucent. Looking at Kit's hands, Annie thought her first assessment was correct and that Kit was quite young. Early twenties at the most.

"I grew up here, went to Silver Valley High, then left for college. How about you, Kit? Have you been in Silver Valley long?"

"Yes. Well, for the last five or six years I've lived here, anyway. Are you the granddaughter Ezzie said works for the police?"

Dang Grandma Ezzie and her bragging. "I am. But I'm not a cop. I'm support staff."

"Oh." Kit nodded, looking anywhere but at Annie. "This new yarn is beautiful!" She grabbed a hank of alpaca variegated and squeezed it, the universal sign of a rabid fiber freak. Annie smiled at the gesture, then froze as she noticed muted purple spots on Kit's upper neck and jaw. Bruises covered with the carefully applied makeup she'd noticed earlier. Her stomach clenched, and she consciously forced herself to remain calm and not reveal what she'd seen. It'd be too easy to scare Kit away, and she'd never be able to help her. Annie couldn't let another person who needed help get away.

It's not all about what happened in New York with Rick. Although after losing her dear colleague to suicide, after he murdered his wife, would it ever *not* be about New York?

Letting out a slow breath, she leaned against the counter. "Yes, that's a lovely blend, isn't it? I have to say that my grandmother only picks the best for her customers. I happen to knit, too, and even if this wasn't my grandmother's shop, it'd still be my favorite shop in town. It's better than any I've ever found in the city."

There were one or two yarn shops in New York City that she frequented, but none gave her the sense of being at home and safe as Grandma Ezzie's.

Kit looked around. "Yes, I'd like to make a new shawl. Ezzie said some new alpaca linen blend was shipping in, too. Is it here?"

"Absolutely. It's been our best seller this week." Annie led her to the antique washstand that had the new hanks splayed out in a rainbow of colors. "With the heat, everyone wants to knit lace."

Kit ran her fingertips lightly over the fiber, then picked up a hank and clasped it before rubbing it between her fingers. Annie realized that she missed being around other knitters like this. Even though she hadn't pursued Ezzie's passion for fiber as a career, she still relied on knitting to keep her grounded at the end of long, hard days working at NYPD. Days she cherished, but needed space from, for the time being. Work she'd taken a three-month sabbatical from in order to help Grandma Ezzie. And to escape the media surrounding the murder-suicide of one of NYPD's finest, an officer who'd come to the end of his coping skills while dealing with his opioid addiction. Rick had been Annie's friend and client, and she'd failed to save him or the young wife he'd taken along with him. She wondered if the raw wound in her heart would ever heal.

"You are a good granddaughter to come here and help Ezzie out." Kit wore a frown, but Annie knew the sad look was for Ezzie's predicament, and saw the warmth in Kit's eyes that conveyed her admiration for Annie's choice. Annie wanted to ask, to know, where and how *exactly* this young woman had come to the States but again, the fear of scaring Kit off stopped her.

"Are you staying in her apartment upstairs?" Kit's question seemed casual, but Annie knew better. This might be the olive branch that Kit sought.

"Yes. It's the easiest solution as it keeps the place occupied, and I'm used to a smaller place in New York, so it's like a real vacation for me." Minus the emotional baggage.

"I'll take three of these." Kit picked out three tonal shades of blue. Annie thought the hue matched Kit's countenance. The woman was struggling with despair, if her training was putting the cues together correctly. But something else about Kit seemed to be triggering a memory in Annie.

Why else was Kit sending alarm bells through her?

Kit held a sky-colored hank to her cheek, sighing dreamily. And leaned a little over to the left, exposing a sliver of her neck above the mock turtleneck she wore. On a blistering summer day the top was out of place, but not for a woman like Kit. All at once Annie knew why Kit had set her police psychologist sirens wailing, beyond the bruises. She reminded her of a witness the DA had asked her to vet. Another woman with a Russian accent whose husband had a penchant for harming her. Her testimony had helped put the abuser behind bars.

Annie made out another mark, this one a definite deep reddish-purple bruise that peeked above Kit's collar. It looked as if it had a fuzzy filter over it, and the beige-toned stain on the turtleneck's fabric confirmed it was concealer. If Kit were a teenager, it'd be easy to think the mark was a hickey. But combined with the other bruises, how Kit was dressed, her skittish behavior and the fact that she had wanted to talk to

Ezzie, Annie knew that she was dealing with an abused woman. Ezzie was known for helping women out of tight spots and had in fact made it her life's purpose since she'd fled her first husband after being battered by him in a drunken rage. Ezzie had been lucky—she'd met Annie's grandfather after that and enjoyed a long, happy marriage. But Ezzie never forgot her ordeal.

"So you and my grandmother are friends?" She kept her demeanor purposefully chipper, casual. Annie made a show of reaching into the drawer of the antique table and pulling out skeins to replace the yarn Kit was purchasing, displaying them in perfect symmetry.

"Yes. She is my friend." Quietly, with certainty.

"I'll see you ladies later. Don't you dare miss tonight, Kit!" Ginny gave them a wave as she gathered up her bags and walked out of the shop, the large front door opening and closing with the familiar sound of the squeaky wood that surrounded the stained-glass window.

"That doorjamb needs to be trimmed. It's swelled every summer since I can remember." Annie looked at Kit, who'd taken her skeins to the counter and still looked like a rabbit ready to bolt into the nearest bush.

"I love the old feel of this place." Kit's words were softly spoken, wishful.

"You strike me as the contemporary type. Your sense of style is beautiful." Annie referenced Kit's chic urban style, from her sleeveless silky turtleneck, long linen cardigan and flared crops. Her stacked sandals revealed perfectly manicured toes, and her designer bag cost more than Annie's New York City rent.

"Thank you. I do like modern things, but there's nothing like the comfort of the familiar." Kit gazed at the balustrade that followed the stairs behind the counter up to a peekaboo corridor above the built-in bookcases that led to Ezzie's apartment.

"You know, Kit, if you ever need anything, you can stop in, or call me. I'm not my grandmother, and you don't know me yet, but you can trust me." Annie rang up Kit's order and added her personal cell phone number to the back of the shop's frequent-buyer card that she handed to the woman. It was far less incriminating than if she gave Kit her NYPD business card and her abuser found it. "My number's on the back. You're one skein away from a free one."

"I don't keep these cards." Kit frowned at the punch card. Silver Valley was like any other American town in that the local business owners did everything financially possible to reward repeat customers. Annie wasn't surprised that Kit didn't save them. Abused women learned to leave no trace of where they'd been, what they'd done. It made fewer waves at home from a prying husband who wanted to control their every move.

"Oh, well, I didn't know. I'm still getting to know all of the regular customers." Ezzie would have known, and she'd know why Kit didn't keep the cards. It was probably because she didn't want her husband to know where she shopped, in case he went through her wallet. Annie had heard every breach of personal boundaries in her career with NYPD.

"No, you didn't. But I feel you do. Know." Kit's eyes dropped all previous defenses, and for a long moment she stood at the counter, emotionally naked to Annie, who saw fear, trepidation and an unexpected emotion.

Determination. Kit was going to fight whoever was hurting her.

Annie handed Kit her bag of yarn, "I'm here."

Kit's hands shook as she took the bag. Without another word she turned and walked out of the shop.

Annie might not have expected to bring her law-enforcement therapy skills to bear this soon into her stint at Silver Threads Yarn Shop, but having a sense of purpose related to something she knew allowed a sliver of light to slant through the veil of doom she'd carried here from New York.

Joshua Avery walked through the Silver Valley Police Department, trying to remember that for the time being he was Officer Avery again and not Detective Avery. He'd asked for a temporary demotion so that he could be around more for his younger sister.

The building was unusually quiet, especially for a Friday morning. Everyone was either off, out on patrol or attending a law-enforcement conference in the next town over. He had to admit he was a little disappointed no one was around to see him back in his working blues. As a detective he hadn't worn his Silver Valley PD uniform in more than a year, and he was grateful it still fit. He'd gotten used to his civilian clothes while he served as an SVPD detective, but had to admit that being back in uniform felt good.

"Morning, Josh." SVPD Chief Colt Todd motioned to him to enter his office. "Don't get too comfortable in that uniform, Josh. As soon as you get your sister settled, I'll need you back as a full-time detective." Tall with graying hair, Colt still looked like a man in his prime, fitness-wise.

"Yes, sir." Josh, along with the rest of SVPD, would follow their leader through fire because of exactly this—Colt's ability to be compassionate while still letting an employee know he thought the person was the only one for the job. Without hesitation, he'd given Josh a reprieve from the near-24/7 routine of detective work. Josh's younger sister, a disabled adult, needed to be placed in a full-time care community, and Josh needed time to pick the right place for Becky. But Josh couldn't afford extended leave, so going back in uniform was a good compromise for both him and SVPD.

"As for this weekend, I'll need you to man the fort while most of the department is in Carlisle for the ROC strategy session." Colt referred to the Russian Organized Crime deterrent conference, run this weekend at the county seat.

Josh nodded and listened as Colt ran down the issues he wanted him to keep his finger on. Since ROC had come to Silver Valley, the entire department had been putting in extra hours, scouring the community for any evidence that the criminals had sent yet another group of trafficked underage girls to the area. ROC had initiated a shipment to Silver Valley a couple of months ago, and SVPD had played a role in saving the girls, freeing them from the degrading work, legal and illegal, they'd been enslaved to before they ever touched American soil. Like the flow of ROC heroin into the area, the sex trafficking trade was relentless.

"You're also going to be the top guy here while I'm at the conference all weekend. I'll be back on Monday morning to check in, and of course call me with anything you need to."

"Copy that, Chief." He hoped the station would stay

quiet so that he could go home for dinner with Becky. And to continue his search for an apartment for her, as much as he didn't want to think about it.

"Look, Josh, I know you'd rather be in the thick of the ROC problem with everyone else right now. And I'd love to have you there. It hurts like hell to lose you as a detective, even if it's only for a few weeks or so. I'm sorry about the setback with your sister. You'll be working as a detective again soon." Colt looked at him. "It'll be no longer than a few weeks, right?"

"I hope not, Chief. The more regular hours on patrols and at the desk are better for Becky and me as we adjust to our new reality. It's coming together. We were spoiled when she went to school every day, and then all the day camps she was eligible for in the summer. Since she graduated from high school, her requirements have changed. I'm close to finding her a more permanent living arrangement." It killed him to say it, but he forced the words through his teeth. Becky didn't need him as much anymore, didn't want him as much. It was time to let her become as independent as any mentally challenged young woman could. She'd drawn a sucky hand with being deprived oxygen at birth, giving her lifelong mental difficulties that were umbrellaed under the description of Pervasive Developmental Disorder, PDD. They included developmental delays, attention deficit disorder and anxiety. To make matters worse, she'd been dealt another horrible hand when their parents had been killed in a car crash a decade ago. But she'd made the best of it and was happy, as happy as a nine-year-old in a nineteen-year-old body could be. Josh couldn't ask for more. Except for a promise that nothing bad would ever happen to her, which he knew was impossible.

"For what it's worth, I'm proud of you, Josh. You've done a fine job of raising your sister, and your parents would be pleased."

"Thanks, Chief." Josh stood up. He didn't like it when people complimented him on what he'd done. It was what any other brother would do, and he never felt worthy of the praise. He did his job—he took care of his sister. "Is there anything else?"

"No, Josh. Only the usual—let's keep it rolling and do what we can to make Silver Valley the safest place possible." Colt dismissed him in his usual easy yet professional manner.

"Yes, sir." Josh thought that Silver Valley's days of suburban serenity might be over, shattered by the opioid epidemic and now ROC's entry into the area, but he kept those thoughts to himself. And he hoped against hope that he was wrong. If it were up to him, Silver Valley would again be the low-crime-rate town it'd been when he was a kid.

After a few hours of administrative work, Josh headed for the small break area. He sent up a silent thanks for the full pot of coffee on the heating plate, and he noted the plate of cookies someone had dropped off. There wasn't enough coffee to keep him going today. Chief Todd wasn't someone he'd want to whine to about how the paperwork for Becky's needs had plowed him under these past months. He'd been up all night working out the finances for Becky to be able to leave home and live in her own apartment. It'd be possible in a community with other mentally challenged adults, and he was pretty sure he'd found the perfect one for her. She'd have supervision with autonomy. It was a fine line for his nineteen-year-old sister, who still asked about their parents, long dead. Becky knew they were gone and understood that part, but she didn't understand why she had to still feel sad about it. Life-long sorrow was too adult an emotion for Becky. Her pain crushed him.

Josh had been at the Jersey Shore on a spring break beach getaway when he'd received the phone call that had changed both of their lives forever in that split second. There were no adults named to take guardianship of Becky, so he stepped up to the plate. Instead of continuing the scholarship to Penn State, he'd transferred to a local private school for criminal justice, allowing him to take care of Becky once she was released from the hospital. She'd miraculously survived the accident that had taken their parents. Fortunately the college had given him a hardship scholarship, and their parents had left enough to help them survive. Becky received state and federal aid, too.

Becky had suffered developmental delays almost immediately and still had emotional difficulties from time to time, but her motor skills were intact. Becky functioned completely normally, for a nine- or ten-year-old girl, socially ahead of her mental capacity, which was closer to seven years of age. She'd never grow older, emotionally. Mentally, she grasped just about everything, but lacked the practical judgment to be able to live completely on her own. As he poured a large mug of the steaming coffee, he acknowledged that it was a blessing he'd found a local program. Upward Homes would handle her disabilities, emphasize her abilities, give her a job, friends to spend time with and a chance to enjoy whatever further education she was capable of. He sipped the coffee and told himself he didn't need the cookies. The younger officers would appreciate them more, and they wouldn't take an extra fifteen minutes to burn off in PT as they would for him.

He knew thirty wasn't old, but he also knew his limits. The paperwork for Becky's application was daunting, and his protective urges were hard to let go of. But if he ever wanted to freely work as a detective again, he needed to know Becky was taken care of round-the-clock. Worrying about her being on her own at home, no matter that he had a neighborhood friend to check in on her, was stressful. For both of them.

"Officer?" Cali, one of the SVPD's receptionists, walked into the break room and stopped in front of him. How long had he been daydreaming about how to fix Becky's problems?

"Hey, Cali. How's the weekend looking for you? Because I'm going to be right here at my desk."

She flashed a quick grin, nodded. "Been there. Hey, there's a woman here who's asked to talk to one of our detectives. Says she's with NYPD and showed me a badge."

"What about?" Cookie temptation evaporated.

"A possibility of domestic violence."

He quickly added some French vanilla creamer to his coffee, one indulgence his six-foot-four-inch frame could still handle. He was painfully aware that at thirty, his fast metabolism days were quickly fleeing.

"Send her back to my desk."

"Will do."

He carried the navy ceramic mug with SVPD's gold logo stamped on it. Before he sat down a tall, willowy redhead walked up to him. His body immediately recognized who his mind struggled to believe was standing before him. The woman he'd never expected to see again. The one who'd got away. The woman his eighteen-year-old self had thought was his one true love.

Annie Fiero.

Chapter 2

Josh thanked his stars he had the seat to catch him because the sight of Annie after all these years sent him reeling. As soon as his ass hit the leather padding he shot back up, ingrained respect having nothing to do with it.

Josh wanted to be on his feet for this reunion. "Annie."

He took her in, from the crown of her head still framed by her flaming-red hair, her catlike eyes luminous in her beautiful face and her lips—hell, her lips. He licked his own as he allowed his gaze to meander farther south, seeing how her formfitting white T-shirt under her open ivory cardigan clung to her breasts. He wished the sweater was off and he could tell if her nipples were hard, if she felt what he did. Her curves were nonstop, evidenced by how she filled out her dark, tight jeans. Pink polished toes in sandals underscored her femininity. And his reaction to it.

Damnation. He needed to get Becky situated so that he could start dating properly again. Ever since he and Christina broke up, he'd been afraid to bring another woman home. It was too hard on Becky when they left.

"Josh?" The incredulity in Annie's voice hit him in the solar plexus. Her tone, the soft quality of her speech, was the same. As were her startlingly blue eyes. "Josh." It wasn't a question as she said his name the second time. The pulse at the base of her throat danced under her smooth skin.

Apparently he'd caught her by surprise, too.

"Annie." He took his time to look her over again. Since they'd once been best friends, she wouldn't misconstrue it for unprofessional police behavior. And damn it if he didn't check her left hand. Bare as his. Not that it meant anything, necessarily. It didn't matter either way. He wasn't available, and if Becky were already situated, Annie would be the last person he'd risk his ego with. "I didn't recognize you at first."

She ran her fingers through her hair, flipped it lightly over her shoulder. A smile as she looked up at him. "Time marches on, right? You've grown at least a foot!"

He couldn't help it, his chest puffed up at that. Not that he was immune to a woman's admiration, but this was Annie. Her opinion had meant so much to him in high school. And still did, to his surprise. And maybe a little bit of alarm.

"Six inches is all. Had a spurt after we graduated." He froze when he saw her eyes narrow. Oh hell... "Annie, we didn't leave it on very good terms, did we?"

"If you call telling each other we were done, never wanted to ever see one another again…" She leaned against the edge of his desk, her long, lean lines seeming to underscore how very aware of her each inch of him was. Too aware. He maintained eye contact, hoping like hell she would, too. That she didn't notice what she was doing to him, because if she looked at his crotch she'd know. He hadn't had his uniform on for a day yet, and already he wanted to shove it off, show Annie just how much he'd changed. How the years had taught him how to be a man who could give her more than he'd been capable of on their bungled prom night. Her eyes studied him, too, and he forced himself to mentally detach from his reactions.

What the hell was going on with him? So what if Annie was hot? It wasn't like he didn't see attractive women all the time.

But none he had such a deep history with. "Yeah, we left it on crappy terms. I am sorry for anything I did that might have hurt you. We were kids, though, right?"

She sighed. "We were, but I'd like to think we shared more than the typical teen friendship."

"I'm sure I was old enough to be more polite. I remember myself as a bit of a blockhead." He indicated the chair next to his in the cubicle, and as she sat down so did he. "How are you doing, Annie? What are you doing? The last I heard you were in New York City."

Her face, briefly open and almost vulnerable, snapped shut as tight as the security around Three Mile Island, the nuclear power facility only a thirty-minute drive away near Harrisburg. "I know you know I work for NYPD. Nothing escapes the Silver Valley grandmothers' network." She paused, an absentminded smile giving her face a soft glow. "I'm back here, though, for the time being. A few months. Running the local yarn shop for my grandmother." She mentioned the name of the shop, one he recognized as being in the same building as a tourist adventure agency. "She recently had a minor stroke."

"I'm sorry to hear that. She okay?" Couldn't he sound more intelligent, come up with more than trite conversation?

Annie nodded. "Yes, she'll have a complete recovery. A longer rehabilitation was in order, though, so my parents packed her up and shipped her to Florida, to their home in Naples. Grandma Ezzie can get whatever she needs there, from privacy to a bottle of her favorite sparkling wine."

"Sounds ideal. But your mother didn't want to run the yarn shop?"

"No, she thought it best she stay down there and help along Grandma's rehab. I couldn't argue with her. Besides, Grandma Ezzie is her mother-in-law, so the yarn shop hasn't ever been something my mother felt particularly attached to."

"I remember you always loved to knit when we were kids." He couldn't stop the chuckle that burst out of his chest. "Remember that sweater you made me in school colors?"

She blushed, and it was as if his dick felt the heat on her skin, too. He vowed to never go this long without a date again if it would keep him from making a fool of himself in front of Annie.

"I meant for you to be the envy of all the other kids, but instead made you a laughingstock. I am so sorry,

Josh. You really took one for the team there. Wasn't the body of it too short, the arms waaay too long?"

"All I remember is how warm it was at the freezing football game." An immediate visceral image of them taking each other's clothes off, including the sweater, in the back seat of his parents' station wagon assailed him. And sealed his fate for blue balls.

Annie might have felt the same, but he couldn't tell as she immediately shut down, went back into the shell he'd noticed the rare times they'd seen one another on her trips back to Silver Valley. They'd never even spoken, at most waved across a crowded mall or nodded during a Christmas church service.

"The receptionist says you showed her your badge?" He needed to make a copy of it.

"Yes, here." She opened a leather case and showed her NYPD credentials. They looked like a badge but were in effect identification cards for her assignment as a law-enforcement psychological expert.

"So you're a shrink to the cops?" He fought against the incredulity that bubbled deep in his chest. Because if he let her see his surprise, he had the distinct impression that Annie would clock him. Or else turn and leave with no explanation. And he couldn't handle that, not when he'd just got her back again.

Wait, where had that come from? He'd never really had her, had he? And he wasn't looking to "get her back."

"I'm sorry, Annie. 'Shrink' is inappropriate."

"Yes, it is. But it doesn't surprise me that you have that kind of attitude. A lot of officers are threatened by psychology."

He snorted. He wasn't threatened by anything except for the real-deal feelings toward Annie that were surfacing from parts unknown. From his heart. All at once he wanted to know if she felt the heat between them, if his erection was one-sided. As he watched her, she licked her lips and softly chewed on her full, pink glossed lower lip. Yeah, he was pretty darn sure she felt it, too. Like if they didn't crawl into bed this instant he'd spontaneously combust in the Silver Valley PD office.

How had he forgotten, shoved the memory of her to the far recesses of his mind? How had he sloughed it all off, thinking that what he'd had with her as a teen was just that, an adolescent crush? Because the fact remained that they were twelve years older, full adults, and yet Annie Fiero was the only woman he'd ever known who could make him feel like this.

Annie watched Josh's attention shift from being totally on her to someplace over her shoulder. As much as his intense scrutiny had been flattering, it was also a relief to be able to breathe. This man was the same Josh she'd known, had the same smile, but he was far more potent. Heart-lethal, because she was already imagining what it'd be like to kiss him, and she didn't even know if he was available. The brief thought of him involved with someone else made her inexplicably sad. *Crap.*

"Josh? You okay?"

His eyes were sexier than she'd remembered, shrewder, but had glazed over a bit. As if he didn't believe her professional choice, didn't accept the damn proof in front of him in the form of her IDs. Was it that crazy to think she'd become a police psychologist?

And since when did she get so aroused by talking to a guy? Her hormones had been conducting rapid-fire drills since the instant she'd seen him across the office bay. Since before she realized it was the same Josh Avery who hadn't been able to get the condom on after prom, giving her time to back out of their plan to lose their virginity with one another and thus ending their planned night of passion. An awkward end to an otherwise emotionally intimate relationship. He'd been the first boy she'd ever loved.

Maybe the only man, but he'd been so young. Not like he was now, all sexy muscle and deep voice conversation meant to make a woman drip with want.

"I'm great, Annie. Just thinking. You look a little peaked, though, if you ask me." Wham. Without warning he turned the tables back on her. This was a new skill of Josh's, because the teen she'd known was too sweet, too kind to play mind games. She shook her head.

"I'm fine. I came in here—"

"On a suspected domestic violence. Who's hurt you?" His last word ended on what sounded like a feral growl.

"Not *me*. A woman who came into my grandmother's shop." She forced herself to calm down and stick to her purpose. "I know what signs to look for." She didn't have to remind him it was her job, did she?

"She told you she's being abused?"

She recognized the practiced neutral expression, knew it intimately. He was used to people throwing accusations around, claims that if true could be lifesaving. If false, they could ruin a person's reputation and potentially waste police time and, worse, risk an officer's life.

"Of course she didn't. If she'd be willing to tell me, she'd be willing to come to the police, right?" She leaned back in the chair and shoved off her thin, summer-weight sweater. It'd kept the chill of the AC off her shoulders but no air-conditioning unit could keep up with the heat wave. She rubbed her shoulders, trying to undo the myriad knots that had sprung up at the top of her back. "I do this for a living, Josh. I know you have no reason to believe me, other than you knew me a long time ago, which is why I've brought these." She took out her credentials for the second time in ten minutes and handed them to him. "Feel free to call it in and talk to my boss. I'm the real deal. I see this all the time. And I saw finger marks on her throat. She'd covered them with makeup and was wearing a turtleneck. It's ninety degrees out, Josh. No one wears heavy clothes in this heat unless they have a reason. I only got a glimpse of the bruises because of the way she leaned over. But I also saw some higher, on her jaw. Probably older ones."

"You're sure?" His direct look was focused, his demeanor professional. Unlike her reaction to his nearness, which was chaotic as heat rushed to her face and her nipples tightened under her lightweight T-shirt. If his gaze moved lower, he'd see her physical reaction to him, and it wasn't from the air-conditioning.

"I'm sure." She paused, not wanting to tell him how to do his job but needing to know Kit would get the help she needed.

"I hear you." He nodded. "But she's not reporting it. So even if you have her name—"

"Kit Valensky."

"I need more information. I prefer to talk to her directly if at all possible and—wait, what did you say her name was? Valensky?"

"That's right. You know her?"

"Not personally." His mouth was a straight line; his fingers drummed his desktop.

"But?" She'd wait him out. He knew something he didn't want to tell her. Or maybe couldn't, if it was a confidential police case. She was privy to whatever she needed to do her job in New York, but Silver Valley wasn't the jurisdiction she was assigned. Josh didn't have to tell her anything.

"But." He blew out a breath and looked up from his desk, his eyes back on her. "She may be related to another Valensky in town. One we keep an eye on but never seem to have enough on, if you get my drift."

"Maybe if I could talk to one of your detectives…" She looked at his badge, his uniform. She thought Ezzie had mentioned he'd been promoted, but maybe he didn't like detective work.

"I am your detective, Annie. All of our officers and detectives are overcommitted right now, working a big case that's spilled over from Harrisburg and Carlisle. Silver Valley's caught in the middle of an ROC op."

"Ouch. That's a lot of work for a small force." She knew what ROC meant. They had more than their share of it at NYPD. Organized crime of any type weighed down the caseload, pushed the officers to their limits as they fought not only to keep the streets of Silver Valley clean but human trafficking, the inflow of heroin and countless other ROC-related crimes. She looked around the station. "What do you have, thirty, maybe forty officers?"

He nodded. "Thirty-seven officers, three detectives. Four when I work as one."

"I wondered about that—I was pretty certain Grandma Ezzie had told me that you were a detective. Why aren't you now?" She waved at his uniform.

"Personal reasons. I needed the more regular hours for the short term." His tone was tinged with regret. Based on the energy that vibrated off him, she suspected he liked to be in the middle of a case, solving it.

"Oh." He must have a family. She didn't see a ring, but a lot of officers didn't wear them. It was for practical safety as a wedding band could lead to a severed finger in the midst of an operation, and to protect their loved ones from the vilest criminals who'd stalk their families. For some reason her stomach sank, and she experienced her first wave of defeat since returning to Silver Valley. Not that she'd hoped he was single, like her. His chuckle shook her out of her emotional pothole.

"What's so funny?"

"I'm not married, Annie." Oh, no, was she that freaking obvious? "What about you? Are you with anyone?"

"It's none of my business if you're single or not." She bit her lip. "For the record, I'm not married, either. Or with anyone."

"Ever been?" His teeth were so straight, so white, so sexy in that strong face. His lips were full for a man, yet only heightened his masculinity. "Annie?"

"Hmm? What?" She blinked. "No, never married. A few close calls." One in particular that swore her off serious relationships for a long while after college and probably doomed the other, longer relationships she'd had. And made her extra sensitive to women like Kit. "You?"

Josh shook his head. "No, but I came close, too. I was engaged for a few years." His face was unreadable. She wondered if he'd been hurt, why the relationship didn't work out.

"That's a long time. What ended it?" Shame sent warmth into her face again, and she held up a hand. "Wait, nix that. Sorry, it's none of my business." She'd come in here to help out Kit, possibly save her life. Instead she was flirting with a man she didn't know, not anymore, not as the man he was today.

A tall, sexy length of police officer.

"That's all right, Annie. It didn't work because of a number of things, but mostly me. I wasn't willing to commit to anything other than…" He trailed off, his eyes misting over but not with tears. Memories.

"Other than your job. I get it."

"It wasn't, wasn't… We weren't right for each other is all." He cleared his throat, and she watched the smooth movement of his Adam's apple, looked at his clean-shaven jaw and almost groaned when she noted the cleft in his chin. She had to stop this. She wasn't in town for a fling, and a relationship with any man she met in Silver Valley would be short-lived. Her heart couldn't deal with that right now. It was achy enough, thank you very much. "What about you?"

"Me? Oh, I'm pretty much a career girl." She hated how much of a coward she was. Here he'd admitted some pretty private stuff, and all she gave him was a cute Mary Tyler Moore reply? "And my job at NYPD is all-consuming. As I'm sure you can imagine. Do you have a psychologist on your force?"

"No, but we contract out as needed. Whenever there's a shooting, suspicious circumstances around a case that might be due to an officer, or when we have a rough accident or other first response scene."

She nodded. "That's what my job was meant to be, originally. But now we have so many cops who are military veterans with PTSD, and who've seen the worst here at home, too."

"You mean like 9/11."

"Yes. And the human trafficking."

"We've got our share of the sex trade here in Silver Valley, believe it or not. This past year we had a local strip club employing underage girls from Ukraine. ROC brought them in. We're working a huge case right now, as a matter of fact. There's another suspected ROC group of underage women en route to Silver Valley. We've been able to stop these shipments before, miles away, but each time it's getting closer to Silver Valley proper." She saw the enormity of it in the lines etched between his brows.

"That reminds me—when I spoke to Kit, I got the feeling that how she came to the States might be questionable."

"Hold that thought while I look a few things up." His fingers flew over his keyboard, and she had to fight the urge to stare at his masculine hands. A man's hands had always been one of her weak spots, and Josh's would have made the throb between her legs pulse even if they weren't. Guilt hit her in her gut. She was here to help out an abused woman, not get all sexy on an old crush.

Josh frowned as he read an open file. "The woman

you're talking about, Kit Valensky, is married to Vadim Valensky, the scumbag we suspect has dealings with ROC but never have been able to nail. We're fairly certain he has ties to Dima Ivanov, but since the death of the number two guy in that chain of command, Yuri Vasin, there's no connection we can prove. Did you know that we took out Vasin right here in Silver Valley two months ago?" He waited for her to shake her head. Heck, what had happened to her hometown? "We were thwarting a human trafficking operation the ROC ran. They're up to it again, I'm afraid. Valensky's a dangerous character if a fraction of what we suspect he's responsible for is true." Josh's smile was gone, his intention clear. He wanted Valensky off the streets as much as she wanted to make sure Kit was safe. And Annie knew who Ivanov was—everyone in East Coast law enforcement did. He was the head honcho for ROC on the Eastern Seaboard.

"Kit's in danger, then. We have to get her out of there." Would waiting until the knit and chat night be good enough? Annie didn't want to think about what could happen to Annie between now and then.

"*There* is a six-bedroom mansion on the top of Silver Hill, on the way to the mountains. The Appalachian Trail traverses right alongside its eight-foot wall. It's a veritable fortress." Frustration laced his words.

"You sound like you've tried to get on his property."

"Maybe." He stayed silent on the topic, and she respected that. She didn't need to be privy to all the workings of a local case. But she still wanted Kit in a safe place.

"Josh, look, you don't need to give me any details, but what I do need is a report filed that I witnessed those bruises on her. She's supposed to come to our knit and chat tonight, between six and eight."

"What's that, a knitters' meeting?"

"Yes. My grandmother has built quite the community with her shop, and the women as well as some men take care of one another like family. One of the regulars was in the shop earlier, and she was very friendly to Kit when she came in. Actually, you know the woman— it's Ginny Vanderbruck." They'd gone to school with Ginny's granddaughter. "It's clear to me that Kit is well liked and that the other knitters feel protective of her."

"Let's say she comes in tonight. Are you going to ask her point-blank if she's in danger?"

"Absolutely. It's my job. The only reason I didn't yesterday is because I didn't want to frighten her into not coming back. I gave her my number."

"That's good, all of it. I'm impressed, Annie. You've done more for Kit Valensky than anyone local's been able to do in a long while. I don't need her statement to press charges against Valensky, but if we can get her to confirm he did it, all the better."

"So you're saying she's asked for help before?"

Josh's expression stilled, and she knew the minute he trusted her. He shook his head. "Not here, not in Silver Valley. There are reports from where they lived before, though, out of state, in a rural area. The neighbors called in the loud noises, shouting. She and her husband told the responding officers that it was a mistake, that she was fine. She refused to press charges. They lived in a smaller house in a subdivision, according to the records. We only have them because we've been watching Valensky. At that time there were repeated complaints from the neighbors of angry shouting, the sounds of fights. But each time, she showed up at the front door with Valensky and said she was fine, and the local officers let it go. Which as you know, means they didn't do their damned job. If it'd been an SVPD officer, he or she would have handled it the right way. We would have separated the two and got statements. They would have been recorded on the officer's police cams. Charges would have been pressed." He sighed and ran his fingers through his chestnut hair. It was short cropped but just long enough to remind her of the looser curls he'd sported in high school. God, how many times had she tugged his hair when they'd made out ad infinitum in that beat-up station wagon?

"What are you thinking, Annie?"

"Uh, nothing. Sorry—I drifted."

His eyes were warm, and the crinkles at their edges teased her. "I've been doing some of that myself since you walked in here."

They stared at one another, and it was like being in a bright tunnel, only the two of them, the years melting away. Except her body was feeling very adult responses to his every glance, each sound of his voice.

"Why didn't you ever come back, Annie? Really." He wasn't asking for her résumé.

"I got involved in school, and then graduate school, and then this job." And she'd been too wrapped up in her own hurt, needing the time to work through and heal from the abusive relationship that had flayed her soul and broken her heart. "And, well, I had some personal reasons, too, I guess." Shame rushed her. "I should have come when your parents died. I'm so sorry, Josh."

"It was a long time ago." He shrugged off her too-late amendment and looked at her. "I wondered. About your personal reasons for staying gone so long."

"You never tried to find me." She didn't mean for it to sound so accusing. "I never blamed you—we agreed we were done after prom night."

His mouth hitched on one side. "What a freaking disaster, right? Again, I'm sorry, Annie. I was a bumbling teen, and I blew the best relationship I've probably ever had."

"We were kids."

"That doesn't mean our feelings weren't adult. We were pretty precocious, wouldn't you say?" Was that a twinkle in his eyes?

"*Precocious*. That's not a word you hear in police work every day." She couldn't help but tease him.

"I'm not used to a police psychoanalyst coming in here every day, either." His grin was pure magnificence.

"Psychologist, thank you very much." She mirrored his grin, and felt a warm glow that she'd thought had been eradicated from her emotional repertoire years ago. Was it possible to heal so much later, in such a spectacular way?

"Roger." Josh spoke the police word for "I hear you." He twisted his desk chair as he angled his long, lean frame to face her, their chairs next to one another. His forearm brushed hers in the cramped space, and the tingle it sent through her was positively delicious. It was at once sexy and alarming, as this police department felt like her workspace at NYPD. She'd learned early in her career to not get involved with another officer on the job, but she wasn't working as a cop right now, not really.

She inched her chair away the small bit his cubicle allowed and chose to ignore the sexy smile on his too-handsome face. He knew he turned her on, a worse crime than the fact that she was getting so hot and bothered in the middle of trying to help a victim.

"Josh, I can't..."

He coughed, loudly, stopping her weak protest.

"The problem we have, Annie, is complex. You've reported what you think is a sign of abuse, yet the woman was in your store, perfectly healthy and normal in her behavior, correct?" His brow rose, and she knew what he was getting at.

"Except for how frightened she seemed, yes. And the bruises."

"That's your interpretation. I'm not saying I doubt you at all, but without Kit coming forward, we don't have a lot. We've never had any complaints since they've lived here, but their house is also out of earshot of anyone but the bears."

Annie swallowed and nodded. She knew everything he said was true. Still, she wished it could be taken care of more quickly, without the added risk of each hour Kit lived with that bastard.

"I knew you'd say that, and I do understand the legal issues. And there are problems with going to their home without her requesting help, and no reports of any noise or disturbance. Right now it's my word, my observations only. But I also know you can go check things out, interview Valensky."

The lines between his eyes deepened, and her fingers itched to smooth them. "We could. As I said, I'd prefer to do it with her corroboration, and when I know she's not there. It's admirable that you're willing to help her, Annie. We're far from at the end of the road for solutions. If she shows up at your knitting circle tonight, talk to her. Earn her trust. Get her to confide in you, to come in with you or at least agree to speak to me, and we'll be able to move forward."

"The odds of that…" She ran her fingers through her hair, her frustration familiar but no less dismal. Domestic abuse remained the toughest nut to crack.

He touched her forearm, a gesture of assurance that grounded her. "Normally, yes, the stats are against us in this type of case. But with you on her side, the odds of her opening up are high. That is, if you're half as good a listener as the girl I knew." His eyes blazed with the same heat that simmered in her belly and zinged straight to the intimate spot between her thighs, begging for release. If they weren't in the Silver Valley Police Department, would he kiss her? She wasn't sure.

Annie was absolutely certain, however, that she'd lean in and kiss him. Heck, who was she kidding? She'd straddle him in his chair and lay the hottest, sexiest, all-tongue kiss on him she had to give.

"Avery! Chief Todd's called in a DUI on Silver Valley Pike." The receptionist's voice echoed through an intercom.

"Roger. I'm on it." His gaze never left hers as he replied to the request and his mouth lifted in his signature half smile. "Until we meet again, Annie Fiero."

Chapter 3

Annie was still thinking about Joshua Avery long after she left SVPD, and later, as she closed the shop Friday night. It was as if he'd personally stayed with her all day, but whether it was the sexy edge to his humor or her reaction to him, she couldn't tell. He'd believed her story regarding Kit, and he had enough police information on Vadim Valensky to validate Annie's concerns. She'd hoped to have more information for him after tonight's knitting circle, or better, to bring Kit into SVPD to file a report. But Kit hadn't shown up, much to Ginny's and the other knitters' dismay. Annie was the most disappointed but unable to share it.

The night hadn't been a total wash, though, as a newer couple to the group, John and Jacob, were happy to announce their engagement and the night turned into a double celebration, adding to Lydia's birthday party.

Three new knitters had joined the festivities, as well. Annie had to hand it to her grandmother. Just as she'd told Josh, Ezzie had not only formed an entire community around the shop, she'd created a unique family of fiber crafters.

Annie turned the Open sign to Closed against the stained glass and locked up the store. She climbed the worn cherrywood steps to the apartment above the shop, running her hand along the timeworn banister. Silver Threads Yarn Shop was one of several businesses in downtown Silver Valley proper, but its Victorian architecture was rare. At some point it had been divided, and the other side had been remodeled into a dentist's office, which it had remained until recently when a local had returned to Silver Valley after serving as an FBI agent in Washington, DC. She'd turned the dentist's office into an outdoor adventure travel agency. It was especially busy this time of year, as groups of tourists came to the area to hike the AT, canoe the Susquehanna River and its tributaries, and enjoy day trips to surrounding attractions such as Gettysburg Battlefield and Hershey, Pennsylvania. Annie had met the owner, Abi Redland, only once but had liked her immediately. They were around the same age, she guessed.

Annie remembered when Ezzie had surprised her family by announcing she wanted to convert her library and living room into a yarn shop, move the kitchen upstairs and remodel the bedrooms, many empty, into an apartment. Annie marveled at her grandmother's intelligence and, more importantly, her determination to make a life for herself after her beloved second husband of forty-five years had passed away suddenly, when Annie was in high school.

The roomy upstairs apartment had always been the perfect place for Annie to lick her psychological wounds, too. First when she'd broken up from an abusive boyfriend, during college. She'd only ever told her family the barest facts of her harrowing escape from the man who'd abused her regularly, who'd emotionally battered her until she was but a shell of the young woman who'd graduated high school with dreams of traveling the world and becoming an artist.

They all knew why she was on sabbatical this time, though, and supported her need to heal. And run her grandmother's shop.

"Meow." Ezzie's cat greeted Annie at the door, wrapping his warm body around her ankles.

"Come here, Bubba." She lifted the large orange tabby into her arms and was surprised that he didn't try to claw his way out of her hug as she walked them both to the sofa and sat down. "Thank you, sweetness. I need a little TLC right now."

Bubba purred as he rubbed his head along her chin. As she accepted his feline ministrations, she was reminded of the scary bruises on Kit's jawline she'd spotted. Her stomach hardened at the brutal violence that she believed caused them. "We're going to get that bastard and see that he's locked up, aren't we?"

Annie looked around the living room that was piled with various knitting and crochet projects, the baskets heaped with yarn, the doilies under each and every knickknack. Grandma Ezzie had managed to pack two lifetimes' worth of stuff into the homey apartment. She wondered what she and her parents would do if

Ezzie decided to stay in Florida for good. It would take months to clear the clutter.

It was "clutter" for many, but to Annie it was pure comfort. She set Bubba next to her on the sofa and stood. His tail twitched. "I'm going to make a cup of chamomile. Would you like a kitty snack?"

At the word *snack*, Bubba's purr turned into an all-out drone. "You sound like you're revving for the Indy 500, sweetie."

Annie padded on bare feet into the kitchen and rummaged around in the cupboards for a tea bag and the aluminum pouch of cat nibbles. Two definite raps sounded on the apartment's front door and she jumped, but then stilled, her heart calming along with her mind. All part of police training to help her ascertain if there was indeed a threat, or if raccoons were in the garbage bins out back again. Silence settled over the tiny kitchen. Nothing. Bubba twitched his tail from where he sat atop the table, and she shooed him off.

"I hope those cute raccoons aren't back. They're handsome, but we don't want to risk rabies, right, Bubba?" She shook the kibble bag at him, ready to offer the cat his treat, but Bubba darted to the front door, tail held high.

Annie blinked. Pets never lied about something different going on, or about intruders. She made her way to the door as quietly as she could, and peered through the peephole.

The top of a head was all she could make out, but the shade of hair and approximate height of the person was all she needed. Before she opened the large wooden door, the person looked into the peephole and knocked, more loudly this time.

"Annie, it's me, Kit. Please. I need you."

* * *

Kit wasted no time telling Annie that she feared for her life and wanted Silver Valley PD protection. Annie didn't think twice; she called Josh. She spoke to Josh from the privacy of her bedroom while Kit waited in the living room.

"Where is she now, Annie?" His concerned tone reached through the phone.

"Here, with me. I'm staying upstairs from the yarn shop, in my grandmother's apartment."

"I sent an officer to her house earlier today but we didn't get very far. She denied all possible charges and Valensky did, too."

"The officer's visit probably triggered Valensky."

"Yeah, not unusual. If she's ready to move forward, though, I can have charges filed against him by tomorrow. Not sure how you do it at NYPD, but at SVPD, the police officer files the charges. It's to protect the victim and to prevent the all-too-common dropping of charges by the same victim."

"I understand. What should I do now, besides wait for you?"

"Stay put and I'll be over as soon as I have Becky's sitter come over. If I can't make it within twenty minutes, I'll send another officer. Keep her comfortable and take note of what she tells you. I guess I don't have to tell you that. You're a professional."

"Got it. And, Josh? Thanks for picking up."

"You did the right thing by coming to Annie's." Josh's voice reverberated around Ezzie's living room. She'd been back in touch with him for less than twenty-four hours, and yet he'd come when she'd called, agreed to help her with Kit's situation. Annie wanted to act quickly since Kit could decide against telling the police everything at any moment. She'd reached out to Josh, hoping he'd send an officer right away. He did—himself. Annie's shoulders immediately lowered as the tension left her. Josh could put the most feral cat at ease.

"Vadim will kill me if he finds out I told anyone. He was so angry when that cop showed up at the house today, asking questions." Kit shivered under one of Ezzie's hand-knit afghans.

"You don't have to go back there. There's a women's shelter in Cumberland County, right, Josh?" Annie's confidence in Josh and SVPD's efficiency were boosted by Kit's words. But Josh hadn't told her that he'd sent someone to Valenskys' house. Not that he reported to her.

Josh nodded. "Yes, there is, but to be honest I think Kit would be safer either staying here with you or going to a shelter in another state." He gave Annie a meaningful look and mouthed the letters *ROC*. Of course. She should have thought of it. If Valensky was part of ROC, he'd have connections everywhere and find out where Kit was without much effort. It was the sad truth about organized crime. Its effectiveness depended on networking. Nothing happened in an area the ROC claimed without the ROC knowing about it.

"He'll never know if we play this right, Kit." Annie wrapped her arm around the other woman's shoulders. "You can tell him that I called you, or that my grandmother did, for help with the shop. Or, if from what you told us, he's still passed out, he'll never know you left."

"Is that true, Kit? That he drinks so much on a regular basis?" Josh's tone conveyed authority but more importantly, compassion.

She nodded. "Yes. His drinking is much worse these days than in the beginning." She started to cry again. "He used to be much nicer to me. The beatings didn't start until the last couple of years. First before we moved here, and then once we were in this big house."

Annie met Josh's gaze over Kit's bent head. Anger, determination and compassion were reflected in his eyes. The realization that they were a team working this case together hit her. So much for her sabbatical.

"I'm only the yarn shop owner, as far as your husband is concerned, Kit. You already know from my grandmother that when I'm in New York I work for NYPD on their staff as a psychologist." Annie braced herself, waiting for Kit's reaction.

Kit sniffed. "I knew what you did when I came into the shop. Ezzie told me all about you. She's so proud."

"My point is that I'm obligated to report any evidence of possible abuse that I witness. I went to Josh with my suspicions after you were in the shop earlier." Annie waited for Kit's response. This was always the tricky part—garnering trust while in fact working without the victim's tacit permission.

Kit looked Annie in the eye and nodded. "I know what you do, and while I don't like it that you went to the police without telling me, I understand. I suppose I'm the fool for not coming forward sooner."

"You're no fool, Kit. You're one brave woman." And Annie meant it. Because she understood more than Kit knew she did. She'd been the victim of an abusive boyfriend in college.

She caught Josh's eyes as he stared at her. Hope reflected in his expression. Somehow, they were going to save this woman and put the man who'd basically enslaved her behind bars.

As they gazed at one another, the connection moved from solely professional to a level of intimacy.

Sensual awareness hit her in the solar plexus. Annie knew the feeling—she was swimming in the deep end of the relationship ocean with this man. It was going to be all or nothing, starting with her agreeing to serve on this case while she ran her grandmother's shop. It seemed incongruous to be on sabbatical from such a huge personal and professional loss at NYPD, then be called to serve on a dangerous local case while she did something as mundane, as far from law-enforcement ops as possible, as run a yarn shop. Annie fought the urge to speak up and say she couldn't help, not this time. What if she screwed up, missed another warning sign like she had in NYC? But Josh's expression kept her silent. He needed her, Kit needed her.

Being in Silver Valley was supposed to be her respite from NYPD and losing her friend. Instead she was in the middle of what could potentially become an ROC revenge case. Because ROC protected its own and she was helping Kit take down its senior-most point of contact in Silver Valley.

Instead of a respite, she'd walked into an asp's den. No amount of fuzzy skeins of yarn could take away a lethal threat.

Josh allowed the heat in Annie's gaze to stoke his desire for her, but not so much that it would be creepy in front of Kit. As quickly as the fire was there between them, it blew out, the shadows in Annie's eyes indicating she was struggling. He got it. She'd arrived in

Silver Valley to take a break and instead found herself facing a lethal ROC operative, via his abused spouse.

He was grateful, and not a little glad, that she'd trusted him enough to reach out again. She could have called it into SVPD dispatch, but she'd texted him. He'd almost banged his head on the headboard when Annie's text dinged on his nightstand and he'd grabbed his phone.

Kit's here. Come now.

Annie's place was actually her grandmother's, but he felt Annie's imprint all over the space. How could he not when she sat across from him, next to Kit on the small sofa? If he were honest, he'd admit he hadn't shaken the sense of warmth and charged energy she'd left with him at the station.

First things first.

"Annie's going to be your right hand through all of this, Kit. You have nothing to worry about. First, are you physically okay? Do you want a physical exam?"

Kit shook her head, much to Josh's regret but not surprise. She looked at him with a hard expression. "He hasn't hit me in almost a month. These bruises are old—I have very fair skin. I've been thinking about reporting him for a long time, ever since I came to the United States."

"How long have you been in the States?" His records reflected she'd married Valensky five years ago.

"Six years. I was brought to New Jersey and introduced to Vadim at a strip club. He said he was going to give me a new life and he took me home. I trusted him, as much as I could, because he protected me from getting pimped out. I only ever had to dance in the club. We were married a year later."

"How old were you then?"

"The records will say I was eighteen, because that's what my fake passport says. But I was only sixteen when we married."

Josh saw Annie's chest visibly rise and fall, her shock evident. He got it. As many times as you read about these cases, it was always tough to see the victim, any victim, in person.

"So you were underage and forced into a marriage." He pictured his own sister being treated so horribly, and knew he was going to do all it took to put Vadim Valensky behind bars. Along with his cohorts. The perfect timing of this wasn't wasted on him. A chance to take down the Silver Valley rep to ROC, just as SVPD was assigned to help intercept and prevent another group of women smuggled from a former Soviet bloc nation to be sold into sex slavery. His nape tingled the way it always did when he was onto something valid in a case. He leaned in and listened to Kit's every word.

"Vadim is a product of how he was raised, and his alcoholism. He's never known any different. So this part I can almost forgive, as I've learned to avoid him when he's drunk. If I wanted to see Vadim go to jail for hurting me, I could have already done it, but I have to save anyone else they want to hurt."

"Other women, and whatever else Vadim's doing, aren't your business, Kit. He's a threat to you. He could kill you with his bare hands if he decides to." Annie's professional skills were obvious as she tried to make Kit see the danger she was in.

Kit nodded. "I know that. But he's involved in something far worse, and I want him and the men he works with to all go to jail. That's why I'm here. To help get Vadim and his friends caught. They are horrible human beings."

"Your safety has to come first, though. If anything happens to you, we won't have a case. Right, Josh?"

Annie's blue eyes saw through to his soul, and he wondered if she realized she'd said "we." As if they were a team and working a case together. Which, practically speaking, they were.

"Yes and no. I'm going to file charges against him." As the reporting officer, he had the right and obligation to press charges against Valensky. Standard SVPD procedure was for the police to press the charges in order to protect the domestic violence victim and ensure the abuser met justice. Too many victims recanted after their abusers once again intimidated and manipulated them. He silently damned the Podunk cop or sheriff who'd known what was going on with Valensky years ago but never pressed charges. It would have saved Kit from untold abuse.

Annie rubbed the place between Kit's shoulders. "We're going to keep you safe, Kit. It's our job."

Annie looked at him with determination and expectation.

"Exactly. What Annie said." The bond between him and Annie was palpable. It made him feel like he was agreeing to more than Annie's promise to help Kit. As if she wanted more of whatever they shared than working a case together.

Annie had never been so attuned to any other officer or colleague she'd worked with as she was to Josh as he sat in Grandma Ezzie's feminine living room, his attention on Kit. Was it wrong to revel in the pure male beauty sitting right in front of her?

Kit waved her hand at both of them, as if Annie and Josh were naive. "Trust me, I've made it this far with Vadim. And I'll outlive him as long as he keeps drinking like he does. He's never used a weapon on me, and only hits me when he's drunk. He doesn't remember in the morning and is ashamed for what he knows he must have done. He's not a total monster." Kit spoke with the wisdom of an old woman, yet she was only twenty-one or -two. Annie disagreed with her on the monster part, but kept silent.

"Can you tell me a little more about what you meant, Kit? When you said Vadim's involved in something you don't like?" Josh's tone was professional yet incredibly compassionate. Annie mentally stopped adding his sexy points up—he was off the charts.

"I'm not exactly sure because he hides everything from me. But I'm almost positive he's helping other women get tricked into coming here." Kit looked first at Annie, then Josh. "He treats me like a little girl who can't handle anything except getting her nails done and buying the latest designer purse. He only allowed me to go to SVCC because he thought I might be interested in learning English better." Kit referred to Silver Valley Community College. "I can speak it well enough, from watching television, but I still need work on my writing."

"He lets you go to school?"

"Oh, yes. I was bored and wanted to get a job, but he was dead set against it. No woman of 'his' ever needs to work." She made air quotes around *his* and scrunched up her face in distaste. "When I told him I needed something to engage my mind, he understood. I had to time it between his blackouts, of course. I didn't want to come home to him drowned in his own vomit." Spoken with such ease, as if dealing with a blackout drunk was a normal part of life. For Kit, it was.

"Are you still taking classes?" Annie had met so many domestic violence victims who had zero self-esteem left. Going to college would seem beyond them, even if they had the financial ability.

"Yes. And I've taken whatever I wanted to take." Underneath the layer of wariness Annie had witnessed earlier, Kit was incredibly strong and driven. A woman with a purpose. But Annie didn't want that strength to become her downfall, either.

"That's brave." Annie meant it.

"I've finished all the classes for an associate's degree in Criminal Justice. Vadim won't allow me to go away to Penn State, but he agreed to allow me to take more classes. I needed his permission to pay for them, of course. Now I'm working on a second associate's degree, in computers." She shrugged. "I want to be able to help other women who were brought here against their will. One day I'd love to work in law enforcement myself." She said the last shyly, her eyes downcast. "But as far as Vadim's concerned, I took the classes for him, to be able to help him with his business. I never, ever told him my hopes to escape and start my own business."

Annie's insides plummeted with her hope. "Wait—you've helped your husband in his work for ROC—Russian Organized Crime?"

Kit's eyes widened. "No, no, I will never help him in what he's doing. He's not asked me to yet, but I've let him think I will. That I don't have a problem with what he does. Of course, I don't let on how much I know, and I tell him I'll help him with his pawnshop. He thinks I'm book smart but life stupid. Sometimes the only way to survive is to go along with the flow, as you say."

"What exactly do you think your husband is involved with, Kit? Besides the pawnshop?" Josh spoke up, and Annie knew that he already had his suspicions of Valensky, but needed Kit to share what she knew. She tried not to hold her breath, as the entire crux of what Josh hoped to accomplish here rested on this moment.

"He's been working with his criminal colleagues and bringing in shipments of women to the Silver Valley and Harrisburg area. Women from all over Eastern Europe and Asia, young women. They are told they'll work in a home as a nanny and be able to go to school. But they…they never do. They have to work in a strip bar, or as escorts. Some get sent out to be married, like I was."

"Escorts, as in prostitutes?" Josh needed Kit to give him the truth, but Annie hated that Kit had to feel all of these emotions again. Because she had no doubt that Kit had been one of these women six years ago when she'd come over.

Kit nodded. "Yes. But not on the streets, not like you see on television. This is in private men's clubs, where the girls are never seen in public, only by the customers. He had a good friend, a criminal contact he worked with exclusively. But he's disappeared, and now I'm not sure who Vadim's working with."

Annie's jaw started to ache, and she realized she'd been clenching her teeth. It was one thing to be exposed to the sickest parts of human nature in a huge metropolis like New York, but to be faced with such ugliness injected into Silver Valley was sad. Her hometown, the place she went to in her mind whenever life on the city streets proved too much, had been infected with the same vile human behavior.

"Did you know the name of Vadim's contact?"

"Yes. It was Yuri Vasin. I saw in the paper that he died in that crash a couple of months ago." As Kit spoke, Annie watched Josh's expression. It remained neutral, but when he looked at her, she recognized the gleam of determination. Josh had just confirmed that Kit's account matched the police records. Annie gave him a quick nod before he turned back to Kit.

How was it possible to be thinking about saving Kit and her overwhelming emotions regarding Josh at the same time?

"I'm going to need you to give me an official statement about what you know of your husband's actions, Kit. Who he talks to, where he works on a regular basis."

Josh's voice only increased her confusion. How could she feel so comfortable with him when she hadn't seen him in over ten years? She'd worked with NYPD colleagues for years and still didn't enjoy the immediate sense of trust she did with Josh.

Dare she trust Josh as she had no other? If she wanted to be an asset to SVPD as they faced down ROC, she'd have to.

Chapter 4

Kit cleared her throat. "Vadim's always in his pawn-shop during the day, but that's not his real work. His real work he does from home, in his safe room in the basement." Kit wiped her nose on a tissue.

"Are you willing to come into the station with me to file a report?" Josh hated to ask her again, but it would be better for them all if she could come in. He'd need every resource and means of recording her statement as possible. This was the center point of a huge ROC operation. An op he longed to be in the middle of but had to make sure his sister was permanently situated first.

Kit grasped Annie's hand and looked at her. Josh's heart constricted. Annie was so damned beautiful, her attractiveness only rivaled by her infinite strength.

"You're not alone." Annie squeezed Kit's hand. "We'll be with you each step of the way."

Kit nodded. "Okay. Yes, yes, I'll come in. I can tell Vadim that Annie here got caught driving after too much vodka. That's real enough, right? And that I had to come help her, get her out of custody. That's only if he finds out I was gone."

"You're talking like a cop now, Kit." Annie's smile radiated confidence, and Josh couldn't help but wish it was directed at him, too. "But it's not your job, as we've said. It's ours, and you'll be best in a safe house."

"Annie's right, Kit. You're a brave woman. You're going to help a lot of people, more than you know. And we'll keep you safe. You have my word. But the only way I can promise that is if you let me call the social worker who manages the shelter we're sending you to." Kit stared at Josh for a long minute, and he prayed she'd agree to go. As much as a part of him wanted to incarcerate Valensky—and Kit was the most direct way to do that—he didn't want to risk her well-being. Finally Kit nodded.

"I'll go to the shelter." She turned toward Annie. "Will you be able to get my things that I need, to keep studying?"

"Of course, but we're going to recommend you don't go to class for a week or two, until we make sure you're not being followed," Josh stated, and too late realized he'd spoken for Annie. He looked at her, expecting her censure. Instead, she smiled at Kit.

"What Josh said. Do you happen to have your computer with you now?"

"I do. I packed my laptop and some clothes, just in case I needed to go to the shelter. I need to take my car with me, or you have to hide it."

"Smart thinking. You'll make a fine law-enforcement official, if that's what you hope to do."

"I'll put a call in to the shelter coordinator now. She'll show up to take you there. We'll take care of getting your car to you later." Josh pulled out his phone and scrolled through his contacts. He stood up and walked down the hall, out of earshot of Annie and Kit.

He needed the space, too. In that small living room he could feel every time Annie's gaze landed on him. Whenever he met it, looked into the depths of her eyes, his heart threw itself into overdrive. They were going to do this. They were going to work the case together. And he didn't think the only actions they took together would be professional. There were other things they could do, would do, once they were alone.

He had no illusions of what else he planned to do with Annie, when it was safe to do so, when she invited him to. Not that making love to Annie would ever be good for his heart.

Kit looked at Annie the minute Josh was out of earshot, her gaze beseeching. "I can't miss that much class time. I'm sure I'll be safe. I would know if Vadim had me followed."

"I'm sure you can arrange to take your classes online or at least do your homework remotely. You can't risk your husband's temper."

Kit didn't answer her right away, tearing at the tissue she held. "I told you, I can handle him. The most recent bruises were because I was stupid and got in his way. I didn't realize how drunk he was."

Annie stared at her and knew that like every other

abuse victim, Kit wasn't going to heal overnight. "Let's talk to Josh about it, okay?"

After Kit left with the social worker, Annie and Josh agreed to share a pot of tea and go over a to-do list. Kit had left with both of their phone numbers memorized and put into her cell under pseudonyms in case Valensky was able to remotely access her contact list. Annie was relieved for Kit but also anxious for both herself and Josh. ROC was notoriously efficient and invasive. The odds of Kit being discovered in the shelter, no matter how far away, were good. Annie would be surprised if Kit weren't being surveilled all the way to the shelter, even under police protection. If Valensky found her, there'd be no telling how much danger she'd face.

The thought made Annie shiver.

"Cold?" Josh's voice wrapped around her, causing an explosion of warmth in her chest.

She shook her head. "No. Worried. This is going to need to be cracked more quickly than most cases, isn't it?"

"You've already confirmed you're familiar with ROC. You know how vile they are, how quickly they infiltrate an area."

"Yeah, unfortunately. Since you mentioned it in the police station, I've been fighting my anger that it's seeped into Silver Valley. Is no place sacred?"

"You already know the answer to that." Josh's eyes were so bright, so intense.

"I'm willing to do whatever you need me to, Josh."

Annie sat across from him at Ezzie's miniature dining table, a fold-down contraption that made sharing a pot of tea seem more intimate, as if they were on a date having champagne in a New York City bistro.

"Thanks for coming in on this, Annie. I know you're on sabbatical and are busy enough with Ezzie's shop." Josh's strong face was inches from hers, his motions efficient and reflecting latent strength. She wanted to all at once embrace the moment, throw herself at him, or flee. "I admire you for looking out for Kit. Because it's butting up against our bigger concern that I told you about when you came into the station. SVPD's primary objective right now is to intercept a group of women heading to Silver Valley and prevent them from being put to work against their will in the sex trade. Valensky is involved in it, we're certain. We just haven't had enough to arrest him, or break up their op."

"I'm not afraid of Valensky, Josh. As I'm sure you understand, it's my job. Whether on duty or off. Have you ever turned your back on a crime victim? Whether you're on duty or off?"

"No." He took a swig of tea, the bone china cup minuscule in his large hand. She had to stop obsessing over Josh's physicality. "We'll have to let NYPD know you're working this, of course."

"I've already emailed my supervisor about it, but yes, you'll need to call it in, or have your chief do it. To make it official. And to provide whatever other details you need—I wasn't fully aware of how deep in with ROC Kit's husband is, of course." She'd thought she'd been dealing with domestic abuse, period.

His eyes narrowed. "I'll do that, but first I'm going to go out to Valensky's place and charge him with domestic abuse." Josh's eyes blazed with conviction. "He's done with hurting her."

"Will you go over there tonight?"

He shook his head. "No. We know Kit's safe, for now. It'll wait until tomorrow. The way it works in our county is that we, SVPD, press the charges—the signed statement of the officer who either spoke to the victim or witnessed her injuries is all we need to move forward." The lines between his brows deepened, and Annie wanted to smooth them. Wanted to do a lot more to him, in fact. Was something wrong with her, that in the middle of a very serious case she wanted nothing more than to explore her attraction to Josh?

"It never gets any easier with a domestic. I'm always asking myself if I'm doing enough."

"Oh?" *Please, please say you want to kiss me.* Where the hell was all of this coming from? It had to be the combination of being back in her hometown, in Grandma Ezzie's place and in the company of a man she'd once tried to lose her virginity to. She choked on a gulp of tea as laughter gurgled up her throat.

"You okay?" His brows lifted in a classic "no matter what you say I know you're nuts" expression, and it set her into a gale of giggles.

"I'm so sorry, Josh. I'm obviously overtired, and it's been a long day. You've handled all of this as well as I've ever seen it done—better." She wiped her eyes with a napkin that had cat paw prints on it, in a rainbow of colors. All Grandma Ezzie had in the kitchen cupboard were cat-themed paper products. "I was laughing at my thoughts. I was thinking about how we know each other, well, *knew* one another…before."

"Before prom night?" It was his turn to laugh. "We were the best of friends, weren't we?"

"Until we weren't." She vividly remembered the

debacle they'd made of their after-prom plans, neither of them having had any sexual experience beforehand. "I'm sorry I never tried to contact you after that, Josh. It was stupid of me."

"And I'm sorry, too, for letting you go so easily. It was totally expected for our ages and time frame, though. We both went to college and learned how to do it, right?" The twinkle in his eye got her pulse pounding in all the right places again and she knew he saw the flush she felt on her cheeks.

"Yes."

"So you're still single."

"I am." She added milk to her tea, needing the distraction. Her hands were shaky with need. "We already went over this."

"I want to make sure I wasn't dreaming." He stared at her, his expression neutral but his eyes, his eyes made her want to close the distance and kiss him for the umpteenth time since she'd first seen him again in the police station. So she did.

Josh was no fool. When a beautiful woman placed her lips on his he was happy to oblige, maybe even throw some tongue in for added effect. He liked kissing. A lot. But when Annie's lips hit his, his mind shut down and his body woke up and went full throttle. He placed his hand on her nape and pressed her to him across the sorry excuse for a table, wanting to toss the tiny piece of furniture to the side and pull her onto his lap. Instead, he settled for a taste of her lips, taking extra time with her lower lip, sucking it into his mouth ever so gently.

Her groan undid him, and he growled in response as

she opened her mouth fully, allowing his tongue complete access to the sweet softness that was Annie Fiero.

"Josh." She spoke his name against his mouth, and he loved the way her lips moved, her breath felt. Annie even smelled, tasted the same as she had, but with more spice. And her abilities had vastly improved. As had her passion.

"Come here, babe." He stood up and she followed suit, her arms going up onto his shoulders as he wrapped his arms around her waist. "God, you feel so good, Annie."

"You're feeling mighty fine yourself." She smiled up at him and he lowered his lips to taste her again, not stopping until his erection became almost painful.

"God, Annie, I want to—" He grasped her ass and pulled her to him, allowed her to feel his erection.

"But we, we can't—oh, Josh." Her eyes closed and she pressed back against him.

"I'm not saying we can't ever." He had a hard time keeping his words even. His breath refused to stop hitching.

"We shouldn't, though. Especially if we'll be working together." Her voice was husky, and he knew that it wouldn't take much to convince her. And he wanted to convince her, to show her that he wasn't the nervous teen she'd tried to sleep with prom night.

But not here, not now. She deserved more than a quickie after a particularly emotional event. And he wanted more than that with her.

"I don't care about any of that, Annie. If we do work together on this case, through to its end, we're both professional enough to keep our personal feelings out of it."

"But—"

"No buts. I want you, but I'm complicated. I can't do serious, and you're, you're definitely a serious kind of woman, Annie."

Oops. He felt her stiffen an instant before she pulled back. "What the hell does that mean? 'Serious' woman? Who says I need anything more than a good time in bed? And why would you even assume I'd want anything but a casual time with you? I'm headed back to New York at the end of three months. The last thing I need is serious when it comes to a relationship."

Like a cold dowse of mountain spring water on the Appalachian Trail, her words stopped him dead. She wasn't going to be here forever, and the last thing he needed was to be involved with another woman whose departure could hurt his sister like Christina's had. Because in a small town like Silver Valley, it'd be tough to date Annie even casually without having to introduce her to Becky.

"Wait—" She had her hand on his forearm as he turned to leave. "That was incredibly rude of me. I'm sorry, Josh." She ran her fingers through her fiery locks, tousled from their embrace. "Maybe we need to start over?" Her full lips and brilliant eyes begged for him to resume where they'd left off. To take her to bed tonight and each night while she was in town.

"I'd love nothing more than to get to know you better, Annie. To appreciate the woman you've become, both in and out of bed." He saw her pupils dilate when he said "bed," and it was a total test of his self-control that he didn't back her up against the kitchen counter and make love to her here and now. "But I can't afford to do casual. I have someone else to worry about."

She tilted her head. "Is there something I'm missing? Do you have a child?"

"No, a sister. You remember my younger sister, Becky?"

She nodded and smiled. "The Beckster. I loved her. She was always such a sweetie pie!"

He couldn't help but smile back. "Yeah, well, you might remember also that she had some developmental delays from being deprived of oxygen at birth. The official term for it in the school system and for living placement is PDD—Pervasive Developmental Disorder."

"I do recall that, but your mother was always so positive about it, and I don't remember Becky having any major issues, at least not physically."

"That's right. But mentally—that's the catch. She seemed okay when she was seven or eight, when you knew her, because that's closer to the mental age she'll always be. Somewhere around ten or eleven. She's a grown woman of nineteen now, and she still behaves and acts like she did when you knew her."

"Oh, Josh, I'm so sorry. I didn't know you were the one taking care of her. I should have, of course."

She didn't know. But how would she? He kept his responsibilities on the down low right after his parents' fatal crash, and now that he'd been taking care of Becky for over a decade, they were invisible to the Silver Valley community. He and Becky were a pair, a family. No one saw the effort it took on his part to care for her because it was none of their business as far as he was concerned.

"That's just it, Annie. I was named Becky's guardian as they'd neglected to pick anyone else. I changed my entire life to fit Becky. So you see, I don't come as a solo package."

He saw the light dim in her eyes. Annie understood. There would never be a long-term commitment where he was concerned.

"I admire you and all you're doing for Becky. That doesn't have to affect a casual relationship, though."

"Maybe." He wanted to agree, to throw in his resistance and fear of taking on too much. But first he had to address a startling observation. He was disappointed that Annie didn't make a case for a more lasting commitment.

It had to be the long hours affecting him.

"Before I go, let me get something for you out of my car." He was back within three minutes and Annie froze at the sight of what he gave her.

"I don't want this, Josh." She took the SIG Sauer from him, though, knowing that the .45 handgun could save her life if Valensky came after her.

"There's a lot to what we do that we don't want. This is my spare—please take it. I take it you have a license to carry?"

"Of course." It was all part of being in law enforcement. "And this is my favorite, on the range." She'd never had to fire a weapon in New York City. Would she in Silver Valley?

"If you want, I can get you a gun safe."

"I'll take care of that, no problem. It'll be a write-off for the shop." She tried to muster a smile, because it was terribly important to her that he remember her in a positive light. No matter how disappointed she was that a relationship wasn't happening.

"Okay, well, I need to get back home and then clock

in at the station. Call me if you need anything, okay?"
He hadn't been looking at her, his gaze bouncing from
the gun to his phone to the floor of the apartment entryway. When his gaze finally settled on hers, she saw
everything she needed to know.

Desire. Dedication to duty. Disappointment.

Yeah, she and Josh were on the same page.

"Will do. And, Josh?"

"Yes?"

"Thanks."

He nodded and turned, his steps quick and certain
down the stairwell as he left her standing at the apartment door.

Josh was never fond of making a house call on a
Saturday morning, but as he pulled up to the Valensky
fortress he didn't give a chipmunk's butt what day it
was. Vadim Valensky had beaten Kit, and it was Josh's
job to apprehend him.

"You expecting trouble from him?" Lieutenant Rachel Hollenbach sat in the passenger seat. He'd grabbed
the first officer he'd seen when he'd gotten into work.

"Not sure, but we'll find out. Let's see if we get past
his security to start with."

He wasn't expecting to get past the locked front gate
as quickly as he did, as it opened right after he held his
badge up to the security camera. As soon as the sound
of the gate's motor started, he got back into the cruiser.

Vadim Valensky stood at the top of the imposing
front porch as they pulled up.

"He looks real friendly." Rachel's crack was accu-
rately inaccurate as he took in the dark expression on
Valensky's worn face.

"We don't need friendly. We need to charge him. Let's go."

They got out of the car and walked up to Valensky, who started to visibly shake.

"Mr. Valensky, we're here to follow up on yesterday's visit about your wife. She has filed a complaint with SVPD that you have abused and assaulted her." Josh spoke first.

Valensky's face crumpled, and to Josh's surprise, fat tears ran down the man's cheeks. "Oh my God. Is she okay? What has happened?"

Josh realized that Valensky could easily not have any idea that Kit had left voluntarily. He might think she'd been in an auto accident or even met foul play while away from home. Or the monster could be playing both him and Lieutenant Hollenbach.

"Can we go inside?"

"Of course." Valensky turned and led them through the most ornate front door that Josh had ever seen in Silver Valley. The inside of the house was no less opulent, with fancy looking knickknacks on every surface. But Josh wasn't here to determine whether Valensky's belongings were legit pawnshop finds or stolen. Or worse, bought with ROC-earned funds.

"We can talk here." Valensky pointed to a sitting area, where he sank into a huge leather chair while Josh and Rachel remained standing. Rachel began the questioning, as they'd agreed upon.

"Mr. Valensky, it's come to our attention again that you have been harming your wife. It'll go much smoother for you if you don't repeat what you said yesterday and admit to whatever you've been doing."

"I didn't say anything yesterday because I was

afraid. I'm all Kit has and if something were to happen to me, she'd be alone. She relies fully on me. I would never hurt her, not on purpose. Do I drink too much sometimes? Sure. Who doesn't? Does she get on my nerves? Of course. But I've never touched her, unless of course she's asked me to." His smirk earned him a steely look from Rachel. Seeing her lack of understanding, he looked at Josh. The smirk melted away.

"Do you keep any weapons here, Mr. Valensky? Licensed or otherwise?"

"Only one handgun, in a lockbox on my nightstand. All the rest of the weapons I own are in the pawnshop, legally locked up." Josh knew that this was true, at least the pawnshop part. And Kit had verified that she didn't know of any other weapons on the property other than the one Valensky mentioned. Though, as he looked around the ostentatious room, he knew he wouldn't feel safe living here with Valensky, not with the line of medieval bows on one wall or the trio of battle axes on another. And they didn't have a search warrant, so he wasn't going to pursue this. He wanted one thing from Valensky today: compliance.

"Where's your wife?" He took over the questioning. He watched Valensky for signs that he knew Kit was in a shelter, under police protection.

"I have no idea. Sometimes she's gone for a long time, the whole day, at her college library. Why she can't study here in this nice home I built for her, I don't know."

"When's the last time you saw her?" He knew Valensky was worried; it was in the deep furrows of his jowls. Josh trusted his investigative gut. Valensky had hurt Kit, and would do it again. But Kit had most likely told the truth. Her husband was a blackout abuser. And he seemed to be genuinely confused about why the police were at his home.

"Kit was here on Friday morning before I left for work."

"You're telling us that you haven't seen her in over twenty-four hours?"

"No, no, I haven't."

"And that doesn't give you cause for concern?"

"I thought maybe she's mad at me. My wife, she's young. When she gets very angry, she goes to her sister's." Valensky sighed.

Josh silently swore. He didn't know if Kit had a sister, but if she did, he'd have liked to know about it from her.

"Where does her sister live, Mr. Valensky?"

"In New Jersey." Spoken with resignation, as if Kit had done this before. Josh looked at Rachel and raised his brow. She picked up on his cue.

"For the record, you admit to assaulting your wife, Mr. Valensky? On the date and time listed here?" Valensky looked at the report Rachel gave him and after a long beat, nodded.

"Yes."

"Go ahead and sign here, and I'll need your initials here and here." Rachel handled the task like the professional she was. After Valensky finished, she continued.

"We're going to verify all you've told us, Mr. Valensky. If none of it fits, you can expect us to return." Rachel proceeded to charge Vadim Valensky with assault and battery. Josh observed, but not because he had to—Rachel was an extraordinary cop and she'd proved her expertise not only on domestic calls like this one but on the streets of Silver Valley, taking down drug dealers and apprehending criminal suspects. As he watched Valensky, he saw what he prayed was resignation and maybe the beginning of remorse in the man's eyes. It was the most Josh ever hoped for—that the abuser would pay for their crimes, and find help to never do it again.

Rachel wrapped up the formalities after obtaining Valensky's signature. There would be no arrest because it was his first officially charged offense, and because Kit was safe in the shelter.

"One more thing, Mr. Valensky. If for any reason you think you have a problem with your anger, and how you express it, I suggest you seek help. Voluntarily is always better than being forced to do it in a jail cell." Rachel reached into her back uniform pocket for a pamphlet that she left on the coffee table. "There are links and phone numbers for you to utilize. Please do."

Valensky didn't get up as they walked out of his house and drove off the property. Only after the gates closed behind them did Josh speak. "You did great in there, Rachel. I thought he was going to piss when he saw your expression. And that was before we charged him."

"After he tried to brag about his sexual prowess when he said he doesn't touch her unless she asks him to? Gag." Rachel's profile was resolute. "He's like all the other ones, isn't he? He'll never admit he has a problem even after he's broken her bones or worse."

"It's our job to prevent that. Charging him is sobering, no pun intended. When he gets the charges and court summons in the mail, it'll be another reminder to him that he risks jail time. That'll be the judge's decision, not ours." Josh hoped that they'd be able to arrest Valensky on his dealings with ROC and put him away for the longest time possible. "But I think we shook him up enough that he'll think about it."

"I'm glad his wife wasn't there. Made our job easier. She going to stay in the safe house?"

"No telling. That's the toughest part of this at times." He hated even contemplating that Kit would return to Valensky, but he wouldn't bet against it. At least they had been able to charge Valensky.

So where was his satisfaction at a job well done? Nonexistent, as long as Valensky was free to walk the streets. He couldn't control the law, or the fact that there was so much domestic violence that not every perpetrator could be arrested, at least not as often as Josh liked. Still, they'd done what they'd come here to do, and Kit was safe, for now. Why wasn't he surprised that his first instinct was to to call Annie and tell her they'd taken care of Valensky?

Chapter 5

A few weeks after Kit had been taken to the women's shelter, Annie came up for air from the cloud of fiber, needles and knitters that she'd thrown herself into. She wanted the shop in order in the event she was needed to help with Kit's case. It helped distract her from thoughts of Josh and what they'd both said no to in her apartment the night Kit came for aid.

She hadn't been able to shake the sense that a reckoning from Valensky was imminent. If he found out her involvement, he'd level her and the yarn shop. She'd worked too long at NYPD to not know how quickly ROC doled out revenge. Nevertheless, she relished a chance to assist in keeping ROC out of Silver Valley, no matter how small her part.

If she were brutally honest with herself, though, she'd hoped that working the long hours would also help her forget about her attraction to Josh. Or at least put it on a back burner.

Tell that to her body, which reacted every time she thought about his hands on her, his mouth on hers.

The chimes on the front door roused her from sexy thoughts of Josh and the pyramid of red yarn she was stacking.

"Hi, Annie." Carla, Grandma Ezzie's backup store cashier, walked up to her. Annie looked at her watch.

"Wow, I had no idea it was lunchtime already. Thanks for coming in, Carla."

"Anytime. You should call me more often. You've been here a month already and I'd guess you could use a break."

Annie stepped away from the display and went to get her purse behind the counter. "Careful, I may take you up on that."

Her best friend, Portia, had suggested they meet and Annie agreed to come up for air. A visit with the bubbly woman she'd known since they were kids was the best antidote to her ROC worries. She enjoyed the walk along Main Street to the Silver Valley Diner. She needed girl time with her bestie.

But she questioned her decision when she found herself at the receiving end of her grade school bestie's interrogation.

"You're nuts. There's no way you're going to survive three months in Silver Valley. It's snooze-ville compared to New York!" Portia DiNapoli's brown eyes were wide as she sat across the booth table from Annie.

"I'm fine. And it's almost a month since I got here, so only two more." And unbeknownst to Portia, Annie was involved in something besides the yarn store. Or thought she was. Even though she'd only had one text from Josh over the last few weeks that told her Valensky had been charged with assault and battery.

She'd hoped to be more involved. So much for the promise of a high-profile case to help her days fly. But that wasn't fair. She knew that cases, especially sensitive ones that impacted many people, took a long time to piece together. Josh would call again, when he needed her. And if she felt a little sad that he hadn't needed her for more personal reasons, that was her problem.

"Fine isn't good enough, Annie. Every time I've visited you in the city, you've said you'd never move back here, not even for a week. I know you'd do anything for Ezzie but this is a huge favor. Three months! Not that I'm complaining. There's so much we can do together."

Annie listened to Portia's voice over their meal with one ear. Her mind was preoccupied on how exactly she was going to help out Kit without getting herself completely mired in thinking about Josh. *Face it, you already are.*

She'd lain awake for hours after Josh left. Even though he'd dropped that shocker on her about his sister, Becky, they'd managed to sit back down, albeit in the living room and with a little more space between them, and hammer out what they had to help Kit with.

They were both certain Valensky had no clue where she was. Annie told him everything Kit had mentioned, no matter how insignificant it seemed. She knew from working with NYPD that what seemed silly to her could lead to a big break in a tough case.

Josh had been so complimentary of how Annie had handled Kit's case, it had been disconcerting. She'd reminded him again that not only was it her job, it was part of who she was. Josh seemed to understand that. But what he didn't understand, what no one in Silver Valley knew, was that Annie was haunted by Rick's death and a serious case of low self-esteem.

"Have you heard a word of what I just said?" Portia stabbed into a thick slice of Texas French toast, the maple syrup pooling on the diner's ceramic plate. They'd both ordered from the 24/7 breakfast menu. "And have you given any more thought to the book group tie-in I suggested? I've been putting books aside at the library."

Annie picked at her spinach omelet. "I have, and I think your idea to do a combined book study–knit group is brilliant. Grandma's groups have read books before, but with your expertise they'll get more out of it. You'll probably bring in more customers to the shop, if you advertise in the library." Annie shot her a grin, and laughed when Portia raised her brows.

"I'm a librarian, not a wizard. The whole key is in picking the right book to read. I'll come by this Friday's group and bring several, and they can pick one." Portia's excitement painted her cheeks red. She loved her job as the elementary school librarian and also worked in the local library on a part-time basis.

"That sounds great. Thank you, Portia. I'm in a little bit over my head here." She didn't mention that a big reason was that she'd found herself in the midst of a high visibility case. Or even more importantly, that she'd found herself with a serious case of the hots for one of Silver Valley's finest. She'd gone over their old relationship and her instant attraction to Josh at least a hundred times over the last weeks. Each hour.

"I hear you. Between the library and my volunteer work at the Silver Valley shelter, I feel like my hair's on fire."

"You still spend a lot of your evenings there?" Portia had served at the homeless shelter since right after college. "I'm surprised you're not running it by now."

"That would require a social worker's degree, and getting my MLS was enough, thank you very much."

"You do so much for Silver Valley, Portia." How would her best friend feel if she knew ROC was threatening the very peace Portia spread by helping the homeless?

"What's really going on with you, Annie? You're usually a lot more excited about life and things in general. And while you came home to help out your grandmother, you have to take care of yourself first. If you want to talk about your loss, I'm here."

Annie smiled at her friend.

"You know there's more, a lot more, to my sabbatical than the death of a friend. I'm looking at my life, what I'm doing at NYPD. I'm not ready to talk about the feelings around losing a work colleague, one I was assigned to care for. Not in depth, not yet. But if I were, I'd talk to you—you know that." But she didn't think she'd ever want to go over it again. Annie had confided in Portia about the murder-suicide when she first returned to Silver Valley, but she hadn't shared her worst feelings on it. She didn't want to face her deepest fears, that it was her fault Rick hadn't made it, hadn't stayed sober. Or worse, find that she couldn't help Kit any more than she'd helped Rick. And her main objective in Silver Valley was supposed to be keeping her grandmother's yarn shop going, not fighting off the strongest physical attraction she'd ever experienced.

"Losing Rick, and his wife, in the worst way isn't going to be easy to get over. I need a time-out."

Portia's eyes grew huge and filled with tears. She blinked. "Oh, Annie, I know, honey. I'm so, so sorry. That absolutely sucks. Whatever you need, I'm here. And if I'm overwhelming you with all of my plans for us, ignore me. I'm the last person who'd ever put more pressure on you."

"I could never ignore you." She smiled at the one friend she'd kept for all the years since leaving Silver Valley for college and her big-city career. "But tell me something. What do you remember about Josh Avery?"

"Josh? The boy you obsessed over all of junior and senior year?" Portia wiped her mouth. "Oh my gosh, Annie, that was so long ago. I remember you wanting to make the relationship more, but being afraid to. And then the prom thing…"

"So you do remember that." Annie grimaced. Some things were best left to an adolescent past.

"I felt so bad for both of you, but then we all went to college, and I trust that none of us are virgins any longer, right?" Portia grinned and Annie laughed.

"We all drifted so far apart, considering how small a town Silver Valley is." Annie heard the regret in her voice and realized she'd missed her hometown more than she'd admitted to herself.

"Your grandmother kept you up to speed, too, though, didn't she? After your parents moved to Florida?"

"Yes, she's always kept tabs on anyone I knew. When Josh's parents died, she told me, but I never put it together with him needing to take care of his younger sister."

"That's right. I used to see them at the library together a lot. Not so much the last couple of years. She's what, eighteen or nineteen now?"

"Nineteen. It took her a couple of extra years to get through high school, I guess. And she's got special needs, always will have. Josh said it's called PDD."

"Pervasive Developmental Disorder." Portia nodded.

"Wow, you know about it?"

"I've had more than one or two parents come in to research it over the years. And it makes sense that Josh is stressed, because I've seen plenty of parents scramble to find 'what's next' for their mentally challenged children once they're adults. The library has an entire section on Pennsylvania law and benefits for disabled adults." Portia's sincerity was reflected in her clear tone. "Josh was a great guy and still is. He used to come in and do talks for the elementary school kids on career day. They ate it up. He hasn't done it for a while since he was promoted to detective, but he was a regular for many years."

Annie didn't say anything about Josh's move back to a uniform, even if it was at his own request for lighter hours.

Portia's eyes widened and she slapped her hand on the table. "Wait. Why the interest in Josh? Have you seen him again?"

"Hold on there, Portia. We, er, we're working on the same case. Nothing I can talk about, though."

"Uh-huh." Portia eyed her over her empty plate. "What did you think when you saw him again?"

The flush she felt creep up her face was obviously

visible to Portia, who crowed with glee. "You still have the hots for him! I can see it stamped all over you." She sipped her water before leveling Annie with a sincere gaze. "You're both single. And as previously stated, no longer virgins. Seems to me it's the perfect time to pick back up together."

"First, there's nothing to 'pick back up.' I knew him in high school—okay, he was my high school crush, but as you have so brilliantly described, we never took it far enough to talk about."

"I'm sorry, Annie. I didn't mean to be so in-your-face. You've been single again for a while, though, and I think anything to break that spell is good, you know?" Portia shrugged as if Annie's feelings for Josh were no big deal. And they shouldn't be a big deal, but kept popping back up, refusing to go away.

"Yes, change of scenery of any kind is never bad." They both laughed. "Thank you. You've always understood me, sometimes better than I do myself."

"It's mutual."

"What about your love life, Portia?"

She rolled her eyes. "Puh-leeeze. You know my luck with men—it's nonexistent."

Annie studied her friend. Portia was classically beautiful and had been ostracized in high school because of it. Instead of seeing her as the brilliant young woman she was, their classmates and even some of the teachers couldn't see past her looks. Annie remembered the long, tearful conversations when Portia confided she hated being seen as only a pretty girl. Yet Portia followed her calling and went on to be the youngest librarian in the state to run her own branch, and she contributed more to her community than most.

Annie knew that Portia would make the best partner for the right man, but Annie was in no place to play matchmaker. She sucked at fixing her own love life; how could she help Portia?

"This case you're working with Josh—will it keep you from getting bored? Or will it add to your stress? You're supposed to be home taking a break from an awful experience, right?"

"I'm not going to have time to be bored, and not because of the case Josh and I have stumbled upon. Grandma Ezzie needs the full three months, at least, to rehab from her stroke, so my parents took her to their place in Florida. I have no idea how to run a yarn shop, yet here I am. No time for boredom." And now she had the case of Kit to keep her occupied.

"You're an excellent knitter. Didn't you win all those county fair contests in school?"

"Like, when I was twelve. Maybe a little older." Annie sipped on her iced tea. "Hey, what else do you know about Josh, besides what you've told me? I mean, since I'll be working with him, I don't want to put my foot in my mouth over anything that's common knowledge."

"Ha! What you really mean is 'is he attached?' Or has he been recently?"

"I know he's single."

Portia stirred her iced tea. "Sounds like you know more about him than you're admitting. You'd stay in touch with people better if you'd get with the rest of the century and join social media."

"That's not wise in my profession."

"His either, clearly. He posts under a variation of

his name, to protect himself from the crazy criminals he chases down, I imagine."

Annie paused. "I know it's in the past, but it bothers me that I never heard about his parents' accident until a week after it had happened, and I didn't reach out to him."

"What would you tell me, Annie? Let it go. We were a lot younger back then. Immature. And wasn't that about the same time when you dated that creep, freshman or sophomore year of college?"

"Don't remind me." Said creep had been the driving factor in her going for her psychology major. She'd made a great career out of what she'd learned surviving an abusive relationship.

"I know it was a rough time, Annie. I'll never get over how you've made the best from it, going into counseling yourself. You're my hero."

She squirmed again. "Stop." The ghost of that abusive relationship must have passed over her face, as Portia leaned over and grasped her hand.

"I'm so proud of you! That took so much courage. And now you help women in worse situations. Look at that!" Portia had always been her biggest advocate besides her parents and Grandma Ezzie. If she couldn't share her attraction to Josh with Portia, what kind of friendship was it?

"Thank you. And, Portia?" Annie waited for her friend to look up from her meal. "You're right. I do have the hots for one of Silver Valley's finest."

Annie spent the rest of the weekend organizing new inventory that had arrived in her first couple of weeks at the shop. She'd gotten all but a few packages stocked, which she found herself doing to keep up. It was quiet, repetitive work that allowed her mind to wander and figure out how she was going to proceed with Josh. In the hush of the living room and library-turned-store, it was almost meditational. She loved how the tall library shelves were filled to the brim with skeins of yarn, yet still housed books in various locations.

Of course, she and Josh had agreed to not proceed with their personal relationship, but they were still both vested in Kit's case. And she hadn't heard any more on the case, but that wasn't unusual, either. She knew how her involvement in the ROC issue could go from absolute quiet to mind-numbing, in the thick of things, with a single phone call.

Sunday midmorning her stomach was beginning to growl, and she thought about leaving the remaining two boxes of merino wool sock yarn for later. A harsh banging on the front door of the shop startled her, and her awareness immediately shifted into hyperalert.

A large, burly man stood on the other side of the stained-glass window that covered most of the front door. His face was partially obscured by the faceted multicolored glass, but his heavy brows were visible through a pale yellow rectangle, drawn together in the universal frown of anger.

"Open up!" His shout rent the air, and she felt the reverberations of his pounding through the floor and her feet. Her heart felt as though it was in her throat and she froze. Feelings of cold helplessness clawed at her, slid over her skin. *No.* She breathed in and out, made her world shrink to her breath.

"I'm okay, I'm okay, I'm okay." Annie drew on the techniques she'd learned in therapy and taught to others. Almost immediately she was grounded and ready to fight back. In quick movements, she grabbed the SIG Sauer Josh had lent her from under the counter and then dropped to her knees to hide behind shelving. She plucked her cell out of her back jean pocket and for the second time since she'd returned to Silver Valley, called Josh.

Josh sat in his patrol vehicle, grateful for the quiet Sunday after the long hours at work as well as home. He'd put Becky's name on a waiting list for Upward Homes, but he'd wait to tell her. He'd been searching for a place for Becky to live while waiting for the ROC hammer to drop. Because it would drop. ROC was determined to bring in this shipment of girls and all at SVPD was on tenterhooks about it. But instead of emptying his mind for a relaxing meditative moment, a vision of Annie, her eyes wide and lips wet, haunted him.

As if his thoughts summoned her, his phone rang. He picked up immediately when he saw Annie's ID. He wouldn't mind playing with their attraction, taking it further...

"Avery."

"Josh! Thank goodness." Her voice was raspy and alarm in her tone clenched his gut.

"Talk to me."

"I've got a very large, angry man pounding on my shop door. Any chance he's Vadim Valensky?"

"Where in the store are you exactly, Annie?" He pulled out of the SVPD parking lot, ready to go wherever she was.

"I'm hiding behind stacks of yarn. The cubicle shelving unit." Her breath caught, and he heard more noise behind her. "He's trying to get in. I may need to use my weapon."

"Do not hesitate to, Annie." He turned onto the main highway toward the center of town. "It could be anyone, high on whatever. If it's Valensky, he's violent. Especially if he's been drinking." He put her on speakerphone and immediately called into dispatch.

"I was there when Kit told us, remember?" Fear ratcheted up in her tone as the man kept pounding. If he could put rocket boosters on his SVPD sedan, he would.

"Can you sit tight until a unit shows up? I've called it in and two are on the way. I'm close behind."

"I'll try." He heard her soft panting and it was from fear, not his touch, damn it. "Josh? Please hurry!"

"Keep me on the line, Annie."

He didn't have to tell her. Didn't he realize he was her lifeline?

Chapter 6

"Open this now!" the man yelled, and Annie prayed Josh would show up soon. She was trained to diffuse the most agitated suspect and had no desire to use her weapon if she didn't have to. And in the event this man had a gun, she wasn't wearing any body armor. She'd talk him down but he was far too agitated, the risk too high. Since there were no other customers or citizens in peril, she made the decision to wait him out. She hunkered down below the stacked display cubes, each slam of the man's fist on the door frame shuddering through the antique Victorian hardwood flooring.

What if Josh didn't get here on time?

Stern words from a loudspeaker or bullhorn let Annie know the first SVPD unit had arrived. The fist thumping stopped, and she wondered if the man would surrender easily. As she crouched in her hiding place, she saw his arms rise and he turned around. As soon as she saw two uniformed police officers escort him down the porch steps, she unfolded herself from behind the yarn stacks. Her muscles were taut, and she stretched as she watched the action through the huge picture window that ran the length of the front of the store. She wouldn't open the door until the police, or Josh, told her to. One thing being a civilian in a police department had taught her was to trust those on the call. While Annie had advanced defense tactics training, at the end of the day she was support staff, not an operative.

A second patrol car pulled up in front of the shop, next to the patrol car, and Josh got out. He nodded at the cops who were talking to the man they'd led away. They acknowledged him and spoke for several minutes, after which he headed straight for the shop.

Annie couldn't play the cooperative staff psychologist or victim any longer. Adrenaline coursed through her system and propelled her to the front door and she unbolted it, opening it at the same moment Josh arrived at the top steps, his tall body shielding her from anyone on the street. Several neighbors had started to spill out onto the sidewalk, watching as the police officers took their time with the would-be trespasser.

"Josh!" Annie threw her arms around his neck, needing to feel the warmth of his body against hers, needing the reminder that she was okay. She breathed in his scent through his uniform, hating that there was a layer of body armor between her and him.

"Damn it, Annie, you should have stayed inside." His voice was gruff as he spoke into her hair, but his arms held her super tight for a split second, so tight she couldn't breathe. She loved it.

"Is it Valensky?" She pulled away enough to look up at him, soaking in every ounce of his energy. The relief in his eyes was palpable.

"Back inside. Now." He spun her around and gently but firmly shoved her across the threshold, closing the door behind them.

She stepped away and held on to the customer counter. Her knees shook, and she fought to calm her racing thoughts. "Sorry. I need a minute." Her jaw hurt, and she knew it was from the stress but couldn't stop it.

Warm hands on her shoulders, kneading out the knots. As if he knew her better than she knew herself. "It's all right. It's the adrenaline. You've experienced it before, I'm sure. It'll pass."

She nodded, unable to turn around and face him. She'd just thrown herself at him, as if she hadn't told him weeks ago that they needed to keep their distance, keep things professional. No personal relationship allowed. His hands were like liquid comfort as he stroked her muscles, easing the tension that had built from the physical exertion of stocking the store today and then the shock of the thug pounding on her door. When the heat started to become more than what she'd expect from a massage therapist, she shrugged out of his touch and turned to face him.

Mistake. He stood only inches from her, his chest at her eye level, his tight T-shirt leaving little to the imagination. This was a man who took good care of himself, in a gym and out. He radiated a sense of health and vitality that fortified her attraction to him. His skin was tanned from what she imagined was hours of outdoor time, and she wondered if he hiked or biked the Pennsylvania trails.

"Annie." His voice reached her, his hands on her shoulders, as he helped her stay grounded. She met his gaze. He knew she'd been checking him out, and she suspected he'd been doing the same, from the heat that simmered between them. "You okay?"

"Yes. Sorry that I, um, jumped you." Wrong word—jump was what she wanted to do. Embarrassment flared and she felt eighteen again, not knowing exactly how to help him with his condom after the prom. "I was a little freaked out, I guess."

"Come here." He enveloped her in a hug, a very safe hug as he didn't try to press her against his chest or grind his pelvis against hers, which was quite a shame, really. But very gentlemanly. Very Josh.

"You always put others ahead of yourself." She spoke to his badge and uniform pocket, her cheek pressed against his shirt again.

His hands stilled, impressing comfort on her back. "What did you say that night a couple of weeks ago, Annie? When I thanked you for reporting what you thought about Kit? It's my job."

She didn't reply, just soaked up the reassurance that only a man who knew what she'd been through the past weeks and months could give. He didn't know everything about her, though. Josh had no clue why she'd come back to Silver Valley, besides Grandma Ezzie's stroke.

"Thanks. I'm good." She pulled back and he dropped his arms. "Was that man screaming for me to open the door Valensky?" She had to stay focused on the case. Couldn't spend one extra minute on Josh, on how he made her feel. She'd almost told him about Rick and his wife. That kind of confession was for a best friend or long-term lover.

You're leaving after only two more months. Drop it.

He shook his head. "No. It's one of his thugs, though. But we don't have anything else on him. Even today, all he's done is shown up and made a public nuisance of himself on a Sunday morning."

"The shop is closed. The sign says as much. There was no need for him to pound like that." Anger rose and she clenched her fists. "Who does he think he is?"

"He was testing to see if Kit's here. Valensky's realized she's not at school and he's panicking, is my guess. We pressed charges, and he's trying to regain control." Josh walked over to where the single serve coffee maker sat and raised a brow. "May I?"

"Sure, go ahead. There's milk in the mini fridge."

"It's a typical scare tactic, Annie. If you'd opened the door, I doubt this loser would have hurt you. He would have said he was looking for Kit maybe, maybe not. But he'd have gotten the message across to you that Valensky knows she's gone and knows she was here."

"Hell. Is the ROC that entrenched in Silver Valley that they've taken to intimidating local business owners? And why didn't Valensky send someone sooner?"

"No, but they want to be. And remember, all Valensky knows is that Kit is gone. He has no idea where. My guess is that he found a receipt from the yarn store or somehow linked her knitting to here. He might think you're keeping her in your grandmother's apartment. Who knows? He may be nervous that she's either turned him in or…" He paused as he stirred a drop of milk into his coffee.

"Or?"

"Or that someone higher up the ROC food chain has nabbed her. It's cutthroat. I don't have to tell you that."

She swallowed. "No, you don't. But we know Kit's still in the shelter, right?"

"Yes. I haven't received word to the contrary."

"You don't check up on the women you send to shelters?"

"No, because we, and I, don't send anyone anywhere. Kit went to the shelter of her own volition, as was necessary. She has a social worker and legal counsel, at her request. I'll see her again when Valensky's arraignment comes up, if she still agrees to testify."

"Will you arrest this man who was pounding down my door?"

"Doubtful. My officers are on it, but there's nothing to do, save for them to write him up for public disturbance. He hasn't committed any other crime, as we can't charge him with scaring the crap out of you. And he's not Valensky."

She looked at him. "You really want Valensky locked up. For more than the domestic."

"You picked that up, eh?"

She laughed. "I want you to get him, too." Of course, she wanted every man who'd ever abused a woman or child behind bars. As for his involvement with ROC, that was more Josh's territory.

"And you're still not having any doubts? About helping out when needed?"

The look in his eyes let her know he meant more than doubt about helping SVPD out during her sabbatical from NYPD.

"No, no doubts."

"That's good to know." But he didn't look happy about it, showing he understood what she meant. She was happy to work with him but not willing for it to be more, no matter how much he promised her there would be no strings attached.

There was no such thing with Joshua Avery. It'd been a lifetime and several life lessons ago, but she'd known from the moment she'd spied him in her tenth grade physics class that he was special. They shared a unique bond and chemistry all those years ago when they were too young to do much about it. Now that they were adults, doing anything about it was too dangerous.

"What, Annie? Tell me." He sipped from a paper cup, his eyes missing nothing.

"You already know, Josh." She stared right back, unwilling to show a sign of her vulnerability.

"That we're still in the middle of an attraction that's bigger than both of us?"

Bam, right to the hot spot in her center. He made her legs shake more than the adrenaline had. Josh's voice was no longer what she'd remembered. It had the same sincerity and tone, but years had matured it, made it sexy as hell. Josh was sexy as hell, was more like it.

"Annie, I started to call you so many times over the last few weeks."

"Stop. We've already gone over this." She couldn't handle rehashing the fact that a relationship between them was such a bad idea. The thug's violent display still had her shaken.

"Josh, is there anything you want to ask him before we let him go?" A female officer stood in the door, her gaze moving from Josh to Annie, back to Josh. Annie felt exposed, raw. Where was her professionalism?

"Yes." Josh threw his cup into the garbage and strode out the door. The officer looked at her. "Annie, this is Officer Nika Pasczenko. She'll handle it from here. Nika, meet Annie."

The officer nodded. "Nice to meet you. I'm sorry it's under these circumstances. How's your grandmother doing?"

Annie couldn't stop the laughter that bubbled out. "She's improving, thank you for asking. Let me guess, you're a knitter, too?"

Nika smiled. "Of course. And I adore your grand-mother. And this shop."

"I'm glad. Please know it's still open, and I'm receiving new stock every week while Grandma's in Florida."

"We'll need you to make a statement."

"Of course. Although, you should know I'm working on the Valensky case, as well." Annie walked around to the back of the service counter and reached into her purse. "Here are my credentials. I'm with NYPD, but I'll be working with SVPD for the next couple of months. I've notified my supervisor at NYPD and he's sent the requisite permissions and releases to Chief Todd at SVPD." It sounded natural, as if she did this all the time.

Nika read the card. "Annie Fiero. Finally I meet the legend Ezzie always talks about."

Annie inwardly groaned. "Yes. So you already knew who I was?"

The officer grinned. "I was pretty sure but not certain." Spoken like a true cop, Annie thought. "I'm in here knitting every Friday, normally. Except recently it's been impossible to get away from work—we're swamped right now."

"I know. Josh filled me in." Annie wasn't sure how much she should reveal she knew.

"Glad to have you aboard, Doc Fiero."

The cop was astute and hadn't missed the PhD after Annie's name. Of course, Grandma Ezzie's bragging had probably been what drew notice to her degree.

"Nice to meet you, too, Officer Pasczenko."

Josh stopped home on the way to the station, mostly to check in on Becky. Her regular sitter, Tonya, was with her but it didn't matter; he needed to see his sister. Truth be told, he needed a break from work, too. Becky was fine for up to half a day alone if need be as she rarely strayed from either watching television or playing video games, and she knew how to handle an emergency like a fire, but Josh hated the thought of her being without him for too long a stretch. Even though it was the house they'd grown up in, and Becky was being watched and was comfortable there, he worried.

"Hey, Becky. Hi, Tonya." He spoke to them from the front hallway, seeing across the great room that Becky was watching cartoons while Tonya folded laundry.

"Josh!" She jumped up and her unabashed happiness at seeing him poked at his guilt for being away so long.

"Hey, sis." He accepted her exuberant hug and hugged her back, grateful to be able to provide her with any kind of stability and security. "What have you been doing all day?"

"Watching TV. Melissa called and we talked for a while." She loved talking to her best friend, like any other young woman.

"Define 'a while.'" He chucked her under the chin and headed to the kitchen. "Have you eaten lunch?" Judging by the orange peel, open bag of cookies and half-empty glass of milk left on the countertop, she'd not starved.

"She had lunch and that's the mess from her snack— I'll get to it right after I finish this pile. How's work going?" Tonya was a college student who made her tuition by caring for Becky whenever he needed her. It worked well as Tonya's classes were when Becky was in her adult day care program. It would be a relief to know Becky was living in a freer environment with peers her own age.

He had another pang of guilt. Becky deserved more. She deserved her parents, who'd been taken from both of them too soon. He couldn't fix that, but he could do his best to find her a good place to live and thrive. The thought of not having her here every day tugged at something deep. Ignoring it, he set to work in the modernized kitchen, making himself a meal to take back to the station. He had no idea how long he'd work tonight. As he rinsed his hands in the deep, farm-style sink, he wondered what Annie would think of the old house that he'd renovated five years ago. He'd brought her here plenty of times when they were teens, when its most modern decor was avocado appliances.

"Josh, I want to move to Upward Homes."

"Hmm." Becky had walked into the kitchen while he'd been daydreaming about Annie. He hadn't even heard her; he'd been miles away, thinking about the teenaged kisses he and Annie had shared, probably right on this very spot. He'd dated before, lived with a woman who Becky had accepted well enough. But

Annie—Annie would require more from him. She was all or nothing.

He tried to feel bad about the thoughts of wanting Annie in his life as his sister stood next to him in the kitchen, watching him spread the bread with grape jelly. Becky knew all about Upward Homes, as she'd devoured the brochure when he brought it home and did her own research on the internet. She knew its accommodations would give her greater freedom than she had living here with him, which he suspected was her primary reason for pushing it today. She was tired of needing a sitter, no matter how friendly and a part of the family Tonya was.

"Josh!" She grabbed his arm and a glob of jelly flew across the counter. "I mean it. I want to move."

"Becky, please don't do that." He wiped up the jelly. "I heard you, and I told you already, we'll see." He didn't want to give her false hope. Or himself. He'd been working on it, and Upward Homes might be the answer for both of them.

"Melissa lives there, and it's safe and I can have my own apartment and everything!" Her cheeks were rosy, and he suspected she'd been waiting for him to come home to talk about it.

"I'm sure it's a fun place, Bec. But I have to know all about it, and even if we can afford it, we might have to wait a long time for a space to open up." He'd finished the paperwork and in fact, they could schedule a tour at any time. His work had gotten in the way again.

"But we can apply now, and then when the space opens up I can move there." She was as focused as he was on a case, and he couldn't help but laugh.

"Okay, okay. We'll see about getting a tour of Upward Homes. Remember, we just got you settled in your new job, Bec. It's always a good idea to take your time with the big changes." He'd breathed a sigh of relief when the position for her opened up at the local thrift store. Becky was assigned to sorting clothing as it came into the facility, and she was able to talk to her colleagues as she worked, many of them friends from the special needs class she'd moved through elementary and high school with. Becky was a social creature, and she'd never make it in a stricter work environment. He'd sunk to his knees in gratitude when the call to hire her had come in.

"I love my job! I have to be there at 8:30 on Monday morning. I want to be there at 8:21, just to make sure. I don't want to be late, Josh. It's my job!" Becky also had OCD, which, while successfully treated with meds, cropped up as her being a stickler for promptness.

"We'll get you to work on time. No worries, Bec. For now, let's go eat." A meal with Becky was the highlight of his day.

Maybe later he'd bite the bullet and sign them up for a tour of Upward Homes. He sighed as he plated her sandwich and added a cut-up apple. His concerns over her hopes being dashed were selfish, really. Because it was he who would suffer the crushing disappointment if he couldn't get the very best for his younger sister.

Back at the station Josh allowed his mind to return to work, and what had occupied his thoughts more than even Becky these past several days.

Annie.

Frustration made his gut roil in an acidic mix of the crappy coffee in Annie's yarn shop and his reaction to hearing the fear in her voice when she'd called him. He knew she was solid with her police training, and it reflected on how she'd handled the entire situation. She hadn't taken any unnecessary risks, or worse, tried to handle it herself. Annie knew her limits and that was the best quality whether a cop or civilian.

"Josh, I need you in my office." Chief Todd's voice startled Josh. He watched as his boss walked by his desk without another word. Colt Todd rarely pulled people in his office this late in the day as he spent the time cruising through town, keeping his finger on the pulse of Silver Valley. The chief rarely worked on Sundays, but it was an unusual time for SVPD, thanks to the Russian crime ring.

"Yes, sir." He grabbed his phone and followed the chief into the largest office in the building.

"Shut the door and have a seat."

Josh did as ordered and sank into the comfortable chair in front of Colt's massive desk. He looked his boss over for signs of irritation but found none. Phew. The last thing he wanted to do was disappoint the man who fearlessly led their department through thick and thin. Right now was a thick time, with ROC breathing down their necks.

"You've been busy the past few weeks." Colt got right to the point. Josh had provided his boss with both a written and oral summary of the Valensky issue.

"Yes, sir. We're getting somewhat closer to Vadim Valensky."

"How's his wife?"

"Safe." He named the shelter, two counties over.

"But we had a problem at the Silver Threads Yarn

Shop just now. How's the psychologist from NYPD doing? And tell me, do you trust her observations?"

"She's fine, and yes, I trust her completely." He hated telling Colt the rest. "We had to let Valensky's thug go. He claimed he only wanted to see if the shop was open to buy some yarn for his girlfriend."

"But?"

"But we're pretty sure Valensky sent him to warn us to stay clear. This man has worked at the pawnshop with Valensky for over three years. Valensky knows Kit's come to us by now, since we pressed charges. He's covering his ass by sending someone else to do what he wants to do—sniff around for her at the places he knows she frequents, like Silver Valley Threads. He knows we'd take him into custody if he had the least little slipup. So he sent this thug instead."

Colt looked at papers on his desk. "Annie Fiero has an exemplary record at NYPD. Her boss couldn't sing her praises high enough. But he's worried about her."

"Worried?" Josh thought he had the corner on concern for Annie, especially after how he'd reacted this morning. Of course she had other people in her life, people who had known her the past decade while he'd not. He didn't like thinking about it, the lost time between them. He had to stop thinking about it as lost time, too.

It was one thing to worry about his sister, but Annie…Annie was something more.

Colt paused. "Did she say anything to you about why she's here for three months?"

"Chief, full disclosure, I knew Annie well in high school. Our families kept in touch until my folks died. She's helping out her grandmother, who owns the yarn shop. Ezzie had a stroke and has been moved to Florida for her rehab, to be closer to Annie's parents, who live down there."

Colt leaned back in his chair and Josh braced himself. "I didn't know you two had a history. What you've said is true, I'm sure, about her helping out her grandmother. But it's only the surface. She's here because she's on sabbatical."

"Okay." Josh didn't think this was the big deal Colt was making of it. People took breaks from work all the time. He was in the middle of a brief break from detective work, accepting the uniformed officer assignment as his schedule required.

"Apparently she's been through some tough times, work-wise. Her last client was an NYPD cop who was involved in a murder-suicide. Took out his wife before he killed himself." Colt's steely gaze was on him, but not without compassion. "I take it she didn't say anything about it to you?"

Shock rocked him back in his seat. "No, she didn't mention that to me." Shoot. That explained the extra defensive layer in her communication with him that he sensed. Except when they'd kissed. She'd been 100 percent open in communicating her physical desire. The memory made him shift in his seat. "Is it going to affect whether she can work the case with us or not?"

Colt shook his head. "No, it's her call. We can certainly use her, especially if there's a chance of nailing Valensky. She's already cleared with her supervisor and we've filed the necessary paperwork. You know, it might be good for her to be working instead of having too much time on her hands, even with that craft store. None of us are good at taking time from this job."

Colt looked over his desk, his office, before his glance landed back on Josh.

"She's not got a lot of free time, not with running the yarn shop for her grandmother." He sat straighter, his defense of Annie coming from a deep place.

"I'm not saying that running a small business isn't challenging work, but for a person with her credentials, it'll get old quickly. It's too far from what she normally does, which is saving officers as they grapple with the toughest things we all see. She's gifted, if her record is accurate."

Josh didn't doubt it. "Is there anything else, Chief?"

Colt nodded. "Yeah. I'm just back from TH headquarters." He referred to Trail Hikers, a top secret government shadow agency that operated globally but was headquartered in Silver Valley. The name Trail Hikers, or TH as those briefed into the program called it, was a nod to the Appalachian Trail, which traversed Silver Valley in two different places as it wound through the valley and into the mountains.

"And?" Josh prompted his boss, who'd stared off into space. Colt's wife, Claudia Michele, was a retired US Marine Corps General and also the director of Trail Hikers. Josh assumed Colt had unique if not privileged insights on some of the tougher cases that TH took on. ROC was small potatoes for the Trail Hikers, an organization that had taken down a problematic religious cult, stopped a serial killer who targeted female ministers and had helped stymie the ROC human trafficking op two months ago. And those were just the tip of the iceberg, an iceberg that no one but Claudia was completely privy to.

"And…we've got a big problem, Josh. ROC is always looking to expand, like any well-run business. They've been running ops up and down the state, and they keep coming through Silver Valley. TH has intelligence reports that state there's another shipment of underaged female illegal aliens heading into the area. This is larger than the case we closed a couple of months ago. It's clear that Silver Valley is ROC's pick to be their East Coast center of operations. Just five minutes ago we got a tip from the undercover TH agent working the case with Customs and Border Protection at JFK International. Eight to twelve women, all headed for Silver Valley."

"Thinking they'll be employed as nannies?" Josh had gotten educated on the extent of human trafficking in the area as quickly as the rest of the department. In a trial by fire they'd had to help dismantle a network of women who'd been forced to work at the local strip club. Those women had since received the help they needed and applied for T visa status, specially geared to assist victims of human trafficking. The women were supported as they started new lives in college or other professional training. Because of how they'd basically been smuggled into the United States, and the varying degrees of hardship they'd faced in their native countries, they were given an option to seek political refugee status and stay in the States. It had been satisfying to help a group of women who'd been so victimized on to a better way of life.

And now this new trafficking case reared its ugly head.

Colt let out a long sigh. "Who knows what they think? It's crazy. First, it's hard to imagine buying into the promise of a full-paying job once they arrive in the

States, but so many are coming from abject poverty, or are already the victims of the slave trade. They have no hope for advancement out of their situation. Coming here gives them hope, the chance to save not only themselves but the families they leave behind."

"Until they're working the streets or dancing on a pole." Many were younger than Becky, which made his heart hurt. "What can we do to stop this shipment?"

"We have to work hand in hand with TH, and to a lesser extent the FBI. I know your schedule and Becky's needs are paramount, but I need you back as a detective, Josh. What's the soonest you think you'll have Becky placed?"

"I'm working on it. To be frank, I thought she'd want to stay home longer, now that she's done with high school. Except for her mind, she wants everything the same as any other nineteen-year-old girl, or rather, woman, would. She wants her independence and to be with her friends." Josh was not prepared for the sense of deep loss that the thought of Becky moving out triggered.

"It'll be okay, Josh. You've been the best of brothers to her, and you'll continue to be so. But it's time. Let her go do her thing for a while, as long as you're comfortable with the living situation. Of course, I'm being selfish. I want you available to the department, and Claudia wants you working with Trail Hikers more." Josh stared at his boss, wondering how the man kept his wits about him, knowing his wife was in constant danger during an op.

"I do miss TH work." And he did. His involvement in the secret agency's ops were always local due to his responsibilities for Becky, but he loved being part of a team. And there was no team like the Trail Hikers. The best-trained, most integrity-driven operatives on the planet, in his estimation.

Colt's questioning gaze was on him, and Josh nodded. "You're right. I need to help Becky make the next move. This summer has been long enough." Becky needed, deserved more. "I'll check out the living arrangements for her this week and let you know the minute I find a placement for her."

"If you need me to call anyone, just holler." Colt Todd was well respected in the community and seemed to know everyone. He had no doubt his boss could yank a few strings, but Josh wanted to see how it'd play out naturally the first go-round.

"Thanks, sir, I will."

"No problem. As for the enslaved women headed here, we've got some indications that they're being kept at a place in town, and will be placed in the greater Harrisburg area strip joints, to include Silver Valley's, within two weeks."

"So we have to move against Valensky now."

Colt shook his head. "That's just it. We can't go in with guns blazing and roll him over. It'll spook the rest of the ROC in the area, and the girls will disappear quicker than we can click the cuffs on Valensky. We need to take it slow but with certainty. You're still planning to have his wife, Kit, come in here to give an additional statement at some point, right?" Colt knew that Kit had already given a statement regarding the domestic violence charges to another officer, at the women's shelter, within twenty-four hours of arriving there. SVPD wanted more information from her, though, on Valensky's ROC involvement.

"Yes, sir." Also on Monday. Less than twenty-four hours away. It was shaping up to be a hell of a week, and it was only Sunday afternoon. Yet instead of dreading the workload, Josh was buoyed by the realization that he'd be face-to-face with Annie through most of it. Working a tough case had its benefits.

Chapter 7

Annie woke early on Monday and made sure the shop was all set for the first of two clerks employed part-time by Ezzie. Both were trained to open as well as close, which would be critical in her ability to work with Josh and SVPD on Kit's case. Her hope was that by the end of her first month back in Silver Valley, they'd have the yarn shop running so smoothly she wouldn't have to worry about leaving it for longer periods.

The drive to Silver Valley's Police Department was a short one, a quick jaunt up the one main highway that bisected the town. The skies were the unique shade of cerulean that she only associated with Silver Valley, showing off the summer shades of green that dappled from the maple trees that lined the road.

As she pulled into the parking lot, she noticed a tall,

older woman in a dark business suit that contrasted with her slick silver bob walking into the building. Maybe the chief of police was a woman.

"Annie Fiero." She held up her ID to the security camera as she spoke into the intercom, and was buzzed in.

"Good morning." The receptionist smiled at her, and Annie couldn't help but smile back. The familial atmosphere at SVPD was something she hadn't experienced at NYPD. Her colleagues were in many instances just like family to her, and she them, but a sense of congeniality in the workplace wasn't as obvious as it was here.

"Hey, Annie." Josh stood in front of her before she could make her way back to his desk. His eyes were clear, and his gaze cut right through her as he looked her over from head to toe. At least she had on a summer-weight linen vest over her thin blouse. She wore a thinly padded bra but even so, she was afraid her instant attraction to Josh would be evident. They weren't in her apartment, or at an intimate dinner for two. They were in the dang police headquarters, probably the least romantic place anywhere. Except every place had amorous possibilities when she was with Josh. The last thing she needed was for her nipples to announce her private desire.

"Good morning, Josh. Any chance I can grab a coffee before we get started?"

"Of course. But it's not the fancy shmancy roast you have in the yarn shop." She detected an edge of sarcasm and bite.

"What didn't you like about it? You drank a cup of it with no problem yesterday."

He stopped in front of a high counter in the break

area and lifted a carafe of coffee from its machine. "It was nothing compared to this. Allow me." He grabbed a ceramic mug from a hook on the wall and poured from a battered and worn carafe. The rich aroma of fresh-roasted beans hit her and she smiled.

"Okay, you win." She took the mug and reached for the creamer. "It's too hard to keep coffee going at the shop all day—we don't have enough people in there most of the time. And there are a fair number of tea drinkers, so we needed a machine that handles both." She spoke in between sips of delicious coffee and equally palatable glances at Josh.

He stood in full police uniform, his body armor stretching the material tight and reminding her to not look down at his crotch, where his jeans had been stretched unbearably tight during their make-out session a month ago.

"We've got to be in Chief Todd's office—" he looked at his watch "—right about now. You can bring that with you." He poured himself half a cup, and led her to the end of the corridor and into a large executive-style office.

A tall man she placed in his fifties stared at his computer screen while the woman she'd spotted in the parking lot stood behind him, watching the screen over his shoulder.

"Sir, ma'am, this is Annie Fiero from NYPD."

Two sets of incredibly astute eyes were on her, but Annie didn't flinch. She knew better than anyone the value of clear body language to include strong eye contact with law-enforcement colleagues. If they saw the least sign of weakness, they'd have a hard time trusting her out in the field. Or in the office, which was indeed Annie's "field."

"Welcome to SVPD, Annie." Colt Todd held out his hand, and she shook it before she took the woman's.

"I'm Claudia. Nice to meet you, Annie." Her smile was warm, but the woman was clearly an über-professional. Not one hair out of place, and her suit was understated elegance that conveyed power better than a superhero costume. Just who was she?

"Have a seat, folks." Without preamble, Colt Todd launched into a quick overview of SVPD's current operations. "I tell you this not to boast, Annie, but so that you'll comprehend what we're facing. We're not the NYPD, we're a medium-size town's police force. But we've faced our share of big-city problems. Only last year we worked to wipe out a cult that had tried to sink its hooks into Silver Valley. And now we have the ROC playing chicken with us."

As Colt spoke, Annie was aware of Josh's body heat next to her. The leather sofa sagged as they sat side by side, forcing their thighs against one another. Claudia sat in the large leather chair directly across from Colt's desk, and while she didn't say anything, her eyes blazed with intensity. An energy Annie understood—Claudia wanted to get the job done, whatever it was.

"I've worked several cases and helped colleagues deal with the aftermath around the ROC." She didn't mention that it was an ROC op that had driven her client and NYPD officer to pick up a heroin habit after nearly two decades of sobriety. Or that he'd killed his wife before taking his own life, all under her watch.

Colt Todd had done his research on her, and she

had no doubt that her boss had told him whatever he'd asked for.

"Yes, your boss speaks highly of you. And I have to ask, are you completely comfortable with taking this assignment while you're on sabbatical, Annie?"

"Absolutely. I'm not sure how much my boss told you." Seeing Colt's serious glance, she was pretty certain he knew the deal. "I went through a lot these past several months, and that's why I'm on sabbatical. For a rest. But it's more stressful for me to not work. I'm sure you understand."

Colt nodded, but it was Claudia who spoke up. "Annie, I'm on staff here at SVPD as a social media expert. Officially. Unofficially I'm the director of a classified agency called Trail Hikers that is involved in the counter-ROC operation. Would you be willing to be read into our program as needed?"

"Of course." She understood that being "read into" any government program meant she'd have a special clearance and access to sensitive information. She'd also done her share of supporting clandestine ops while in New York. "But I'm only here for the next two months."

"Well, then, don't do too good of a job or we'll try to keep you here in Silver Valley." Colt smiled; she relaxed. If he knew why she was on sabbatical, he wasn't going to reveal it. Annie respected that he recognized it was her story to tell. She didn't miss how Claudia soaked up his presence, either. She made a mental note to ask Josh about it later.

"You don't have to worry about that." Her words fell into silence, and she inwardly grimaced. "Wait—that came out wrong. Of course I'll give you my best while

I'm here. I meant that New York's been my home and where my job has been for over a decade."

"I get it." Claudia spoke, her gaze keen. "I only moved to Silver Valley at the insistence of the powers that be—the government folks who started Trail Hikers. I was perfectly happy in my nomadic Marine Corps lifestyle up until then. My last few tours were in the Washington, DC, area and I expected to retire there. But then this job opened up and believe it or not, while TH is a global operation, I found out there's a lot more going on in Silver Valley than I ever imagined."

"As you probably already know, and stop me if I'm being patronizing, we tend to get a lot of overflow crime because of the three major interstates that intersect through the county." Josh pointed at the map that hung on the wall behind Colt. "I-81, State Turnpike 76 and I-83."

"Plus all of the state roads that crisscross the valley." She spoke as much to herself as them. "You have to understand that I'm not a cop, I'm not a detective and I'm not an intelligence expert. But I'm good at what I do, usually." She faltered, the memory of why she'd needed a sabbatical slamming her confidence. Again.

"Annie, I'm going to speak frankly. I'm aware of why you took a break, beyond coming to town to help out your grandmother." Colt's eyes were kind. "You're among trusted colleagues. You haven't known us long enough to know that, but I promise we'll prove ourselves to you."

She felt Josh's stare and knew he had to be wondering what the heck Colt was talking about. Sucking in a breath, she turned toward Josh, figuring that Claudia already knew what had happened. She'd have to, if she was willing to offer her a position, even temporarily, with Trail Hikers. Annie had no doubt her entire résumé and work history had been vetted before she walked in here, and she was okay with that.

"One of my clients, he'd been a longtime friend, died in a murder-suicide. He was seeing me for PTSD symptoms from an operation breaking up a child trafficking ring. He'd witnessed the worst parts of human behavior, as I'm sure you understand. He was a heroin addict and had been sober for years. Until…until he wasn't. He used, and went off the deep end. His wife managed to called 9-1-1 before he killed her, but we didn't get there in time. For either of them." She squeezed her eyes shut, all the while knowing that nothing could ever erase the memory of seeing the crime scene. "It will haunt me for the rest of my days."

"Each of us has our demons from doing this kind of work, Annie. As long as you're faithfully in contact with your therapist, and promise you'll speak up if this case gets to be too much for you, I'm good with you working with us." Colt regained control of the conversation and Annie nodded.

"Yes, sir. To be frank, this will be a nice break from stashing yarn. Retail sales isn't my talent." They all quietly laughed, and for the first time since she'd left New York she felt a sense of camaraderie with fellow law-enforcement personnel. Almost as if she belonged, which was silly. It'd taken years to feel part of the force in New York; how could only one morning at SVPD in Pennsylvania be so inviting?

After their meeting broke up, Josh caught Annie at the coffee counter. "I can treat you to some even better brew and throw in a scone if you have time. I'll fill you in on how we do things here." The words were out of his mouth before he took the time to engage his filter, and his immediate horror turned to overwhelming relief at Annie's wide smile.

"That'd be great. I have a cashier at the shop and don't have to be back for a while yet."

"Follow me." He didn't want to admit how easy it was to walk alongside her, to have her near. How had a month flown by? He regretted not making time with her happen, the consequences be damned. He already felt the gaping hole she was going to leave when she went back to New York.

Once in his civilian vehicle, he drove the few minutes to his favorite coffee spot.

"It's changed so much since I left." Annie looked at either side of the main highway that bisected town, and he understood her sense of wonder.

"Yeah, I have to say it shocks me and I see it every day. We've had a 500 percent increase in commercial construction over the last seven years, and even more the last two. We can't keep up with the increased traffic, and the school district is scrambling to build more elementary schools."

"What about Silver Valley High?" It was where they'd both gone to school, where they'd met. He detected a note of nostalgia in her tone.

"It's holding its own after the expansion five years ago, but the writing's on the wall. Silver Valley is going to need either a second high school, or two to three additional classroom buildings."

"Wow. It's already what, the second largest high school in the state?"

"Something like that. Silver Valley is growing, and encompasses more land and thus families than Dauphin County." He referred Harrisburg's county as he pulled up to the drive-through portion of the coffee café. "So while we're still technically a town, our high school is a full third larger than most of the Harrisburg schools." He rolled down the window so that Annie could see the menu. "What'll you have?"

Annie's thrilled laugh made tingles go up his back. Tingles. What the hell?

"They sure didn't have drive-through coffee places when I lived here."

"No, this just opened a few months ago when the owners expanded. You've been back several times since high school, though, haven't you?"

Her eyes were thoughtful. "Yes, but honestly I only come to town to see Portia and of course my grandmother. My folks moved to Florida years ago, so I spend my holidays down there, as does Grandma Ezzie. I haven't needed to know the town as well as I suppose I should. It is my hometown."

"It is." He asked her again what she wanted to drink and ordered both their coffees via the shop's intercom, adding in a chocolate chip scone. He paid and retrieved their drinks and pastry, handing them to her so that he could drive. "I'll pull over there, and we can sit on a bench for a few."

"Sounds good."

"Thank you. This is delicious." Annie's pink lips left a perfect Cupid lipstick mark on the plastic drink cover and he bit back an audible groan as his awareness of her shot straight to his dick. His dating life had hit the skids since Becky's school extracurricular activities had disappeared when she finished her public school education last spring. Not that he'd been serious about anyone at the time, but it was nice when he could take a woman out, maybe spend some intimate time together.

"What? Did you say something?" The soft furrow between her brows was almost as kissable as her dang pretty lips.

"No, I didn't say anything." He forced himself to stop frowning. If he told her what he was thinking about, she'd think he was a—

"Phew. I was worried you'd turned into some kind of a perv, the way you were staring at my mouth."

Horrified, he sought her gaze and the twinkle in her sapphire eyes reflected the sunlight and eased his concern, but not his alarm. "Are you psychic or something?"

"Not at all. Just observant." Bold woman that she was, she lowered her gaze to his...crotch.

"New York City taught you some things since prom, I take it?"

She jerked back, and her eyes widened and for the second time in thirty seconds he feared he'd pushed too far. Until she tilted her head and batted her lashes at him.

"You weren't complaining when we were together last month." Her lips distracted him.

"No, ma'am, I sure wasn't."

She sipped her mocha-latte-something froufrou drink, and he took a gulp of his black coffee. It'd been a long while since sitting next to a woman on a public bench had been so tortuous.

"You look really uncomfortable, Josh. No, I don't

mean, your, um, you know, that." She waved her hand in the general area of his pelvis. "I mean more along the way of being here with me. We agreed to keep it professional, but maybe going out for coffee together is pushing it too much?"

"I can't tell if you're yanking my chain again or serious, Annie. I'm a physically healthy thirty-year-old male. Single. And I'm sitting next to a beautiful woman. But I can't do a damn thing about it right now, right here."

"You think I'm beautiful?" The teasing lilt was back in her voice, and he loved it and hated it the same.

"Stop it, Annie." Even he heard the wolfish growl in his response.

"Why did you say you're physically healthy, as if maybe you have other parts like your emotional and mental state that aren't so hot?"

"You caught that, huh? What are you, a psychologist or something?" He stared straight ahead, preferring the safety of their banter to the heated direction their conversation had veered onto.

"Hmm. Not right now—I'm just a friend here. What's going on?"

"I'm questioning my sanity because I can't stop thinking about taking you in my arms and kissing you, making you as turned on as I am. I can't help but imagine both of us naked, and what we'd do if we were naked." At her silence, he risked a glance. "Annie? Your fancy-pants drink too hot? Did you burn your tongue?"

"Not at all." She jutted her chin as if she were about to take on a black bear that'd climbed out of the mountains. The obvious swipes of rosy red on her cheeks warmed him all over. He was affecting her, too.

"You sure about that? You look deep in thought."

"I'm thinking about what I tell my clients all the time."

"What's that?"

"You have the right to change your mind. As in, *we* have the right to change *our* minds. Maybe instead of agreeing to stay out of a physical relationship, we need to be drawing up some ground rules. If we were to decide to take this past collegial."

Her voice and posture were totally professional, friendly. But the heat in her eyes told him what he needed to know. As they stared at one another, she licked her lips, and with a start he understood it didn't matter if it was an unconscious action or deliberate. Josh wanted Annie with the ferocity of the adolescents they'd once been and the knowledge and experience of the adults they were right this minute. Holy mocha-latte.

"This could get dicey. Risky." He couldn't take his eyes off her wet lips.

"Yes, sir."

His phone vibrated and he checked a text. "Oh crap." He ran his hand over his face. "I forgot I've got to be somewhere. Fifteen minutes ago."

"No problem." She stood and threw her empty cup in the receptacle, tossing the crushed paper pastry bag after it. "My car is still at the station, though. I'm still good with time, Josh. If you need me to tag along with you I can, until you can take me back."

It was only a few minutes back to the station, but he liked having her with him. Liked how well they seemed to mesh. "It's to look at a place for Becky. She's eager to move out, and there's room at one of the best places in the state, and it's here in Silver Valley."

"That's great! And I'd love to come along with you."

"Then buckle up, buttercup."

As they got into the car and fastened their seat belts, Josh had to accept that no matter what he wanted to think, no matter how crazy it seemed to be that he'd hit it off with someone he hadn't seen for the better part of ten years, Annie Fiero was getting under his skin. This was the first time in he didn't know how long that he'd actually not been worried about Becky. Or at least wondered how she was doing. Annie allowed him to trust in himself and the choices he'd made for his sister. And whether she realized it or not, she was helping him see that his needs were just as important as Becky's.

Annie had worked a miracle.

Chapter 8

Annie couldn't tell who she'd shocked more—herself or Josh—when she offered to accompany him to check out Upward Homes. Because of her psychology work, she was very interested in seeing a new supported living community created specifically for adults with disabilities. But it was because of Josh's tension that she'd really wanted to join him. He'd seemed overly worried about Becky, and she'd wanted to ease his discomfort. That gave her pause. Compassion was part of the deal for her vocation, true, yet she hadn't felt this connected with anyone else in a very long while. To call it a romantic bond was short-selling it. She'd had two or three long-term relationships in New York but nothing that had stuck. After having such a creep for her first serious boyfriend, she'd been so cautious with other men that she knew she'd stymied her chances at a satisfying, longer-lasting relationship. But being with Josh had her rethinking her inability to form a deep connection. Had she always held Josh up as her standard for all men, somewhere in her subconscious? They'd still been kids themselves when they'd parted. When she thought about the years they'd been apart, her heart hurt. She didn't want to examine that fully, not yet.

Annie looked around the building they were touring. It was a nice break from the concern she had for Kit, and the foreboding sense that the ROC case could explode at any moment, requiring her full attention to life and death.

She and Josh were a half step behind the guide, and Annie fought the urge to hold his hand. He looked a little stunned. She leaned in close to him, just enough to catch a whiff of his sexy scent. "Can you afford this?"

His eyes exuded warmth and appreciation. "Yes, or we wouldn't be teasing ourselves with it."

"Then why do you look so overwhelmed?"

He offered her a weak smile. "I'm sad to see my sister move out."

The tour guide turned around and addressed them. "Here is where Becky will enjoy our group activities." Sandra Deal, the facility coordinator, opened the doors to an expansive clubhouse in the apartment complex. It included a large screen television, kitchen area and lounge furniture. "There are game nights, movie nights, cooking nights. We bring in students from York Culinary Institute to teach the residents different recipes, usually seasonal. This is to keep our residents from becoming lonely in their apartments and isolated."

"Do all the other residents work, like Becky?"

"Yes, all of our residents are high functioning and need minimal life skill instruction or assistance."

"That's Becky. She's fine on her own, but she loves being with other people." Josh's in-depth knowledge of his sister's capabilities and consistent concern for Becky was touching. Annie watched as he looked over every aspect of the facility and the empty apartment that would be Becky's if he agreed to it. Sandra took them through several rooms that were open to the entire community, including a library that had a comfortable sitting area.

"Do any of the residents actually use this library? All Becky wants to do is play video games."

Sandra laughed. "That's not uncommon. We have several university students from the education department who come in to get the requisite community service hours for their degree program, and one of them has had particular success with turning a few of the gamers into readers. I'm not promising anything, but once Becky sees that a story is behind every game she plays, she may show more interest in books."

Annie had remained quiet the entire time, but when Sandra took them into a fully modern gym and pool house, she couldn't help from saying something. "Josh, this is wonderful. Becky can work out with her friends and swim. She still loves the water, I'll bet, right?"

"You remember." He paused, and she knew he saw the same memory she did, of when they'd taken Becky with them to a water park. "It's her favorite thing, to go to the beach. And a pool is a close second."

They wrapped up the tour, and Josh agreed to call Sandra with his decision as soon as he made it.

"Don't wait too long. I can hold the apartment for

Becky for the next twenty-four hours, but then I'm afraid I have to continue down our waiting list."

"I understand."

They walked in silence to the car, but before they got there, Josh grabbed her hand. Annie felt the warmth shoot up her arms and to her heart as she stopped and turned.

"Thank you, Annie. I couldn't have done this without you."

"Are you kidding? You didn't need me—I was just your arm candy." She smiled, hoping to break him out of his serious, older-brother mode.

"No, not true. I'm not used to having anyone around to see the decisions I have to make. It's nice to have a listening backup."

"Anytime. Becky is so lucky to have you as her brother, you know. You aren't giving yourself the credit you deserve." Annie knew she was babbling, and she tried to keep her thoughts where her words were. Professional, friendly. But with Josh holding her hand under the apple tree, with the warmth radiating from his eyes, her attraction was on full steam ahead. As in she wanted him to—

"Annie." He hauled her against him and lowered his mouth to hers. She eagerly met his lips, wrapping her arms around his neck. They were in an isolated part of the facility, in a small parking lot behind the main building. Since the residents didn't drive, there was no need for a large lot and this was more like a garden courtyard, ringed with fruit trees and picnic benches.

His kiss rocked her as his tongue played with hers, his hands moving lower to cup her ass. It felt so good that she swore he was making her butt vibrate, until she realized it was her phone. "Josh," she groaned as she pulled away, beyond reluctant to end the kiss. She reached in her back pocket and withdrew her cell.

"Everything okay?" He stroked her cheek and she closed her eyes, wishing they were somewhere she could toss her phone to the side and make good on her raging hormones. This had to be purely chemical—true intimacy took years to build. *You had years together a long time ago. You have shared history.*

She reread the texts with increasing alarm. "No, everything is not okay."

"What is it?"

She looked up at him, damning the intrusion on their private moment. "It's Kit. She's left the shelter and is back at home with Valensky."

Josh took a step back and let go a string of epithets that Annie hadn't heard since she'd left NYPD. Before she could react, he was on the phone with Colt. The conversation didn't go well and ended quickly.

"What is it?"

"Valensky's checked himself into anger management rehab."

"That's a good thing, at least. But why did Kit go back to that house?"

"I can't say I'm surprised. It's not the first time a victim has gone back to her abuser."

Annie nodded. "I know. I was worried about the same thing. In her texts she says she's okay, that Valensky seems to believe her when she says she made a mistake by leaving and is sorry."

"Until he gets her phone and sees she's texting you." Josh's anger was evident. He was as frustrated as she was.

"She's smarter than that, Josh. She'll immediately delete these. And she can still call me under the pretense of needing more yarn. Although it's hard to imagine he'll let her back out of the house." She bit her lip, trying to think of the best way to get to Kit.

"I know you won't want to agree with this, Annie, but Kit may have done us a favor, as risky as it is for her. It's a long shot, and since she went back it's possible she's gone into denial again about the danger from Valensky, but maybe not. Maybe she was serious when she said she wanted to help us bring him down, along with ROC. With her back on the inside, we may be able to stop the shipment of women coming in next week. We'll go in immediately if she gets into trouble." His earnestness outweighed the danger he'd acknowledged Kit could be in, with no warning. Annie's gut turned hard.

"You're right. I don't agree with that. At. All." What. The. Hell. "Who are you?" She stared at him, trying to reconcile the man she'd started to fall for with the man standing in front of her. Did he really think it was okay to put a woman in danger, for the sake of anything? Dismay washed over her, and she wanted to get away from him, away from what she feared was the end of her possible relationship with Josh.

"Annie, wait, hear me out." He looked straight ahead. "Did you know that Kit has a sister in New Jersey? And she goes to visit her when Valensky gets rough. When I questioned him he thought she was there. He had no idea she was in the safe house. I reached her and confirmed her sister's existence."

"So she probably told him she was at her sister's.

And her sister, assuming she came over here the same way Kit did, would back her up."

"Right." Josh's expression was haunted. "Annie, there's more to this case than domestic violence."

"I don't want to hear it, Josh. There's nothing more important than saving Kit's life." How could she have thought that Josh was different, special? That he'd never do anything but protect women?

"I don't disagree with you. But it's a lot harder to help someone who's not taking our suggestions. And now Valensky's signed up for the counseling he needed all along. It's a better result than we often see." Annie heard the truth in his words but railed against them. She could still feel each verbal cut she'd received from her loser abuser boyfriend in college too easily. And she never trusted that an abuser could be rehabilitated. Sure, it happened, but not for most.

"He's also an alcoholic who needs long-term rehab. What about that?" She went to his car and waited for him to unlock the doors, and she reached for the handle after she heard the locks open.

Two shots rang out and Annie heard the ping of a bullet hitting the patrol car.

"Get down!" Josh's command came as she was already flat on her stomach on the pavement. Two more shots, the sound of running feet.

Annie looked up to see Josh running after two assailants. They crossed the street and ran in between two apartment buildings, with one of the men peeling off to the right. Josh kept chase with the one who went straight. She got into his car, shut and locked the door and called 9-1-1.

As she relayed what she'd observed, dispatch con-

"FAST FIVE" READER SURVEY

Your participation entitles you to:
✳ **4 Thank-You Gifts Worth Over $20!**

Complete the survey in minutes.

Get **2 FREE Books**

See inside for details.

Dear Reader,

Since you are a lover of our books, your opinions are important to us... and so is your time.

That's why we made sure your **"FAST FIVE" READER SURVEY** can be completed in just a few minutes. Your answers to the five questions will help us remain at the forefront of women's fiction.

And, as a thank-you for participating, we'd like to send you **4 FREE THANK-YOU GIFTS!**

Enjoy your gifts with our appreciation,

Pam Powers

To get your
4 FREE THANK-YOU GIFTS:

✴ Quickly complete the "Fast Five" Reader Survey
and return the insert.

▼ DETACH AND MAIL CARD TODAY! ▼

"FAST FIVE" READER SURVEY

1 Do you sometimes read a book a second or third time? ○ Yes ○ No

2 Do you often choose reading over other forms of entertainment such as television? ○ Yes ○ No

3 When you were a child, did someone regularly read aloud to you? ○ Yes ○ No

4 Do you sometimes take a book with you when you travel outside the home? ○ Yes ○ No

5 In addition to books, do you regularly read newspapers and magazines? ○ Yes ○ No

YES! I have completed the above Reader Survey. Please send me my 4 FREE GIFTS (gifts worth over $20 retail). I understand that I am under no obligation to buy anything, as explained on the back of this card.

240/340 HDL GM37

FIRST NAME	LAST NAME

ADDRESS

APT.#	CITY

STATE/PROV.	ZIP/POSTAL CODE

firmed they had a nearby unit that would meet Josh. Annie was to stay put and keep low in the seat of the car, until an SVPD unit arrived. She saw Josh take down the man he chased, just as sirens sounded.

"Officer Avery is in between the apartment buildings at 500 West Third Avenue, with a suspect on the ground. He's disarmed him now. I have no idea where the other suspect went." She watched as Josh, still holding the thug's hands behind him, his knee into the man's back, slid a pistol across the concrete, out of arm's reach.

The next twenty minutes were a blur as police units arrived, the suspect was handcuffed and read his rights, and Josh spoke with the other officers. Annie had nothing to add but support for Josh, but she'd only be in the way if she got out of the car now.

As the suspect was turned around and led to the SVPD vehicle closest to her, she saw his face. Icy dread swirled in her belly.

It was the man who'd tried to break into her shop.

"Annie, unlock the door." Josh was knocking on the window, waiting for her to open up.

She forced her shaking fingers to hit the switch, and Josh hauled her out of the car and pressed her to him.

"Josh, it was the man from the store the other day, with an accomplice."

"They wanted to scare us."

"More like kill us!"

"No, he's one of Valensky's thugs. He admitted it as I was cuffing him. He doesn't want to do time for a loser like Valensky. But he's going to. After we get the information we need from him. I'm angry I didn't get the other one."

She held on tight to Josh, needing to feel the warmth of his heat through his shirt, on her cheek, against her body. "You could have been shot, Josh. It's a big deal that you caught one of them."

"I wasn't. If they'd wanted to take us out, he had a free shot. Their goal was to shake us up, make us want to think twice about fighting Valensky and ROC."

The thugs hadn't succeeded. Anger started to simmer as the reality hit Annie. Her conviction to help keep ROC out of Silver Valley was strengthened, not deterred, by the loser's foul play.

"Thank you, Annie." Josh's hand pressed firmly on her back and he spoke into her ear, his sincerity unmistakable.

"Thank me? You're the one who caught the bad guy!"

"One of them, at least."

Josh pulled back and looked into her eyes. She waited for what he'd say, but instead he kissed her long and hard, in full view of the SVPD officers on-site. And Annie let him. He wasn't injured, the bad guy hadn't managed to hurt either of them, and they could work out whatever else they had to.

For now, that was what mattered.

Josh and Annie drove back to SVPD in silence. Their earlier argument over using Kit to bring down ROC seemed a year ago instead of an hour. She didn't want to look at him, didn't want him to see her vulnerability, but his hand found hers and it didn't feel like it belonged to a man who didn't care about women. Josh was law enforcement and she'd learned at NYPD that solving the case almost always came first. A hard line but necessary. She'd been too quick to doubt him.

Josh was doing his job, nothing less. She grasped his hand back but couldn't look at him, not with the tear that fell down her cheek as she gazed out the passenger window. He could have been killed in front of her eyes only moments earlier.

"Annie. I'm sorry. I didn't mean to sound so callous before, about Kit. If you think we need to get Kit out of her house right now, we will. We can drive straight there and bring her out. I'll support you in making it happen. You're the expert at this."

"You've handled domestics." She considered all police officers experts. They had to be, with the statistics.

"Of course I have. I was 'handling' it with Valensky, as much as it hasn't turned out how I'd wanted it to. I didn't want Kit to go back home. Usually my participation is either in the midst of a brawl or right after a woman's been abused. I've had to convince women to leave when they didn't want to, and I've done my share of wrestling an admission of guilt out of the abuser who's hyped up on testosterone and often booze or drugs. But Kit doesn't want our help right now, and Valensky's awaiting arraignment. And the kicker is that he's voluntarily checked himself into an anger-management course that we can't drag men to most times. There's a good chance the judge will let him go free as long as he continues to comply with his treatment plan." Josh's words caught her up short.

"We both know the chances of him never harming her again." About the same as him learning anything from the therapy he'd volunteered for.

"Right." He pulled alongside her car in the SVPD parking lot and shut off his engine. "Annie, what's this about, other than me being a complete ass?"

She wiped her cheek and turned to him. "It's personal for me, Josh. I've never been at risk for my life physically, but when I was in college, the first guy I got serious with did a mental number on me."

"I'm so sorry, Annie."

She nodded. "It's okay, now. It was the catalyst for me to major in psychology and go on to become a counselor."

"Where did you get your PhD?" His face scrunched up. "Wait—I know where. It was California, right?"

"Let me guess, the Silver Valley connection?" She smiled and he chuckled.

"You know it. Your grandmother has never stopped talking to the parents of our high school friends." His smile straightened into a sad line.

"I know Becky is the most important person in your life, and that it's a risk to have her get attached to me again."

"Yeah, she was torn up the first time you left."

She nodded. "Yes. And I...I understand if you don't want me to see her while I'm here." She did understand, damn it. It was going to cost her. Her selfish attraction to Josh would go unanswered.

"Why don't we take it a day at a time?"

"Sure."

Josh was around to her side before she had a chance to get to her car. His eyes were lit with something knowing she wasn't ready to label.

"What?"

"About taking things one day at a time. How about dinner tonight?"

She laughed. "What about Becky?"

"She likes the snickerdoodle cookies from Silver

Valley Bakery if you don't mind picking up dessert. Seven o'clock okay?"

She stared at him, not sure what to answer. He was offering her too much, too soon. *Liar.* It was all she wanted. To belong, to feel welcome.

To spend more time with Josh. Time without a uniform or a case to worry about.

"There's no knitting class or group tonight, so it's not like I have to be at the shop." She felt like she was on the edge of an outcropping on the Appalachian Trail. What the heck. "I'll see you then."

"Don't you need the address?" Grooves deepened around his mouth. He'd caught her at her own game. As if he saw that her heart and intellect were at war.

"You're in your family house, right?" A peal of satisfaction lit in her belly at his surprise that she'd remembered.

"Yes."

"I'd know my way blindfolded. See you at seven."

It was with no small amount of nervousness that Annie walked up to the front door she used to walk right through, stopping in the kitchen and grabbing a brownie off the counter. Mrs. Avery had made the best baked goods.

She sucked in a shaky breath. "Easy, girl." Just because she was having nostalgic flashbacks didn't give her the right to put her unexpressed grief on Josh and especially not Becky. They'd done their grieving, for ten long years. She was the newcomer to the party.

The door opened as soon as she pressed the doorbell, and she was immediately engulfed in a huge bear hug.

"Annie! I'm so glad to see you!" Becky held her

tight, and it wasn't the diminutive Becky she'd known in high school, who'd only been seven or eight. This was an adult, but with Becky's exuberance and joy. For the second time in the same day, Annie couldn't stop the tears from flowing.

"Let me look at you." She held Becky out at arm's length and looked at the features that were the exact feminine replica of Josh's. Gone was the little girl button nose and missing front teeth; a beautiful young woman stood in her place.

"You're taller than me! Not fair." She smiled at Becky and was rewarded with the widest grin possible. The guilt at not being here in the time after their parents had died tried to press past the happy reunion, but it couldn't surpass the fact that Becky was obviously thrilled to see her.

"Bring Annie in, Bec." Josh's voice sounded from the back of the house, and Becky groaned.

"Coming, Josh." She looked at Annie. "Will you please come in?"

"Thank you." Familiar warmth enveloped her as a tsunami of memories washed over her. She and Josh coming in after school; she and Josh doing algebra, geometry and eventually calculus at the scarred maple farm table that she saw the minute she stepped into the living room, part of a great room that connected with the open kitchen.

Josh stood at a large island, chopping carrots. His figure was as incongruous with her memories of the lanky boy he'd been as the whitewashed oak cabinets and stainless-steel appliances were to the memory she had of the original dark-paneled kitchen.

He looked up and met her eyes. "Hey, Annie."

"Hey." The kitchen might be modernized, but she was awash in pure old-fashioned lust. She walked over to him. "Can I help?"

"There's a baguette in that drawer—can you split it and brush it with the melted garlic and butter in that glass cup?" He motioned with his chin as he chopped, and she got to work. "Becky, please set the table."

"I did!" Becky answered from the sofa, where she appeared mesmerized by the electronic tablet she held.

"She's so grown up."

"In some ways, yes." He paused. "She remembered you." He spoke low and quiet, for her ears only.

"You must have shown her old pictures or something."

"Not at all. She's been excited since I got home and told her you were coming over."

Guilt crept in, raising the hairs on her neck and making her face flame.

"Annie." His hands were on her shoulders, giving her a rousing massage as if she were a boxer in the ring. "No more of that. It's both of our faults we didn't keep in touch." He turned her around, and the butter on the pastry brush dripped down her hand. He handed her a paper towel.

"But I knew. Grandma Ezzie told me, and I didn't know how to deal with it." It had been December, final exam time. And she'd been in over her head with the boyfriend who'd manipulated and verbally abused her to the point she believed she couldn't make her own decisions. He'd been so attractive at first, his famous artist family luring her into thinking he was creative and loving, too. Until he started demanding to know everywhere she went, who she was with. When he tried

to convince her to drop out of college so she could be
with him all the time, she woke up and told him she
was done. She'd been lucky to escape his angry, violent outburst with a split lip and bruised pride. With
time and a very good counselor, she'd healed from the
shame of the abusive relationship.

"Let it go, Annie." They were inches apart, the
aroma of garlic and tomato sauce adding a warmth of
familiarity that she'd missed. Looking up at Josh, the
years melted away as did all the hurts, all the hard life
lessons. It was just them and it could have been fifteen
years ago, with big textbooks on the table waiting for
them to finish their homework as they learned how to
flirt over a cup of hot cocoa.

"Are you two going to kiss?" Becky's voice was
loud, insistent and completely sincere.

Annie jumped back and left the answer to Josh. She
had garlic bread to get into the oven.

They had a lively meal of spaghetti, meatballs, salad
and garlic bread while Becky told Annie all about the
new place she was going to move into.

"You've signed the papers?" she asked Josh as
Annie cleared the table with the promise of dessert
as her reward.

He nodded. "Yes. Thank you again for coming with
me today."

She shrugged. "You would have come to the same
conclusion. It's a great place for anyone, and Becky
will love it."

Becky came back into the dining room with a plate
of the cookies Annie had brought. "What will I love,
Annie?"

"Your new apartment. At Upward Homes."

Becky nodded. "I can live independently there. My friend Melissa lives there and I love visiting her. Our apartments are going to be close to each other's."

Annie couldn't help but laugh. "Becky, you're independent no matter what. Tell me about your job."

"It's so cool! I'm in charge of the children's clothing." Becky went on to describe how she worked each day at a community thrift shop. "When I move into my new place, I'll be able to have more fun at night. They have games and everything."

Annie's skin felt on fire, and she looked for the cause. Josh was looking at her with very hot intention in his brown eyes. She tried to frown at him, to discourage his silent flirting, but who was she kidding? She wanted him more than she ever had. Except, it wasn't going to happen. Not tonight, anyway, with Becky here.

"Becky, it's time to get ready for bed."

"Can I watch television for an hour?" Becky was on familiar territory.

"One hour. Then bed."

"Is Tonya still coming over?"

Annie had no idea who Tonya was but found out when Becky went to change into her pajamas.

"I hope it's not presumptuous that I made arrangements for us to have some time alone. Becky's sitter was available, and I can't wait any longer, Annie." Josh's implication was clear. A thrill of awareness pooled in her belly and spread to her most private parts.

"Um, where exactly will we go?"

"I was hoping your place."

Josh had seen all the signs from Annie and hoped, more like prayed, he hadn't misinterpreted them.

When her chest hitched high, emphasizing her delicious cleavage, he knew he'd hit pay dirt.

And he wanted Annie with all the intensity he'd ever felt for her coupled with his very adult needs. Needs he was beginning to think might only be filled by her.

As they slipped into the building where the yarn shop and her apartment were, he wanted to growl when she stopped to look at the shop's front door. "That was quick." The piece of stained glass that had been cracked by Valensky's thug was replaced with a new, clear red pane. She allowed herself a moment of satisfaction at the criminal's apprehension.

"Didn't it have the shop name on it above the door?" He eyed where a solid piece of unfinished wood rested in the frame.

"Yes, but that's an easy fix. I'll have the painter come and do it this week." She paused, as if she was thinking about going inside the shop instead of up the steps to her grandmother's apartment. "I should probably go and see how the cash flow was today. The funds get deposited right away, but the system has the transactions stored."

"Can't it wait?" His words came out clipped, and he mentally smacked himself. He wanted to seduce Annie, not scare her away.

Her eyes were half-lidded and he knew she was turned on as he, but maybe a little nervous as she softly bit down on her full, plump lower lip.

His dick was so hard he swore it had a pulse of its own.

"What, Josh? Don't you want to see the yarn?" Only after he counted to ten did he realize that she was teasing him.

"You have no mercy, woman."

"Come on." She turned and jogged up the steps, and he thought he'd died and was on the ladder to heaven with the full view of her hips she gave. She'd been so slim in high school, and the curves that had only made their debut then had matured into sheer feminine beauty.

She unlocked the door, and before it was closed behind them he placed his hands on either side of her face and met her lips with his. Annie's reaction was instant and she opened her mouth fully to his exploration as she hooked her leg over his and tilted her pelvis against his erection. Her mouth was hot, wet and as insistent as his, meeting his tongue's every stroke and thrust.

"Annie, where have you been?" He dragged his mouth from hers, reached to cup her breast through her T-shirt. She had a bra on, but thankfully it was pretty flimsy as he was able to skim her nipple with his thumb. Her groan was his crack, and he ground against her, grateful for the wall that was keeping them from collapsing on the floor and going at it like the teens they'd never be again.

"Josh, please don't stop." She leaned her head to the side to give him maximum access to her throat. When his tongue flicked under her ear and trailed down the satin skin, she groaned and reached for him. The pressure of her palm along his hard length, even under his jeans, made him worry he'd come right then and there.

"Your bedroom, Annie."

"Come on." She led him back into what he figured was the guest room, as it was pretty bare save for the queen-size bed in the middle. All he wanted was to be with her, inside her, making her come as hard and fast as he knew she would him.

"You first." He helped her out of her top, and stopped. Annie had taken off her pants, but he wasn't looking there, not yet. Her breasts were perfect, her skin glowing against the pale pink bra. "So beautiful." He reached around her and unhooked her bra, earning a throaty laugh from her.

"You know what you're doing."

"You've no idea." Still, his hands shook as he cupped first one, then the other breast. He savored the weight of them, the feel of her silky skin against his callused hands. Annie made sexy, needy sounds in her throat, and he bent over to suck first one nipple, then the other. He could feast on her all night.

Except his erection was to the painful point. Annie reached down and undid his jeans, shoving them away along with his briefs, and when her hand wrapped around his length, he almost came in her palm.

"Hell, Annie, you've got me so turned on."

"I know, Josh." She shoved on his shoulder, turned him around and pushed him onto the bed. "I can tell." She flashed a grin before she bent over him, taking him into her mouth. She was naked, save for the matching pink thong that only emphasized the hot curves of her ass. He fought from drowning in the sensations of her tongue on him, the sucking sending him too close to release.

"Not yet, Annie." He hauled her up his length and about died when her wet, warm center settled on the base of his erection. He pulled her head down to his and kissed her with desperation. And he was desperate—

he had to be one with her. Inside her. No more fooling around like teens.

"My. Jeans. Back. Pocket." He reached his arm out; he'd thrown his jeans on the bed on purpose. "Condom."

"Shh. You're getting yourself all worked up." Her sexy talk wasn't in her words but how her hot breath felt and vibrated next to his ear. "I've got plenty of my own." She leaned over to the bedside table, leaving her breast in his direct line of sight. Josh was no fool—he suckled the nipple, a charge of pure electric need cutting through him. As his mouth worked her breast, he pushed her thong down. Out of the way of her beautiful femininity.

"Josh!" She was ready, too. He watched as Annie ripped a foil packet off a strip—good, she had plenty for later—and made a slow tease of sheathing him. "You are so hard." She licked her lips and might have said more, but he couldn't wait. Not this time. Not after all these years.

He thrust into her in one single motion, arching his hips to be able to sink to the hilt. Annie's eyes widened, her lips open, as they shared what had to be the hottest sexual moment of his life.

"Okay?" He never wanted to hurt her.

"Incredible." She closed her eyes and started to move, her hips taking them both where they needed to go.

Annie allowed her body time to adjust to Josh, his length filling her as she'd never been before. He took his time, allowing her to savor his width and heat inside her.

"Tell me what you like, Annie." His words, whispered over her lips, made her feel desired. Josh wanted to please her above all else, and was willing to delay his satisfaction to do so.

She moved her hips in slow, deliberate motions, watching his pupils dilate as she encouraged him to start moving in, then out, then back fully inside her.

"I like it like this, Josh. Slow. Deep. Just you and me." She spoke slowly, as if she still had control over her voice, when in fact she was on the verge of losing total control.

"Then that's how we'll do it." She saw the sweat bead on his upper lip and licked it away.

"Am I torturing you?" She thrust her pelvis to meet his push, and the cascade of electric shocks their contact caused took her breath away. And still, she had yet to climax.

"Only in the best way." He kissed her deeply as he entered her again, inch by inch, making her scream in his mouth in frustration.

"Josh."

"Let go, Annie. Give me all you've got."

She'd never let herself go completely with another man. With Josh, she knew she could. She trusted she could.

He licked her lips, teased her with his excruciatingly slow thrusts.

"Oh my gosh." She bit into her lower lip, tried to hang on to sanity.

"Trust me, Annie. I've got you."

At his words, something in her heart burst open and she let the warmth and passion move through her. She was one with her desire as she allowed her body to move in driving need against and with Josh's. Her pelvis met his every thrust, and with each connection to her most private spot, she felt the growing waves of her orgasm. It was right there, so close, yet not close enough as they pounded, kissed and gasped together as if they'd made love to one another thousands of times before.

"Come for me, babe." Josh's face was over hers and she knew he wanted it as badly as she did.

After what felt like forever, she finally felt every muscle relax, then tighten around him as she gyrated her pelvis against his.

"Do it, Annie. Come *with* me."

He didn't have to say it twice, as with a quick shimmy she pressed her most sensitive part against him and her orgasm rose up in uncontrollable spasms, rolling through and over her decisively, mind-blowingly. She heard her scream and Josh's shout answered her, their shudders in tandem as they shared their release.

She collapsed on top of him, the feel of the soft smattering of his chest hair against her bare breasts so welcome. So right.

Annie cherished how they lay as one, she atop him, completely sated, completely at ease. His breath fanned the hair on her forehead, and her total abandon reflected where her heart, its pounding settling down, was. Trust.

She trusted Josh.

"Annie?"

"Yes?" Her cheek was still on his shoulder; her body felt like a tired cat as his fingers traced her back, rubbed on her spine.

"Thank you."

She propped herself up on her elbows, earning a grimace from him as one elbow dug into his chest. "Sorry—wait." She turned onto her bottom and sat all the way up, back against the headboard, and looked at him. "There's no 'thank you' for this, Josh."

"No, not for what we shared. It's always been here between us, even if we didn't know what to do with it." His face was relaxed. He disposed of the condom before he settled in next to her. "Thank you for trusting me."

"Trusting you? You're the one who's in the risky position." She looked him up and down and grinned. "Seriously, though, this is your town, your life. And you let me see Becky again…"

"Stop. No thinking, not tonight. We deserve to enjoy this, no stress about tomorrow."

"Okay. But, Josh, I am going back to New York in a couple of months. This can't, won't, be permanent." She felt like such a liar. How could she say this after the most amazing sexual encounter of her life?

"I know." He shifted, his hand under her jaw. "So let's make the most of tonight." He kissed her, and she marveled at how quickly his touch melted away her worries about Kit, ROC and, more importantly, her concerns about getting in too deep with him.

A soft buzzing reached her ears and she ignored it, deepening the kiss. Josh lifted his head. "Annie. It's your phone."

"What?" Crap, her phone, in her pants pocket, on the floor of the bedroom. She saw the screen light up and scrambled for it. She looked at him before she answered it.

"It's Kit."

* * *

Twenty minutes later, she and Josh were in her foyer and she had to swallow her sadness that they couldn't enjoy their afterglow a little longer. But duty called. Kit had indeed gone back to Valensky in hopes of taking him and ROC down. She wanted to meet with Annie at the shop.

"Let's go over our plan one more time." Josh stood at her front door, and she had to ignore the tug of regret, knowing he had to go. That they weren't going to be more than sexy friends.

And they had at least one life to save immediately, and several over the next week or two.

"Kit will be at the shop an hour before it opens. I'll find out whatever I can from her, then call you."

"No, don't call me. If Valensky's tracking her, he'll tap your shop's phone or intercept your cell conversations."

"Right. I'll meet you no matter what she tells me, at the Roaring Rooster, no later than ten thirty."

"Good."

"But, Josh, what if she wants or needs more help?"

"Unless she wants to come into protective custody or go to another shelter, she can't be seen around the station. And neither can you, not with her or close to meeting her."

She nodded. "Right."

"Annie." He put his arms around her and pulled her next to him. "No matter what happens with this case, you and I aren't done."

"We can't talk about it now, Josh. Tonight was…" She couldn't articulate it.

"Spectacular, a long time coming, fate?" He countered his serious words with a kiss to her temple. She felt his lips form a smile, his breath moist. "It doesn't have to be a one-time deal. It can't be, Annie. Not with us." He gave her a hard kiss on the lips before slipping out the door. She threw the dead bolt and wondered if she'd be able to sleep before her meeting with Kit in the morning. What had happened between her and Josh should be troubling her, too. But to the contrary—acting on her desire for him, without holding back, had been the most freeing decision she'd made. Ever.

That was what she was afraid of.

Chapter 9

Relief soothed Annie's nerves when Kit walked through the shop door, appearing herself, for the most part. She'd never get used to the incessant worry with each client who was in an abusive situation. The statistics were bad enough, but her own experience and how closely she'd come to not breaking free of her bad relationship underscored her anxiety.

Annie did a quick visual skim of Kit and saw that while her expression wasn't haunted as it had been weeks earlier, the woman still appeared on the verge of running back out the shop door. Annie understood. Trust in others was the hardest commodity for an abuse victim to regain.

"Hello, Annie!" Kit's cheerful greeting didn't match the wariness in her eyes. As if she expected Annie to reprimand her. There were still shadows under her eyes, and something plagued her.

"I'm glad to see you're okay. That was a tough decision, Kit." Annie fought the urge to tell Kit she was being flat-out stupid and should go back to the shelter ASAP. She'd drive her there.

"I know, I know. I knew you'd say that." Kit placed her laptop on the large round maple table. "First, I am so grateful for you and Officer Avery, and for the help I got at the shelter. But I had to come back, Annie. We have to get Vadim put away for good. Domestic violence charges won't be enough."

Annie's concern was piqued but she couldn't argue with Kit, not if she was going to help the woman. "Go on."

"I told Vadim I had to be at class early, and if he finds out I'm here I have a good enough excuse, but I'd rather not take any extra chances. Not this soon after going back home. I have to make this short. It's not just about me, Annie." She wanted to press Kit and see if she knew about the ROC's ongoing trafficking op, but remained silent.

"Understood. Here, I've made a pot of tea." She motioned to the tray she'd brought down from upstairs. "I opened an hour earlier than the posted hours so that we'd have privacy." As Annie made her way into a chair at the table, Kit pulled out a half-done lace shawl and held it in front of her.

"As you can see, I need 'help.'" Kit smirked through the hole she'd made in the shawl. She laid the shawl on the table and slid it over to Annie.

"I remember when you bought the cashmere blend for this." Annie frowned. "But you didn't have to destroy your beautiful work to fool Vadim, did you?"

"I don't believe in half measures. It's a holdover

from my Ukrainian roots." Kit's expression faltered, a flash of emotion wrinkling her forehead.

"Have you been able to contact your family since you left, Kit?"

"Oh, yes. They think I live in a big mansion and have fallen in love with a prince. I let them think that. I'm not allowed to go back, of course. One thing Vadim's never done is allowed me to know where my passport is. And the one I had when I came is expired by now— you have to get a new one after only five years if the first one was before age sixteen."

"Yes, I'm aware of the passport regulations." And she was heartbroken that Kit couldn't go see her family. A situation that could change imminently. "I also know that you have a sister in New Jersey that you didn't mention to me or Officer Avery."

"I thought he was a detective?"

"He's both, actually. And stop deflecting."

Kit's positive demeanor deflated, and she didn't meet Annie's eyes. "I didn't think it was necessary at the time. That's where Vadim thinks I was. He knows nothing about the safe house."

"If you had a place to go to, why didn't you tell us?" Annie wasn't going to let up until she got to the truth.

"I don't know how safe it really is at my sister's. Her husband is in the same business as Vadim."

"Are they friends? Vadim and your brother-in-law?"

"No, not at all. Vadim had some kind of falling out with the big guys years ago. I've always had the feeling that he got me as an afterthought, a final thank-you. They're using him again because the stakes are higher than ever, with the women being smuggled in." Kit met Annie's gaze. "Yes, I'm sure he's involved, and that's why I'm here. To get your help. What I know is that everyone gets their cut, and Vadim gets a very small portion."

"Then why does he still do it?"

Kit looked at her like she was a toddler, uneducated in the ways of the big, bad world. "So that they don't kill him."

"Or you, too?" Annie knew that crime rings, whether a drug cartel or ROC, used family members to get their way.

Kit looked up. "Yes. Or me. So you see why I had to come back. If I'm in the shelter, I can't do anything to save those girls. If Vadim goes to jail, then the women he's working to bring in now could die. Then ROC will kill him, and probably me, too. They never leave a stone unturned."

Annie made mental notes she'd pass to Josh as soon as Kit left.

"Kit, what did you tell Vadim when you went home? Did he try to hurt you again? Did he? Hurt you?"

Kit's quick smile was downright cunning, but in the best way. "I did what I've seen on crime television. I told him the truth, as much as possible. Except instead of saying I was at a shelter, I said I was at my sister's. Don't worry, I called her and told her to say I was there if he asks. Her husband was out of town for the past three weeks, so he wouldn't have noticed if I was there or not. Vadim will never know I was at a shelter."

Annie fiddled with Kit's damaged shawl as she listened.

"Since he'd been so crazy and violent the last time he got drunk, he felt very guilty. He was more afraid that I'd gone to the police. When I assured him of course I'd never do that, he believed me. And said that he's getting help for his anger." Kit made a disparaging noise. "Not that I believe that will ever happen."

"Kit, are you sure it isn't a setup?"

"No, it's not. I know Vadim. He's a bad man doing some very bad things, but he's not that clever. He is an intellectual rock."

"He can't be unintelligent, Kit." Annie had wondered if Kit was identifying too much with Vadim and excusing warning signs. Signs that meant life or death.

"Not stupid, but not as fast. And he is stupid on one account, Annie. He thinks I'm shallow, that I only give a hoot about myself and my nice clothes. And he believes he's made me the educated woman I am now—and I allow him to think that. He gets to act the benevolent father when he's sober, and I keep him under control so that I can get what I want and really need. My education and freedom."

"Okay." For now. Annie would stay on her, make sure that if Kit needed an escape partner, she'd be it. It wouldn't be Josh, not with Becky in his life. Annie was free to take off with Kit and hide out if they had to. "By the way, Josh sends his regards. He's not here for obvious reasons."

"Yes, I understand." Kit fiddled with the stitches on the scarf. "Annie, you need to know that I have very important news. Vadim was talking to his business colleagues last night, and I was able to listen. He thought I was studying with my headphones on. He's helping another shipment come into the area."

Annie's stomach sank while her pulse ratcheted up. "Do you know what's in the shipment?"

"The usual. Women. This time from Kazakhstan.

They had a shipment of Ukrainian women stopped at the border last month, so they're being more careful, using different routes. No one knows about this group."

Wrong. Trail Hikers and a few key people at SVPD knew. Annie needed to get to Josh and confirm what Claudia had already mentioned. "Do you know if the woman are here yet? In the US?"

Kit paused. "That's just it. It sounded like they're already here, in Silver Valley. But they're being kept somewhere safe until the authorities stop looking for them. Then they'll be placed in clubs and strip joints, like I was. They are most certainly underage, coming here to have a better life than their country."

"What do you mean when the authorities 'stop looking for them'?"

"Vadim's conversation was very animated, and here's the most interesting thing. Usually he just takes orders and does what he's expected to do. They pay him, and life goes on. I get a new designer bag, and I get to pay off my tuition bills on time. But last night Vadim was the one doing the ordering, and almost counseling."

"Counseling or consoling?" She didn't want to criticize Kit's language ability as it was impeccable, but it was important.

"Both, actually. He was trying to calm down whoever was on the other end, as if they were afraid the entire operation was ready to blow up."

Annie's stomach warmed at the thought of ROC being worried about all the involved law-enforcement agencies, local and federal. And higher than that, when it came to Trail Hikers. The LEAs were all doing their jobs—NYPD, FBI, SVPD and the new-to-her Trail

Hikers—to keep ROC on the run and its members looking over their shoulders.

"Kit, listen. While it's admirable that you want to help, you're not a sworn officer. And you won't be alive to serve in law enforcement if Vadim gets wind of what you're really doing."

"Do you think I'd be able to stay in the States once the courts find out I was smuggled here?"

She could help Kit with a lot of things, including building her self-esteem to the point she'd willingly leave Valensky and never look back. She'd be able to keep Kit safe, with Josh and SVPD's help. She wasn't a lawyer, but knew how the law looked at women in Kit's circumstances. "First, as a victim of trafficking, you'll have options—you should be able to stay here and pursue the life you've started. And don't forget, you're a US citizen by marriage, right? Because Vadim came over legally, during the nineties, and became a US citizen?"

Kit nodded.

"I don't know any judge who'd order you back to Ukraine. You're in America for good, Kit." But Kit wasn't enjoying the God-given American freedom that she deserved.

"My dream is to stay here and work for the FBI or local police and help other women and children who are victims of human trafficking." Kit's resolve was stamped in her posture, with her chin out and shoulders back. "I could translate, too, if they speak Russian or Ukrainian."

"I want to be able to help you make your dream come true, Kit. But I can't help you if you're in the house with Vadim and he goes on another bender. You know you can always call the police, too, but again, no one can help you better than you'd help yourself by not going back to him. And it's not even his behavior we have to worry about anymore. Kit, ROC will absolutely kill you if they see you as any kind of threat." Annie was frankly surprised an attempt on Kit's life hadn't been made yet.

Kit's sober expression conveyed her comprehension. She nodded. "I know the risks, Annie. I'm willing to risk my life, because if I'm not, what has my struggle been for? Fate has placed me in the right place at the right time for this new group of girls coming into the US. I'm the only one who can help blow the entire op, right? By finding out exactly what Vadim's up to. I'm the closest to him, besides his criminal colleagues."

Annie struggled to find argument with Kit's reasoning. It frightened her that Kit was so willing to put herself in a lethal position. "I'm not saying you're wrong, or that you can't help, but, Kit, there are trained professionals who can do this. Without risk to your life."

"It'll be too late for the other women, though. You know that. You work for the police, too, right?"

"I'm permanent with NYPD, but I'm not a cop, Kit. I'm a psychologist. And I know better than most what you're up against with Vadim." What they were all up against with ROC. The warning shots at her and Josh were intended to scare them off the case. A last chance to tuck tail and run.

Annie knew she'd never run from doing her duty, and neither would Josh. Kit had the same commitment to justice, even as a civilian.

"I know you do." Kit spoke quietly, the morning sun reflecting off her cool blue eyes as it streamed through the front picture window. "I knew the minute I met you we shared the same…kind of history."

"How is that?"

"You saw the bruises, and you softened when you talked to me. You didn't treat me like another one of your grandmother's clients. And you didn't pity me—you still don't. You want to help, but you respect my right, my need to make my own decisions here. Please know that I didn't go back home because I'm in denial about Vadim. I know what a monster he can become. Right now, he's staying away from the booze. And I think he's very preoccupied with what he's doing for ROC. That's why I have to strike now, when I can."

"You're very observant, which is a wonderful asset for the career you desire." Sorrow filled Annie's heart. It wasn't a premonition, just plain statistics. Women who went back to their abuser were far less likely to survive.

"You worry I won't live to see my career dreams come true. But I worry that I'll never be able to live with myself if I don't help save these women from the fate I've had. And I've had it easy, Annie. Most of the women I came over with are probably already dead, or still working as prostitutes or strippers."

Annie sighed. "You've done your research, then."

"Research is all I've been able to do since I became Vadim's wife. Now I can take action. Please understand, Annie."

Much as it pained her to admit it, she did understand Kit's need for justice. If she thought there was an iota of vengeance in Kit's motivation toward Vadim, she'd call her on it. But there wasn't anything in Kit's expression but sincerity. Truth.

"I understand that you want to get Vadim locked up. And save the other women. But the only thing that you have control over is how you're going to handle Vadim going forward. I can promise you that all kinds of law enforcement is fighting the human trafficking issue, but no one can ever predict the outcome of these cases. It's one at a time, all dependent on timing in most instances."

"You will tell Officer Josh that we met, no?" Kit refused to answer Annie's request. Sadly, Annie understood. She'd probably do the same in Kit's position.

"Yes. But not here, and I won't go straight to SVPD, either. We're all about protecting you, Kit."

"I know this, and I believe you. This isn't about Silver Valley police or you or anyone but me. I'd never be able to enjoy any independence I may get in the future if I don't do all in my power to prevent other future groups of women from being trafficked."

"Understood."

"Tell me something, Annie. You and Joshua—you are more than friends, right?"

"Did my grandmother tell you that?" She knew Kit and Ezzie were close, but had hoped her grandmother had kept Annie's personal business private. Grandma Ezzie had a tendency to talk a lot about Annie and her other grandchildren, Annie's cousins.

"A little. I know you dated someone in high school that Ezzie thinks you should never have let go of. And I knew he was a cop. She never mentioned his name, but when I saw you and Joshua together it was obvious."

Annie gulped. "Obvious?"

"Oh, yes. You have the roses on your cheeks when he's around, and he pretends he's not noticing you, but you're all he can pay attention to. You were both very professional with me when I came to you that dark night, though."

"'Roses on my cheeks.' That's a different way of putting it. I like it."

Kit smiled. "Americans are so busy, always doing something. I love being an American, but it is much different than how I grew up."

"What made you decide to leave Ukraine?"

Kit pursed her lips. "We had nothing. My father was a drunk—you see, it's not just a new problem to me, men drinking—and my mother worked so hard in the candy factory. Chocolates, like what you have but very different, very unique to Kiev. I was promised that if I took this job, and agreed to come here, I would be a nanny for rich people. I thought I'd be able to send money home, make a new life for my mother and my family." She shrugged. "Can you believe how stupid I was? I really thought someone would want me for a nanny when I was only fifteen."

"You weren't stupid. You were young and full of hope."

"You sound like you know that, too."

"In a different situation, yes." Annie paused. "I was never in as hard a place as you are, not physically or practically. But mentally and spiritually? Yes. I dated someone for too long, someone who robbed me of myself."

Kit was quiet. Annie added a thin slice of lemon to her tea, watching the sheer membranes lighten the amber liquid.

"It seems we both owe our future hope to what we

suffered at the hands of the men who hurt us most, then." Kit stood and picked up her backpack.

"Getting away from my abusive boyfriend taught me that I have strength I never imagined. I still haven't plumbed the depths of it." She stirred the tea, needing the distraction or she might jump up and beg Kit to change her mind. Kit didn't deserve Annie's anxiety on top of what she was taking on.

"I've got to go now." Kit pushed in her chair.

"Keep in touch. I mean it, Kit. Any little thing that Vadim does that makes you wonder or think you're in trouble, text or call, anytime."

Kit's glacial-blue eyes met hers, and for the first time Annie saw a new light in them. Trust.

"I will, Annie. I promise."

Annie drove straight to the coffee shop on the edge of town where she and Josh had agreed to meet. She'd never been there. The business was fairly new, and she liked the atmosphere immediately. The building was historical, and from the official plaque on the highway, the original building was where George Washington had met with spies during the American Revolution. As she walked up the few steps to the narrow porch, she noticed the smaller, uniquely shaped bricks typical of colonial construction. The aroma of freshly roasted coffee beckoned, and her stomach growled.

As the bell dinged and her eyes adjusted to the dimmer lighting inside, she immediately honed in on Josh. He sat at a table in the back, casually sipping a coffee as his eyes lit up when he recognized her.

And she felt like a delicious dessert as his gaze

warmed every inch of her. She walked over to him and he stood, his form tall and familiar. Reliable.

"Hey." Her greeting was muffled against his shirt as she was enveloped in a huge hug, which could be considered friendly, except for her body's very sexy reaction. Josh was more than a friend.

"You okay?" He motioned for her to sit, and she saw he had ordered her a steaming cappuccino and blueberry scone.

"I'm wonderful. Wait—how did you know this would be exactly what I wanted?"

"I figured you ate what, a tiny yogurt hours ago, unable to sleep in as you were anxious about Kit. You're running on adrenaline because she gave you some information that you can't wait to share with me." His eyes twinkled.

"Okay. Well, glad to know I'm a woman of mystery." She sat down and couldn't help herself from taking a huge gulp of the frothy coffee and a chunk of the still-warm scone. "Mmm, this is amazing." She looked around her. "When did this open?"

"Not too long ago. They were going to tear the entire building down, then discovered the front wall was part of the tavern where Washington met with the spies. The owners were able to convince the town and state to chip in funds for preservation, and they were in business." His short-sleeved shirt was tucked into his jeans, and she wished she could take it off. He raised a brow when he caught her staring, and she blushed.

"You're not in uniform."

"Chief told me to switch back to detective, and even if he hadn't, I didn't want to draw attention to us. Better if we look like a regular couple than cops."

"Got it." Did that mean he'd given her the hug for show, too?

"Annie." He placed his hand on hers. "I want us to be a real couple. However that can work out for us, whatever it's going to look like."

She met his gaze, and instead of the sexy heat he'd conveyed minutes earlier, she saw warmth and certainty.

"But I'm only here short-term. And Becky might be hurt again."

"Becky will manage with whatever happens with us. And I'm willing to focus on the time you're here, for now. We can worry about you going back to New York soon enough."

The desire to believe his words, to trust that things could and might even work out, was so strong, but so was her typical reaction to any man who wanted to make things more serious than a casual relationship.

"Well, the city is only a three-hour train ride away." She could picture herself coming back on weekends. Except that her job never gave her that much time off, and when it did, she needed sleep and quiet.

"I know." Spoken like a man who'd checked it all out.

"How's Becky?"

His smile faltered. "She's very, very good. Couldn't wait for me to drop her off today, and she'll move in permanently this coming weekend."

"How's her big brother?"

"You caught me." He drummed his fingers on the table. "I'm okay. It's tough—she deserves to have the most freedom possible, and there isn't a better place anywhere than what we've found. Thank you again for going with me to check it out."

"Stop. Back to you. How are you feeling about letting her go?"

"I keep forgetting you're a counselor." He hugged his cup with his hands. "It hurts, makes me a little sad. She doesn't need me anymore."

"Parents who become empty nesters struggle with grief. Just because your relationship with Becky is a little different doesn't mean you won't go through the same stages."

"What stage is kick-in-my-gut? Let me guess—it's right after tear-my-heart-out?" He made light of it, but she heard the sadness under his words.

"It'll pass. And it's a sign of the connection you both have. If you weren't so bonded, you'd never feel this way." She stared at him, all handsome six feet four inches of him, his profile strong against the antiqued wooden bench seat. Josh was the whole package. A public servant, devoted brother, superb lover. Boyfriend. *Boyfriend.*

"What? You look like you've seen a ghost." He looked over his shoulder and leaned over the table. "This place is supposedly haunted. Did you just see George and his revolutionary spies?"

"Stop it or I'll kiss that grin off your face." She finished her scone, conscious of him watching her slowly chew the flaky confection, lick the crumbs off her lips. His eyes narrowed and his jaw tightened infinitesimally. A surge of lusty satisfaction roared through her. She laughed.

"You're wicked, Annie Fiero." Josh missed nothing.

"I try."

He leaned back. "What did Kit say?"

"A lot. And let me say that we're never going to get her out of that house, not until she gets to the bottom of Valensky's operation." She quickly filled him in, careful to go over every point of Kit's report. "We're lucky to have her, but as we've already discussed, I'm afraid the cost could be too high."

"I hear you." He looked thoughtful. "Too bad we can't bring her into Trail Hikers. She'd be perfect for the op."

"She has zero law-enforcement training. And how can you totally trust her?" Annie was surprised he'd mentioned TH. "I've worked in law enforcement for the better part of a decade, and my clearance with them is minimal."

"True."

"What's next?" She wondered if he'd want her to do anything different in the shop, or even help bring Kit into SVPD to give her statement.

"What's next is that you and I need to make a date."

Color crept into Annie's cheeks and spread to the roots of her hair. Her eyes were luminous in the dim café lighting, and her lips were puffed, slightly open. Her reaction to his declaration was so natural, so hot, that he immediately grew hard as he watched her face.

"Answer me, Annie." It was all he could do to not haul her across the booth and kiss her.

"That's what I was thinking about earlier. When you asked me if I'd seen a ghost."

"Thinking of being in bed with me again frightens you?"

"No. Yes. What are we doing? Dating? I'm okay

with that, and I think it's always a good idea to be exclusive when we're having sex." She lowered her voice and looked around the small room. "I keep forgetting we're not in a loud New York café and that this is a small town. Small-town rules and all."

"We're a larger-size town, and the Harrisburg area is big enough to not worry about it. Except for anything about the case, of course."

"You didn't answer my question." She shook her head. "Never mind. I sound like a desperate woman, don't I?"

"No. You sound smart. And yes, I'd like this to be exclusive." He'd like it to be so much more, but there was no sense in scaring her again. Despite her constant reminders about returning to New York, she didn't see what he did: a woman who'd started to find her way back home. That was how he felt, anyway.

"Okay. Exclusive until I go back."

He laughed. "Your turn to answer my question. When are we going to see one another again?"

"Tonight works for me."

"Can't. I've got Becky. But I could do a lunch date." He waggled his brows at her.

"Sorry, I forgot about Becky still being home." She chewed her bottom lip, and he groaned.

"Annie, don't do that here."

"What? Oh, this?" She did it again, slowly, deliberately. "Okay. I won't. Why don't we see what the weekend brings? After you get Becky moved into her apartment?"

"Sure." His gut sank. As much as he couldn't stop thinking about being alone with Annie again, the thought of leaving Becky anywhere but the home she'd grown up in made his future seem bleak. Maybe he was taking this too fast, too deep with Annie. It'd be excruciating when she left.

"It'll be okay, Josh. We'll have things to do that will help distract you from your empty nest." Annie spoke with quiet confidence, yet the sexual promise wasn't lost on him. Maybe this next weekend wouldn't be so bad after all.

Chapter 10

"The women are someplace nearby. Maybe not Silver Valley but definitely in the county. No farther than Lancaster." Kit spoke with certainty as she sat again at the store's project table. She'd come in after one of her college classes, and fortunately no other customers had been in the store. Shivers raced down Annie's spine as Kit spelled out what they all knew was coming. A reckoning with the deadliest organized crime ring in existence: ROC.

"How do you know this?" The whole time she spoke to Kit, Annie watched the cars that drove by the shop, making sure none made repeat passes. She'd been unable to shake the overwhelming sense of danger surrounding them since she'd spoken to Kit. Since Kit left the shelter, in truth.

"I saw his GPS, on his phone. I couldn't make out

the town, but he'd put someplace in it that said it was thirty-three minutes away."

That wasn't enough to go on, but Annie would pass the information to Josh, whom she hadn't seen since they'd met in the café, and their texts had been completely professional. She shouldn't expect anything more—he was using his work phone, she assumed, to text her. It wouldn't be upstanding to send sexy notes to her, would it?

"Kit, how many times has Vadim been drunk since you've gone back to him?"

Kit's eyes narrowed. "Not at all. Why?"

"He's probably due. And I want you to be prepared." If it was up to her, she'd have Kit out of there the minute Valensky cracked open his vodka bottle.

Kit smiled. "Ah, but this is what I know for sure, Annie. He'll not take one drop of vodka as this operation gets closer to happening. This is his typical pattern. He's afraid to get sloppy and forget what he does in his blackouts. He's always hit me in a blackout before. He never remembers it the next day, and his remorse is almost pitiable. Of course, I do not pity him. I will lock him up as quickly as his belt reaches my back." Kit's eyes were cold and her mouth a straight line.

"Kit, the idea isn't for you to get any kind of physical revenge on Vadim. Let the law, and your testimony, do that. But you have to be able to give your testimony! If Vadim gets any hint that you know what's going down, you're dead. If ROC suspects you're going to betray Vadim, you're dead. They will save themselves above all else." She saw the steel in Kit's eyes and she got it; she had the fire in her belly to stop the bad guys, too. But she didn't want to die, and didn't want Kit to, either.

The shop bell sounded and they both jumped. Annie's throat squeezed tight and she had to force herself to focus on the man who walked into her shop. At which point her heart thudded in dread.

The man closely resembled the photographs she'd seen in his police file. Vadim Valensky never took his eyes off Kit, his eyebrows drawn in a straight line.

Annie's insides froze, and it seemed every second was an hour. She had to get to her weapon, in her purse behind the counter. Slowly, she stood, never taking her eyes off Valensky.

"What are you doing here?" Kit spoke to him as if he were a bug. The bravado was impressive but Annie feared for Kit's life. Valensky was so much larger than her and looked like he could snuff out her life with a solidly placed backhand. Annie watched Valensky for signs of imminent violence, other than his forbidding presence.

"I drove by and saw your car." He looked around the shop, and Annie tried to see it through his eyes. Yup, definitely a yarn shop. Nothing remotely linking it to SVPD. His gaze settled on her. "Who are you?"

Annie wanted to reply *The woman who was with the cop you had your thug shoot at* but remained silent, refusing to break eye contact with the monster.

"This is the shop owner." Kit spoke up first, and Annie's ire rose.

"I'm Annie. And you're?"

"Her husband." He thumbed his finger at Kit and walked around the back of a display, rudeness so much a part of his demeanor he didn't qualify his reply. Instead of walking over to him as she would with any other customer, to see what they needed, she took a place behind the counter, her purse open under the counter, weapon ready.

Valensky stood in front of a pile of baby alpaca wool, picking up a skein at a time, squinting at the label, putting it back. "Do you do gift certificates?" He spoke to a large display of sock yarn instead of facing her.

Annie and Kit exchanged incredulous glances. "Yes, we do."

"I'd like one for my kitten." He named an amount that would pay for the next month's mortgage with some left over for the utilities.

"I can make it out for whatever amount you'd like." Annie walked to the counter and pulled out a gift card.

"Vadim, this is crazy. I don't need that." Kit's conciliatory tone coursed revulsion through Annie's veins. "You do too much for me."

"You do need more yarn. It makes you happy." He looked at Annie. "She doesn't want a new purse, no more new fancy shoes—all she wants is to go to classes or to come here and knit. So she will get whatever she wants here." He thought he was coming across as a nice, generous husband and not the controlling loser he was, putting his stamp on the one fun thing Kit had in her life.

Annie riled at how he spoke about Kit in the third person but said nothing, hoping the smile on her face appeared genuine. Because it wasn't. What was true was how much she wanted to see this bastard caught and locked up for his many transgressions. As much as she knew his basic rap sheet—trafficking of drugs, weapons and possibly humans, what she related to the most was his abuse of Kit.

For that, she'd see him rot in jail.

She keyed in the amount and scanned the gift card, waiting to see that the system had registered the transaction. She told Valensky the amount again, to make sure he was certain that was how much he wanted to spend. "I can do credit or debit."

"Credit is for rookies." He rolled his *r* in a uniquely Russian way and shudders ran down her spine. Not from Valensky's language, but from the way he peeled one-hundred-dollar bills from the wad he'd pulled out of his pants pocket. He was a walking cliché but not in a good or campy way.

Valensky was the walking embodiment of a hardened criminal and abusive husband.

Annie accepted the money and rang up the sale, placing the bills in the cash drawer. Her fingers crawled from where Valensky's fingers had brushed hers. She met his eyes as she handed him the gift card, all neat and tidy, in a gold-foiled box. "Here you go. Thank you for your purchase."

Obsidian eyes stared at her, and when she held out the small box he grasped her hand along with it, his huge paws engulfing hers. Annie stared at him, fighting the instinct to pull free and run for the hills. The son of a bitch was trying to intimidate her.

"Annie. My wife adores your shop. It's nice that you have it, here in Silver Valley. I think you want to keep it running, no?"

She feigned confusion, tilting her head and squinting her eyes. "Of course. Why wouldn't I?"

He blinked and looked away, finally releasing her

hand. Valensky shrugged and gave a small chuckle. "These businesses come and go so quickly. It's nice to see one hang around."

He walked over to Kit and leaned over to whisper in her ear. She batted his shoulder. "Go. I will be home soon—I still need help with this." She held up the sweater she'd been working on, and with a combination of dismay and marvel, Annie saw that Kit had ripped out an entire day's worth of stitches, making it look rumpled.

"See you at home." Valensky's words sounded like a threat, but Annie knew she was adding venom to all he said.

It was natural to do that with a snake.

The door shut behind him and Annie stayed at the counter, sifting through an order of skeins that had arrived earlier. "Are you okay, Kit?"

"I'm good." She grimly nodded, her mouth a straight line. "Did you see him? He was thinking he'd find me doing something wrong, maybe in an affair, and here I am at the local yarn shop, knitting. He thinks he's made me the happiest wife in the world with his extravagant gift."

"Has he?"

Kit frowned. "While even I will not turn down two years' worth of yarn, what I'm happy about is that we've tricked him. He thinks he's so smart and that I'm stupid." She threw her knitting onto the table and held her face with her hands. Annie walked over and handed her the box of tissues she kept on the table.

"He doesn't think you're stupid or he wouldn't be worried about what you're doing." Annie's hands shook. Valensky could have turned on a dime and become violent, attempting to kill them both. And she had the creepiest feeling that he knew that she knew that. Bastards like Valensky got off on control.

"No, but for now he's satisfied that I'm not causing him any trouble."

"How long is 'for now,' Kit? Until you get home and he beats you up again?" Or worse. "The shelter is your best option."

"It would be my best choice." Kit sighed. "If I wasn't so sure he's about to do something horrific."

"When will you come in again? Or do you want to call me?"

Kit shook her head. "No, we can't risk that my cell's not being watched. I'll come back here in two days, same time. I'll text if something happens sooner and say that I have a knitting emergency. Otherwise, we meet in forty-eight hours. Does that work for you?"

"Of course. Kit—don't be a hero. If it gets too dangerous, go to the shelter and I'll meet you there."

Kit didn't respond as she left the shop. They both knew the truth—it was already too dangerous.

After Kit left, Annie took full advantage of Grandma Ezzie's part-time employees and set up the shop's schedule for her remaining two months in Silver Valley, allowing herself full availability to Kit and plenty of time to work the ROC case. And to have some space for free time, too.

Oh, who was she kidding? She wanted more time with Josh, too. She stabbed at the paper calendar with her pencil just as the shop bell jingled and Portia walked in.

"What are you doing here?"

"That's not a nice way to greet your best friend, is it?" Portia walked around the back of the counter and gave Annie a hug. Her brunette curls were massed around her head and shoulders in a halo effect, making her expressive eyes seem all the larger. "Rough day?" She nodded at the mangled pencil, still in Annie's hand.

Annie laughed. "No, not really. I've got the work schedule done early, actually." She couldn't tell Portia a lot about the case. Or that she was terrified for Kit, and the women ROC was moving into the area as they stood here.

"I'm on my lunch break and thought I'd walk down. Just think, if you moved back here this would be a common thing. And it wouldn't cost me hundreds of dollars to visit you in the city."

"It doesn't cost you hundreds of dollars. You take the train and stay with me."

"But I'm forced to eat at the finest restaurants, see every new show if I want to experience your slick city life to the fullest."

"I'm sure that your shopping expeditions have nothing to do with it."

Portia grinned. "Remember this?" She pointed to the short skirt and upscale fitted cashmere sweater that she wore. They'd found the outfit in the basement store of a designer studio for dirt cheap.

"I do. That was a lot of fun." In fact, the only time Annie seemed to have fun in the city was when friends came to visit. Her life at NYPD was hyper-stressed, hyper-speed, all the time. She'd loved the pace during the years after school, but lately all she'd felt was worn down.

"You look tired, Annie. What's going on? Is it the

case you told me about?" Portia wandered over to the project table and took a seat.

Annie watched her thumb through pattern books. "Yes. It's…awful. Human beings are capable of heinous things, my friend."

"Is it possible it's worse because you're still grieving Rick's loss? And his wife's?"

Annie nodded. "Yeah. I mean, this case involves the absolute worst kind of criminals, but you're right, everything is hitting me harder than usual." And not all of it was grief over Rick's death, but cycling through the emotions of getting away from her abusive relationship, too. "It's funny how I can tell a client or colleague to acknowledge their loss, to be kind to themselves. Doing it myself is another thing."

"The library has lots of social activities. We're having a gala fund-raiser for the homeless shelter, too. There's so much you can get involved in. It'd be great to see you more."

"I'll think about it." It would all depend on Kit's situation, and after this morning, Annie was certain it would be a hot mess before it was all over. That was in the short run. As for the long run, when she was done with her sabbatical, it'd be easier to return to NYC with the fewest ties possible. Getting more involved with the local community might make that tougher.

The toughest tie to break was going to be the one she was forming with Josh. The realization made her blink.

"I'd offer to go shopping together for a distraction, but I'm swamped with the prep. If you find yourself with some extra time this weekend, let me know. I have hygiene and snack bags to stuff at the homeless shelter, and we always need the beds remade."

"I will, thanks. But don't count on me—not with this case and the shop. My schedule is full!"

"I know. While I'm thinking of it, I need to pick up what Ezzie donated for the fund-raiser."

"She donated something?"

"Yes. She gives jar lid openers every year, with the shop's logo."

"Jar lid openers?"

"Yes, she said that as she gets older, her hands have been her biggest struggle."

"You're right about that. She only knits with tiny needles now. For socks and lace." Annie wondered how Grandma's knitting would be after the stroke rehabilitation. She'd spoken to her and her parents last night after she closed the shop and while Ezzie's rehab was going well, it was slower than her grandmother wanted.

"It's hard when they get older." Portia stopped at a short cardigan pattern, made with heathered yarn. "I want this sweater."

Annie walked around to the table and peered over Portia's shoulder. "That's a very simple pattern. I can teach you how to make it."

Portia sighed. "I don't have time now. Maybe after the gala. I still remember how to do basic knit and purl, but that's it."

"That's all anyone ever needs. Everything else is a variation of that." As she spoke, Annie's attention was caught by a movement outside the shop's huge antique glass picture window. Through the letters of the store name, she made out the same car that she'd watched Valensky drive off in earlier today. And as she looked closer, she verified it was him in the driver's seat. With someone in the passenger seat, another man, who was aiming a long-lens camera at the shop. At her.

What. The. Hell.

"Do you know that person?" Portia had noticed, too.

"I know the driver." The car moved away from the curb with a jerk and sped off. "Give me a minute." She pulled out her phone. Annie's stomach twisted in reaction. Valensky was after Kit and now in turn, she was in his sights. She quickly texted Josh what had happened.

His reply was immediate.

Thanks for info. Stay safe. See you soon.

"Why were they taking pictures of the shop?" Portia's puzzlement was nothing compared to Annie's distress.

"Not the shop. They're looking for someone."

"This doesn't happen to have anything to do with that case you said you're working on, does it?" Portia's concern was obvious, but Annie couldn't dwell on it. She had work to do.

"Yes, it does, but—"

"I know, you can't talk about it. I don't want you to talk about it, Annie, I want you to stay safe. Whoever that was did not look friendly. It's like it's out of a movie. Silver Valley is a quiet town. Or was."

"It's been a rough year or so here, hasn't it?"

"That's an understatement." Portia stood. "You heard about the True Believer cult that they took down, out by the quarry? And this past summer SVPD was involved in breaking up a human trafficking ring. Can you imagine? A shoot-out happened on the main highway between here and Carlisle, at that huge truck stop. Crazy, right?"

"It's life, unfortunately. SVPD has a reputation for handling high visibility cases." She'd been impressed to read up on the recent caseload. And a little ashamed that she hadn't given her hometown police force more credit sooner. It had never occurred to her to work anywhere but a large city, but that had been because she'd wanted something different than what she'd known.

"You know, Annie, it's okay if you've figured out you want to come back to Silver Valley."

"What, you're a psychic now?"

Portia laughed. "I've known you forever. And you were dealt a bad hand when your folks transferred to Florida and decided to stay there right after we graduated. And then with Josh's parents being killed, you and he had no time to come back together."

"Portia, how have you worked Josh back into this conversation?"

"In case you haven't noticed, it seems to me that Josh never vacated your heart, not fully. You and I never talked about him until now because I saw how much it hurt you when I brought him up. And we all grew up."

"Maybe you're right." She'd certainly had times of wondering: What if they'd had another night, after that awful prom? What if they'd even spent some time together at Christmas?

But by Christmas freshman year she'd been involved with her biggest mistake and most important life lesson.

"Give it all a chance, is what I'm saying."

"We'll see." Annie pretended not to notice Portia's

triumphant smile at her tiny concession. There was a lot reflected in that expression, most of it hope.

Hope scared the hell out of Annie. It wasn't something she was used to, not in her line of work or especially with men. Silver Valley and Josh Avery were changing that.

"Okay, I'll see you later, Annie." Portia left the shop and almost immediately Annie received a text from Claudia Michele. Good thing she'd cleared her schedule.

"I've asked you to come in to Trail Hiker headquarters, Annie, not to become an agent but to give you an overview of what we do. I've been in need of a local psychologist for several months, and if there's any chance you're staying on in Silver Valley, I'd like you to consider working for us." Claudia Michele walked around from the desk chair and sat next to Annie in one of two easy chairs.

Annie took in the posh yet efficient executive office that the director worked in, the several-inch-thick oak-on-steel door open so that Claudia's receptionist could come and go as needed from her outer office. "I do like how clever your cover is—with the Appalachian Trail reference and logo on the building and door."

"Yes, well, it's a good way to keep outsiders away and any enemy agents at bay."

Annie sat up straighter. "Claudia, I don't have any previous military experience. I'm a police psychologist, plain and simple."

"And that's why you're perfect for us." Claudia's face was open, warm, her eyes as sharp as those of the hawks that circled the fields between Silver Valley and the mountains. "No pressure, but I needed to put my offer out on the table. I know you're here temporarily, but I also understand how life can change on a dime."

Claudia's demeanor was casual, but Annie made her living deciphering body language. "I can see that you're apprehensive. Your tell is the way you've adjusted your bracelets. I noticed you doing it at SVPD and again now. And for what it's worth, I've no idea where my personal life is. You know about the loss of my colleague."

"Yes. I am sorry you had to go through that. Losing a colleague under any circumstance is awful." Claudia sat quietly for a long moment, and Annie realized she wasn't alone in her loss.

"You sound like you've been here, too."

"Too many times. Wartime, peacetime, it's all difficult."

"I worked alongside Rick for so many years, so many cases. He was the solid one, the rock when I was losing it and needed extra backup with one of the police personnel who was struggling with their addiction. To have him not only use again, but to deteriorate so rapidly, was shocking."

"Are you out of the shock yet?" Claudia's frank query was refreshing after so many others had tiptoed around her grief.

"I am. And now I'm faced with wondering if that hadn't happened, what other event would have triggered me taking a break. This wasn't an involuntary sabbatical. My superiors totally supported me in taking off but not for as long as I asked for. They're not therapists, though, and they don't know how deeply this affects me."

"I'm not a counselor, either, Annie, but I'm a combat veteran. While I don't go out on as many of the riskier Trail Hiker ops as I used to, I offer backup on many and I've seen my share of casualties. It's never easy, whether someone with a life-altering injury survives or dies. And how your colleague died—going back to heroin—is no less devastating than watching your partner die from a gunshot wound or IED. Especially since he was under your psychological care at the time. I imagine you've suffered from needless guilt. You aren't at fault." Claudia didn't have to open up to Annie and yet she had, a demonstration of deep emotional strength.

"Thank you. Yes, it's been tough, and yes on the guilt. My head knows it wasn't my fault but he was a friend, and it's hard to let go of a sense of responsibility for his death, and his wife's." Annie took a deep breath. "If you're still interested in hiring me after knowing how crazy my life's been, it's only fair that I take your offer seriously. I'll let you know if I decide to leave NYPD."

"Wonderful." Annie waited for Claudia to speak again, her therapist instincts on full alert. "And good observational skills about my bracelet fidgeting."

Annie laughed. "It's part of my job."

"Tell me, Annie. If you did move back to Silver Valley, do you have any idea where you'd want to live?"

Annie shrugged. "I could always stay in my grandmother's place. I spoke to my parents last night, and they're leaning toward convincing her to stay in Florida. She loves her rehab and has made friends. And as much as she loves the yarn shop, she's struggled to keep her energy up the past couple of years. It may be time to sell it."

"There are plenty of women in town, as well as men, who'd love to buy it, I'm sure." Claudia nodded. "The downtown historical area has thrived since we got rid of the cult that rigged our mayoral election."

"You seem to be very invested in the local community, even though TH is global."

"Silver Valley is special to me. I met my husband, the love of my life, here when I thought that time in my life had passed. But it's not only that. Silver Valley represents the best place to have a life for me. Members of every race and religion live here and enjoy the area. The children have the best schools, and we work hard to be a safe town. Not easy with a cult and ROC these past two years. It's what I wore my uniform for. Not perfection, but for the hope of a perfect place to live."

That made sense to Annie. "I appreciate the overview of Trail Hikers. Thanks for taking the time to talk to me, Claudia."

Claudia stood and walked with her to the door. "Thank you, Annie. And remember—the offer is open."

Josh told Chief Todd about Annie's text, and they agreed that Valensky was trying to unnerve anyone he thought might be associated with Kit and the domestic violence charges that had been filed against him. They monitored everything over the next two days, and Josh knew the op was about to go hot when Colt called him into his office.

"Come on in, Josh, and have a seat—I need to keep you up to speed. Claudia's joining us, too." Josh sat in the chair in front of Colt's desk, unable to ignore the deep lines etched in his boss's face. The ROC case was requiring all hands on deck, and Colt had been at the station and on surveillance rounds with his officers for the past month.

"We needed to pull Annie into Trail Hikers to get some preliminary training, Josh. She's spent the last forty-eight hours going through the basics over at TH headquarters." Colt drummed his fingers on his desk. "This recent episode with Valensky coming into her shop, then taking photos from his car, might be too easily interpreted as a precursor to him doing something like killing Kit. And the shooter in front of Upward Homes—he was told to catch your attention, and he did."

Josh grunted. "That thug caught my attention enough to get arrested."

Colt nodded as Claudia slid into the office and took a seat behind the desk with Colt.

"Josh."

"Claudia."

"Colt's filled you in on Annie's brief training?"

"Yes, ma'am."

It bugged Josh that Annie hadn't told him about the TH training, but she hadn't texted since telling him about the drive-by photographer maneuver Valensky pulled. She'd been busy and he'd assumed it was with her yarn shop.

"Good. She should be here soon, and we'll go over what we're dealing with. I'd like for you to work together as a team, as we go forward with the Valensky and ROC op."

He would have liked to have had a heads-up that

Annie had spent the last day or two in Trail Hiker training. Not that she owed him an explanation. It just would have been nice. She was his conduit to Kit since it was too dangerous for him to approach Kit directly. Not with Valensky's suspicions raised.

"TH training seems like a big investment in someone who's not going to be here in a couple more months."

Colt and Claudia exchanged a glance. "She wouldn't be the first TH agent or Silver Valley cop who came here from a bigger agency and was trained." Claudia's statement snapped Josh from nursing his stung ego that Annie hadn't told him about her TH business.

"Wait—has she said something to you about staying in Silver Valley?" Damn it, but he wished she had, that she would. Stay.

It'll never happen.

"Not in so many words, but since you two seem to be doing more together than working the Kit Valensky case, it's natural for us to think that Annie might have deeper motives for staying in town."

Colt's declaration shocked Josh. Holy hell, his two bosses knew he and Annie were an item? "Why do you say that?"

"TH needs a psychologist, and Annie is a perfect fit. She could do the job from New York, on a contract basis, but I want to offer her a full-time position," Claudia said.

"Not if I get her first for SVPD."

Claudia spun to face her husband. "I think TH's needs would be higher priority than SVPD. No offense."

"None taken. Because you're wrong. Silver Valley

is handling everything you and any of the other larger LEAs are. ROC today, a cult last year, the constant influx of drugs. My officers are facing burnout and worse with the workload. Remember the heroin OD you accompanied me on last week?"

Claudia nodded. "You were magnificent."

Colt shook his head. "Not me—the Narcan was the miracle."

Josh knew they were talking about yet another life saved with the medical antidote to an opioid overdose. In Silver Valley, heroin was just as huge a problem as it was in the rest of the country.

"You're right, it's exhausting for the officers. You were shaken up after it, remember?" Claudia looked at her husband with respect bordering on adoration. Josh watched the interplay with fascination. And not a little squirming.

A quick knock sounded on the doorjamb and Josh looked over to see the most beautiful woman in the world enter the office.

"Excuse me. Sorry I'm late." Annie's voice ran through him and reminded him of why he was so uncomfortable seeing his bosses' romantic chemistry in full view. He needed to be with her.

"Sir, ma'am. Josh." She nodded at each of them as she stood inside the doorway, her hand gripping her shoulder bag. "I couldn't call or text what Kit's told me, for security, so…"

"You followed protocol. We have to assume ROC has the capability to monitor all of our communications." Josh slid over on the sofa and she took a seat. Unlike him, all relaxed against the back of the couch, Annie perched on the edge like she was about to go hang gliding off nearby Hawk Mountain, one of his favorite places in the Appalachians.

"Yes. First, Kit showed up again this morning as she promised. She reported that Valensky is definitely involved in the trafficking, and that the women are already here in Silver Valley. But she doesn't know where." She relayed all that she'd learned from Kit.

"That's great work, Annie." Colt typed into his computer. "Claudia, do you think TH can ascertain where these women are?"

All four of them looked at Colt's screen, which he'd turned sideways to enable the best viewing. It displayed a topography map of the area, approximately twenty-five miles surrounding Silver Valley.

"We've already got four teams of two in place in the mountains, scattered along the AT." Claudia spoke of the Appalachian Trail. "I've got them staked out in the most obvious spots, posing as campers."

"You're thinking the ROC will take the women *hiking*?" Annie clearly didn't know all of the history of ROC, but she didn't think of them as willing to take the time to pre-stage the group of women. Wouldn't they just move them as quickly as possible?

"They'll make it look like they're a camping group. Remember, these women are one of the ROC's richest resources at the moment, second only to heroin. They'll do anything to protect them. We've got the latest topography of the area, since TH and SVPD worked together last year to take out the cult that plagued us. The True Believer cult used old mining and quarry caves to hide. When we took the leader out, a lot of the man-made caves were destroyed, but there are still plenty of caves and hiding places in the woods." As

Josh spoke, he watched comprehension dawn on Annie's face and wanted to reach for her, wrap his hands around her head and bring her lips to his. Annie's focus on the computer monitor and what he and Claudia had said was a turn-on. Mostly because it reminded him of how focused she'd been when they'd made love, determined that he get off as spectacularly as her screams had conveyed she had.

Wrong time, wrong place for his dick to get hard. And yet it did. He shouldn't keep being surprised by how much Annie turned him on.

"Will the women be moved directly to their purchasers, like the strip clubs, from camping on the Appalachian Trail?" Annie had a hard time wrapping her head around it and wanted to be clear. To know what her role could be.

Claudia shook her head. "There's good reason to believe the women are moved to a holding building, which we are confirming is on Valensky's compound. This lines up with what you're hearing from Kit."

"We want to get this group of women before they move onto Valensky's property, though." Josh spoke up. "Once they're off the AT on his turf, it gets riskier for us."

"And for Kit." Annie swallowed. "There are women somewhere out there in the Pennsylvania mountains, trying to survive being moved from place to place, treated like cattle—soon to be forced into sex slavery. Your mission, our mission, is to intercede and capture them before ROC disperses them to the winds. And we need to prevent them from getting into Valensky's hands." Annie's voice was pragmatic, her words for her own edification. Everyone in the room knew and understood what they were up against. "I need to be in on the camping stakeout. I can help when the agents free the women. They're going to need psychological support."

"You can't go on your own. You'd need backup." The words escaped Josh's mouth before he gave himself a chance to think it through. *Fudge*, he was revealing his feelings for Annie in the most inappropriate way.

Two sets of eyes on him, both from two of the smartest, most intense people he knew. "That's an excellent idea. Except if Kit needs Annie, she's got to be able to reach her ASAP," Colt said.

"Where we need you is a stone's throw from the Valensky compound. The women are within a half day's hike of it." Claudia zoomed the map onto a satellite view of Valensky's property. "He built his house on this mountain, and you can see the wall line here." She used a pencil to point. "There's more to it than this shows, though. The wall is three feet thick and impenetrable without the largest payloads. Fortunately, it's scalable. We have intelligence reports that point to a holding area on his property, probably in the back, near or in the pool house."

"Why send Annie or risk Kit's passing us information if we know this already? Heck, we could use a drone to see what's going on. As long as he's not home." Josh thought about the latest device the department had procured and wondered if he could carry it along with the needed camping items.

"No drones. You're only going to be the backup. That includes you, Annie. You're there if the women are found and need immediate help. You'll go in as a team. Keep in mind that we aren't in charge of this op in the least. SVPD is support, and TH is clandestinely working with the FBI and other agencies on this." Colt's tone was steady. "FBI is the lead. We offer whatever they need. And they need us to first keep the women off of Valensky's property, and if we can't, we need to go in and get them."

"Annie, you're the only TH female on this case for now, and you're minimally trained because we don't have the time to give you more. Your NYPD weapons handling and defensive tactical training will serve you well. I've got several of our other agents tied up with a larger trafficking operation that occurred in Boston a few weeks ago." Claudia sat next to Colt behind the chief's desk.

Josh stood. "I'll take a drive out to the Valenskys' and see if there's anything unusual going on in the area. Annie, we can plan for the camping stakeout now, if you have the time."

"Sure thing."

"Shut the door when you leave, Josh." Colt sounded like his normal, professional self, but Josh didn't want to think about either of his bosses taking advantage of a quick private respite from police work.

And he didn't want to examine the most definite jealousy that had him by the balls. He was jealous of any time Annie couldn't spend with him. He'd do anything to be alone with Annie right now.

Once outside the station, Josh walked her to her car.

"Where do you want to talk about the camping trip?" Annie's eyes were filled with the same heat he was fighting.

"Let me make you lunch." God forgive him, but he

was grateful Becky was in her apartment and his house was a safe, private place to take Annie.

"You've already made me dinner—it's my turn to cook for you."

"I'm not talking about cooking, Annie." Thank God she responded by licking her lower lip, her pupils dilated in the harsh fluorescent lighting. She wanted him, too.

Chapter 11

They were at his place within fifteen minutes. Annie parked her car behind his and followed him up to the front door. "Has it been lonely without Becky here?"

"Of course. And I'm also enjoying my privacy." She watched his slim hand turn the key in the front door lock and remembered that hand on her breast, the fingers tweaking her nipples.

Those same fingers grasped her upper arm and ushered her across the threshold. The inside of the house was shadowed and cool, the outside sunlight pouring in and cutting Josh's face in two. His eyes were inscrutable but his mouth was slightly open, his white teeth in stark contrast to his tan skin.

"This op is about to break wide open and there's no way of knowing how much time we have. I need you, Annie. Now." He shut the door with his foot and pressed her against the wall with his pelvis, his arms braced on either side of her head. She gazed up at him, and her spine melted against the wall as he gyrated his pelvis against hers, his erection rubbing against her most sensitive parts, swollen from her desire. Their gazes held as he continued the erotic motion, and her breath hitched somewhere between her rib cage and her throat. All she felt, all she saw, all she smelled was pure Josh.

She ran her fingers through his short hair, pulling his head to hers. His eyes remained open as she licked his lips and sucked his tongue into her mouth. When he reciprocated with another exquisite circling of his pelvis against hers, she closed her eyes, unable to see past the raw need he expertly drew out of her.

"Josh." He rained kisses on her jawline and down her throat, his hands shoving her dress up, up until he could reach under and cup her between her legs. She moved with his palm, needing more. It would always be this way with him—never enough.

He covered her mouth with his again, taking all of her need and want in a hungry kiss. She groaned in protest when he lifted his head from hers, a mere breath between them. If she could crawl under his skin she would.

"Tell me what you want, Annie. Show me." His pupils were dilated, and his eyes glittered with the same sensations arcing across her skin, to her most responsive parts. Keeping her eyes focused on his, she lowered one hand from his nape and covered his hand, the one between her legs.

"I want you inside me, Josh."

His breath hitched and he turned his hand, holding

hers. In a quick move he tugged her to him and spun her around to face the wall, his mouth claiming the side of her neck. He sucked on her skin as he hooked his hands on her hips and pulled her backside up against him. "Let's go to my room."

She followed him as he half ran, half walked down the long hallway in the ranch house to the room farthest from the front of the house. All she saw in the room was the giant four-poster in the center. Contemporary and sleek, welcoming their need.

And God, she wanted him to make love to her. Would let him do whatever he wanted. She raised her dress over her head and shrugged out of it, throwing it on the floor at her feet. Her matching bra and thong set was her favorite—dark blue with pale pink lace and ribbons. She was glad she'd splurged on them but just as happy to get them off as she reached to pull down the thong.

"Stop." Josh's gaze scorched her; his unabashed reverence mesmerized her. She felt so wanted, so needed.

"You're quick." Her breath caught as she spoke. Josh had shucked his pants and shirt, and stood in front of her like the most intensely erotic dream she'd ever had. But it wasn't a dream, and this…this was more than a sexual encounter. It was beyond her fantasies.

"You're breathtaking." He reached out and tugged at her bra strap until she was pressed up against him again. "I want to draw this out, make it last, but I swear to heaven if I don't have you right this minute I'm going to explode."

She reached up on her tiptoes to press her mouth to his while her hand wrapped around his length, stroking him into silence. "Then take me."

He lifted her in one sure move, and suddenly she was on her back on the bed with Josh on top of her. She had a sense of him reaching for something, the sound of a drawer being opened, the quiet crackle of the condom wrapper. Only as he sheathed himself did she open her eyes and take in the sheer immensity of him. Not just his erection, which was considerable, but Josh. His shoulders were sheer perfection, wide and chiseled to match his pecs and abs. She lay with her legs spread to receive him.

"Come here, Annie." He stayed on his knees and flipped her around, pulling her ass up so that she was on her knees, facing the headboard. "Is this okay?"

"Stop talking." She ached for him—

He filled her to the hilt and she dug her hands into the mattress, providing the support their love-making needed as he thrust again and again. A roll of pleasure swelled in her and then exploded before she could take in a deep breath. His cries soon followed, and she reveled in knowing he was as lost as she'd been seconds before.

They remained joined together until the last possible moment, when Josh leaned over and, with his chest against her back, rolled them both to their sides, his arm around her waist and nestling her in his embrace.

Annie snuggled into the spoon and let her mind drift.

Josh would have loved to stay here all day with her, but work called.

"Annie?" His breath moved her red locks around his face and they tickled his nose.

"Mmm. Shhhhh. Five more minutes."

He laughed. "We don't have five or even two more minutes. We've got to plan our stakeout, and I'd like to get the supplies together this afternoon." He was going to have to call Becky's community adviser and let them know he'd be out of pocket for a few days.

She turned to face him. Her cheeks had the rosy glow only an orgasm could bring, and a jolt of satisfaction shot through him. He'd helped her look like this. Like a painting.

"I'm not much of a camper, but I'll do whatever you suggest." She softly grinned. There was a light in her eyes he didn't want to name. Not yet.

Annie showered before she left Josh's and made a run to the sporting goods store to get some breathable hiking clothes and sturdy boots. Josh had told her that Trail Hikers would provide the vast majority of the camping gear, so she didn't worry about a tent or bedroll, but comfortable cargo pants and T-shirts were a must. With it being the height of tick season, she wasn't going to be vulnerable to Lyme disease if she could help it. Long-sleeved shirts and pants were a necessity, even in the heat of summer.

She texted Josh to make sure she had all she needed.

You're all I need. Thank you for our lunch today.

He added a smiley face emoticon with hearts for eyes. It made her heart squeeze, but she chalked it up to the newness of their relationship. Although she'd known him for so long.

She drove out to a restaurant Becky had picked,

near her apartment, and found them already seated in a back booth.

"Hi!" She stood at the table, feeling awkward. Should she sit with Josh or Becky? Becky held her hands up for a hug, which she willingly gave. Of course, she had to ignore the tug at her conscience. Becky's feelings were at stake. She'd be sad if Annie left her again. Or even if she stayed, if she and Josh didn't make a go of it. As if sensing her overactive mind, Josh reached out and grabbed her hand.

"Come here." He slid out of his seat and stood to hug her. She'd never tire of Josh's hugs.

"Should we be doing this?" she whispered in his ear.

"We've already done it, honey." His answering whisper sent shivers down her spine and made her laugh. Only Josh had ever been able to set her hormones afire and make her giggle at the same time.

Josh sat back down against the wall of the booth, making room for her on his bench. Becky furiously drew on her paper place mat, the restaurant's logo on the tiny pack of crayons. She wasn't the least bit ruffled that her brother was sitting with Annie.

"How's your apartment working out, Bec? Josh told me you're having a good time so far."

Becky's grin said it all. "I've made so many friends, and I love being able to go to bed when I want to."

"Which means you're tired when you get up for work." Josh tugged on Becky's drawing.

"Hey, stop it." Becky playfully slapped his hand. Her eyes regarded Annie. "Do you love Josh, Annie?"

Talk about straight shooting. Annie didn't feel put on the spot, though. Becky loved her brother and wanted to know others did, too.

"Uh, um, I've always cared about Josh. We've been friends since what, third grade?"

Josh clutched at his heart. "Ow, you're killing me here. It was first grade, reading circle. You grabbed my book because you said yours was boring."

"Sounds like me. But I'm sure it was a ploy to get you to pay attention to me."

"I already was. How could anyone miss your bright red braids and glasses?"

She gave him a playful punch on the upper arm. The waitress came and she asked for iced tea.

"Josh used to love Karen but she went away. It didn't work out." Becky clearly enjoyed telling Josh's story, and Annie couldn't stop herself from smiling.

"That happens sometimes." She counted to three, wondering if she should say something about going back to New York in a couple of months.

"Bec, Annie is only here for a little while. She's visiting and working in her grandmother's yarn shop. She'll go back to New York City after a while."

Wow. Josh's words were nothing but the truth, so why did they cut like dried burrs in autumn?

"Can we go visit her in New York? I love the big Christmas tree!"

"I do, too." Annie made it a point to spend one evening each holiday season battling the throngs of tourists and native New Yorkers alike at Rockefeller Center to see the humongous tree with the thousands of multicolored lights. No matter how heavy or grim her workload, the tree and excitement from the crowds cheered her. It was the closest she came to the real wintry Christmases she'd had in Pennsylvania as a child, as her holidays were often spent in Florida with her parents. Nice beach time wasn't something she regretted, but she did miss a traditional Pennsylvania holiday.

The waitress took their food orders, and Annie welcomed the break from the intensity of emotion elicited by their conversation.

"You okay?" Josh leaned over to her as Becky began to play a colorful, animated game on her phone. His eyes were soft, his smile easy.

"I'm good." She looked away, unable to tell him why it felt like her heart was ripped to shreds.

He'd only spoken the truth about her going back to New York. So why did she want to argue it with him?

Josh dug into his food and watched Annie and Becky talk over their meals. He wasn't running from the conversation, exactly, but more from his self-recrimination.

He'd deliberately said Annie was going back to the city to see her reaction. Sure, he wanted to protect Becky, but his sister had managed fine when he split from his last long-term girlfriend.

"Do you like being back in Silver Valley?"

Annie nodded. "I do. Very much."

Becky grinned as she took one of Annie's fries.

"Hey, Bec, manners." Josh wasn't used to needing to correct her on something so basic.

"I told her she could."

"Annie said I could."

He faced two incredulous women who wore the same expression: you missed it, leave us alone.

"Whoa, okay, sorry." He looked at his pile of fries, and then at Annie's and Becky's plates. "You usually share mine. You didn't have to ask Annie."

"I wanted to," Becky said.

He looked at Annie, who watched him with interest. "Did I miss something? Is Becky not supposed to have french fries?"

"I can have fries. I can't have soda except on special occasions." Becky spoke for herself, and pride welled in his gut. He'd do anything to keep her safe, protect her from the realities of life that crashed in no matter how hard he tried.

"What happens when you have a soda? Do you turn into a soda monster or something?" Annie's laughter was infectious.

"No, but I can't stop when I have a soda. Root beer is my favorite. I have it on Christmas and my birthday."

"That seems fair. Can I tell you something about me? I have the same problem with cookies. I can't have just one. So I try to limit how often I eat them."

"That's reasonable." Becky nodded sagely.

"What's your weak link, Josh?" Annie's shining gaze was on him, and he wished they were alone again so that he could be the sole recipient of her attention. He really was a selfish bastard.

"You." Her reaction was worth the risk as her pupils dilated and her lips parted. Yeah, she felt it, too. Even in a family restaurant in a public booth with his sister watching their interaction.

Potent stuff.

He shook his head. "What's my weakness, Becky?"

"Licorice! Josh is only allowed to have licorice on special occasions, too."

"You have a lot of rules in your house."

"Do you think I follow them all?" He lowered his voice, but Becky's hearing was like a bat's.

"He doesn't. Josh breaks the rules all the time."

"And why can I break the rules, Becky?" He grinned at his little, grown-up sister.

"Because you're an adult."

"That's right."

Annie laughed, and he joined her while Becky giggled as if the whole conversation had been her idea. A part of him saw the three of them from afar, as a stranger.

They looked like a family.

Annie left the restaurant no more settled than before the meal, but definitely with a full belly and heart. Time with Josh was never boring, and sitting and having dinner with him and Becky had seemed so natural and comfortable. It should scare her, how easily she'd fallen into her relationship with Josh, but she'd worry about it later when she had to make a decision. Josh knew she was here temporarily, and if he expected their relationship to end inside of three months, it didn't matter whether she stayed or went back to the city. Not that she wanted to think about being in Silver Valley and not being with Josh. But the truth was that she could make a life here, regardless of what happened with Josh.

She didn't know what she was going to do at the end of her sabbatical, and she didn't have to. At least she had a couple of options, including the yarn shop and the offer from Trail Hikers.

A loud knock on her front door startled her from the monotony of packing her new clothes into her backpack. She peered through the peephole. Kit.

"Hi, Kit."

"I'm sorry to come over here so late, but it's important."

"Come on in. Can I offer you something to drink?"

"No, no. Here, I've written down some notes." Kit held out a piece of paper with several bullet points written in neat, legible handwriting.

"Where will you tell Vadim you've been?"

"He thinks I'm at the library doing research for a paper, and stopping here can always be explained with my knitting."

"Do you think you're being followed?"

"No. I don't know. I'm not sure. I haven't seen anything that could be certain, but I get the feeling that Vadim is being watched." Kit wrung her hands and her voice shook.

"Why do you say that?"

Her eyes widened, her fear palpable. "Think about it. He's responsible for this new group of women, keeping them safe wherever he's hid them. He disappears all the time, which, trust me, he doesn't usually do. His routine has always been to do the work in his home office whenever possible. He's at the pawnshop on a hit-or-miss basis, as he has an entire staff running the place."

Annie watched her carefully, assessing Kit's stress level. While Kit had obvious enthusiasm for her perceived mission, it was taking a huge toll on her.

"But you still don't know where he's going?"

Kit shook her head. "No clue. I could follow him, but that would end in disaster for the women. If I found out where they were, and couldn't tell you where, it'd be their last chance. And if he catches me following him, or even gets a whiff of me snooping, I'll lose my chance to help."

"Here. Let's sit down." She was glad she'd packed in her bedroom and not out here, where she'd typically spread things all over the dining-room table and sort them. Kit did not need to have any idea about the Appalachian stakeout.

"How long do you think it might take him to get wherever he's going?"

"My guess is that it's not very far, as he comes and goes frequently, instead of being gone for long stretches. I swear it's in my backyard and I don't know it."

"Could it be? Do you have a shed back there?"

Kit laughed. "A shed? We have an entire indoor pool house, and there's a guesthouse, too, for when his Russian big shots come up from the city. I hate those times most, by the way."

"You never mentioned any of this before." At least not to her.

"I didn't see how it was important. And no one is in the back of our house—I swam this morning and spent time in the hot tub before class."

"Keep your eyes peeled. If you see anything, of course tell me or Josh right away."

"I only text you. I can't risk texting anywhere but this shop, or to your number."

"You really believe Vadim's watching you this closely, Kit?"

"If not Vadim, the rats he works for. They watch everything. Even Vadim is paranoid about being listened to, tracked everywhere."

"What has he said about it?"

"That it's always prudent to be careful about who you speak to, what you talk about. And it's not only to me, when he says that. He knows he's being monitored. It's what those thugs do best." Kit looked like she was going to go off on another tangent, and Annie wanted to know why she'd come here in the first place.

"What have you come here to talk to me about, Kit?"

"I think the girls are in trouble. One of them, anyway. Vadim asked me who my gynecologist is, and told me to look up the symptoms I have listed on the paper."

Annie read the list of medical descriptions, which included sharp pains in the lower right pelvic region. "Is this one of the girls he has in captivity, you think?"

"Yes. If they're the same age I was, they are around fifteen, sixteen. Waiting to get their periods if they haven't already."

"Usually women start their periods around age twelve," Annie thought aloud.

"When you're healthy and your next meal is a guarantee, yes. But for someone like me, who never had enough to eat until I moved here, it's different."

"Are you going to be okay going home now? Are you safe?" Annie had to get moving. She had to get to Josh's and tell him what she'd learned.

"I'm good. If he's already home, he'll think I've been out studying."

"What if he's drinking?"

"He's not. Not yet. Once he stops, he can't quit and he knows that. So he's keeping away from the vodka. This is what concerns me the most. Like I told you before, he only stays sober when he has hard work to do."

"Do you think he'd ask you to go with him, to try to help one of the girls?"

"No. He'll pay someone to treat them privately. I just hope he doesn't try to bribe my doctor. It took me a long time to trust any medical professional after moving here, and of course needing to hide how I've been hurt."

"You're an amazing woman, Kit. Remember, call me or 9-1-1 at the first sign of trouble. If you can, get out."

"Trust me, Vadim's afraid his time's running up since the police pressed charges against him for domestic violence."

"He's not predictable, Kit. That's what you have to keep in mind." Annie knew, as did Kit, that if Kit faltered, if she thought for a nanosecond that Valensky wasn't a threat, it could be the end for her.

Chapter 12

Josh had no sooner arrived home from leaving Becky at her apartment than his doorbell rang. His heart felt like it was on his damned T-shirt as he opened the door to Annie.

"You're the best medicine ever." He motioned for her to come in.

She stood before him in hiking pants, T-shirt and a plaid, long-sleeved camping shirt, her red hair a beacon to his desire.

"What's wrong?" Her lips had glossy stuff on them, and he wrenched his gaze from her mouth.

"It sucks leaving Becky on her own, Annie."

"Come here." He willingly went into her arms and pulled her to him, her head on his chest as he stroked her hair. Her arms were tight around his waist, and he made like the old sponge in his kitchen sink: he soaked it up. "Tell me what's going on."

He moved his hands to her shoulders to put some distance between them, but when those pink lips reflected the overhead foyer light he caved. "In a minute."

She let him kiss her with no resistance, except for the soft insistence of her tongue as it met his in a long, savoring gesture. Her hands gently pushed at his chest, forcing them apart. "Let's go into the living room, at least."

He followed her to the sofa and only then noticed the backpack she'd brought with her. "I like a woman who knows what she wants."

She looked at him and then where his gaze was, and let out a quick laugh. "It's not what you think." As he continued to stare at her, she blushed, and he loved that he did that to her. It was only fair, as his erection strained against his jeans. "Or maybe it is. Tell you what. I'll sit over here for a bit." She took the easy chair that faced the sofa. Her expression was somber as though she had to tell him something. Shoot—Kit must have contacted her again. The police officer in him grimaced. Since when did he let his need for a woman trump his law-enforcement training?

Since Annie Fiero came back to Silver Valley.

"What's going on?"

"Kit came by. She's fine, as safe as she can be while still living with her husband. But she believes the girls are holed up somewhere close by, as Valensky is coming and going frequently. And he asked her for medical information. It looks like one of the captives is sick." She pulled out the sheet with Kit's notes. "Here, you can keep it. I took a photo of it."

He read the notes and swore. "This validates information TH just reported, too. Kit's telling us the truth about all of it, Annie. And now one of the women could have appendicitis."

"Or an ovarian cyst."

"We need to find them sooner, then. Although I doubt Valensky would risk losing one woman—they place big dollars on each one successfully brought in."

"Right. What I learned at NYPD, though, is that ROC puts ROC first."

"They'll let a woman die before risking their exposure, yes. But if Valensky doesn't have a clue that Kit or TH is tracking him, he's likely to try to seek medical help. He doesn't want ROC asking him for reimbursement on a lost delivery."

"He asked Kit for her gynecologist's name and contact information."

"I know him—he's also Becky's doctor. He'll never take a bribe from organized crime." He said it with more certainty than he felt. Even the slightest link to Becky in any of this made him cringe.

Annie's hand was on his, and she sat next to him on the sofa. "It's okay. Becky's safe. This has nothing to do with her."

He groaned. "Easy to say, Annie, but she's my sister, and I will allow nothing like this to touch her if I can prevent it."

"She's safe where she is, Josh. Is this more about the case or about leaving Becky tonight?"

It felt like thorns from the rosebush his mother had planted before her death were stabbing his eyeballs. A solid throbbing started in his temples. "She deserves more."

"Josh, what more can you give her? It's not practical

for Becky to stay here with you anymore, except for the weekends she wants to come home. And you know yourself that she's thriving—you saw it. She has a job, she's making friends and she has her independence, or at least the sense of it, more than she would staying in her childhood home." Annie started to rub his back.

"Wait—I can't do this now. I have to report to Claudia, because I can't let it wait until morning."

"Okay. But you need to chill out before you go anywhere." She pointed at her backpack. "I brought my stuff for camping in case you thought we needed to leave tonight."

He shook his head. "TH has agents all over the mountainside. We need to look like we're legit trail walkers, doing a couple of days' hike. Not a couple of bumbling idiots heading out at night, which by the way, would be a complete tip-off to us being part of a surveillance effort."

Her hand stilled on his back. "I didn't think about that. I'll leave shortly, then. What time do you need me here tomorrow morning?" She dropped her arm, and he immediately missed her touch and damned himself for it. He had no right to impose his needs, his desires on her. What could he offer her? A lifetime of him always needing to care for Becky? The chance that if anything happened to him, Becky would become her responsibility?

"I'll need to meet with Claudia and Colt first thing, to give them this latest bit. I'll call in the highlights to the team working the case tonight, so they have a heads-up. We're going to have to have EMTs standing by, without telling them why."

She went to stand and he stuck out his arm, keeping her next to him. "Wait."

He heard her exhalation and felt her tension. She was afraid he was going to call it quits with her right here, right now. And if he were worthy of her, he would. If he had any damn sense left in his brain, he'd tell her to get the hell out and he'd get another officer or TH agent assigned to the ROC human trafficking case. He looked at her while maintaining his wide-leg stance, elbows on thighs.

"I'm a complicated man to be around, Annie."

"And I'm easy?" Her brows raised, her eyes sparkling with her conviction. "It's not always about you, you know."

Awareness unwound in the dead cold center of him—the part that only she'd been able to warm up as of late. "Meaning?"

She blew out an exasperated breath, making her red curls float around her. With the backdrop of the living-room lamp she looked like an angel. But this angel had a heart that he wanted to believe was big enough for both of them, hell, for all three of them, including Becky.

"You think you have the corner on complicated? I worked with a cop for five years, a good man who ended up being a family friend, along with the woman he fell in love with and married. He'd been sober since before I knew him, and he was so excited to be married, looking forward to becoming a father. And yet the drain of working the worst kinds of cases, day after day, got to him. It was an ROC case that brought him to his bottom, in fact. He went back out there, started drinking and quickly escalated back to heroin. He was so despondent about it he took out his newlywed wife and himself on a beautiful, sunny Sunday morning in Brooklyn. And he'd been under my care for PTSD from one especially difficult case. He'd witnessed his partner being tortured by a sadistic drug lord. It had pushed him too far. So even though he'd walked into my office for his weekly session only two days prior, he still lost it and killed himself and his wife."

"I'm sorry, Annie." He was more than sorry. He wanted to be able to reach back in time and change all of this. Protect Annie from the deep hurt she'd suffered. He wasn't a stranger to bad outcomes; they came with his job description. And normally he was very good at putting things in perspective. But with Annie he lost perspective. His awareness shrunk to her and whether or not she was happy. He hated that anything made her sad, and sad didn't begin to describe what she'd gone through.

"I'm not done." She turned on her bottom, hitching one knee against the sofa back and crossing her outside leg in front of her. "I haven't been able to hold a long-term relationship in forever. I can always blame it on an awful, abusive relationship I had in college, but that's not true. It's because my job swallows up all of me at times. And I feel too responsible for everyone else. It's easier to keep it on a sex-as-you-need-it basis, no strings attached. Convenient, but soul sucking in its own way."

"Annie, you don't have to tell me all of this." But he was glad she had. His eyeballs were getting those stabbing jolts of irritation in them again. He blinked. "We're not, we haven't agreed to be, the friends we once were to one another."

"Screw high school, Josh. I'm glad we had each other, and as excruciating as it was, I'm grateful for the hot mess our prom night became." She turned beet red. "I wouldn't have wanted to experience that with anyone but you. And we've, um, come, oh man, that's the wrong word. We've both learned how to enjoy ourselves in bed."

He grabbed a long red curl that fell on her cheek and slowly wrapped it around his index finger, the tips of his fingers touching her hot cheeks. Was there anything softer on earth than Annie's cheeks? Her breasts. Her ass. Her...

He swallowed as he watched her. "We have. Learned what to do with our best parts." He ran his thumb over her bottom lip and was rewarded with the shudder he felt and saw go through her. "We share an unparalleled chemistry, that's a fact."

"Chemistry won't prevent us from hurting each other. Or Becky." Annie spoke succinctly and with a clarity that didn't reflect how vulnerable she appeared to him in this moment. Vulnerable and totally trusting.

"No, it won't." He let go of her hair and turned to fully face her, knowing she could see how much she aroused him. How much he needed her. "Tell me something, sweet woman. Is there a chance we're doing more here than enjoying the moment? More than showing off how much we've learned between the sheets since senior year?"

A single tear swelled in her eye and slid down her cheek. She swiped it away. "I want to think so, Josh, but I don't trust myself."

"What don't you trust?"

"That I won't bolt the moment this gets too intense between us."

"Oh, babe, we're way past that."

Annie looked at him as relief and hope warred with a potent dose of fear in her gut. "I might stay in Silver Valley, Josh. But if I do, you can never think it's because of you. If I stay, it's because it's where I want to live and work."

He smiled, and she wanted to cry and laugh and bang her head on the sofa pillows.

"Really? You're thinking of staying?"

"I told you, it has nothing to do with you."

"Does *this* have anything to do with me?" He leaned over and kissed her, deeply. She stopped worrying about being embarrassed or how they'd work through the possibility of a relationship that was more than sex. Right now sex seemed the best option.

But it wasn't going to be like anything he'd experienced before, not if she could help it.

"Stand up for a minute, Josh." She tugged on his hands and unfolded her legs so that she could stand in front of him, still next to the sofa.

"Whoa—are you getting kinky on me here? You have a look in your eyes." He teased, but she saw his chest quickly rise and fall, felt the heat coming off him.

"Shh. Don't you know it's impolite to turn down a gift?" She looked him straight in the eye as she unbuckled his belt and unzipped his pants. His eyes widened, and a slow grin spread across his face as comprehension dawned.

"This is a surprise."

"I told you, shh." She kissed him firmly on the lips

before devoting her entire attention to the rest of his body. She ran her hands over his shoulders, on his chest and allowed them to linger as she lowered herself to her knees. She shoved his pants and underwear down and then grasped his hard length with one hand, her other hand on his ass.

"Annie." His throaty plea emboldened her, and she'd never wanted to please a man more. It was a wonderful way to break the heaviness of what she'd just shared, too.

"Sit down, Josh." She gave him a second to sink back into the sofa before she bent her head and took him fully in her mouth.

Annie didn't know who was more turned on, her or Josh, as she sucked and stroked until he found his release with one loud shout.

"Are you okay? Did I do something wrong?" She nestled up next to him on the couch as Josh rested, his head back, catching his breath.

"You're going to be the death of me, babe." He turned his head to make eye contact. "That was amazing. Thank you."

"My pleasure. And yours." She giggled.

"You don't think that you're getting away with this, do you?"

"What?" She batted her eyes at him.

Josh leaned forward and kissed her fully on the mouth, his tongue deep and searching. "Your turn, babe."

"Oh." Heat flared along with anticipation because this time she'd be enjoying her release.

Josh kissed, licked and tasted his way to her throat,

lifting her shirt over her head and getting rid of her bra with practiced efficiency. Annie loved a man who knew how to get her naked with little effort. There was so much else to pay attention to.

"Oh!" He sucked on one nipple as he tweaked the other between his index finger and thumb, sending mini quakes through her pelvis, radiating over her hypersensitive skin.

"You like that?" He undid her pants. "Lay back and help me get these off, babe."

She complied, arching her back to allow him to skim the cargo pants off her hips, along with her panties. It was an excruciatingly intimate moment, with her most private parts angled for his personal viewing, and she held her breath, as if a mere motion would make Josh change his mind.

His expression stilled, and after a long look at her, he raised his head and met her gaze. "Pure beauty. Annie."

Molten heat pulsed through her, starting at the place between her legs and making her limbs heavy with lust. Josh wasted no more time on preliminaries and seemed in fact a starved man as he bent his head between her legs and made love to her in the most intimate, erotic manner she'd ever experienced.

Annie wanted to freeze this moment to savor over and over again for the rest of her life, but her body's unabashed sexual response to Josh's insistent tongue sent her over the edge and into a pulse-pounding orgasm. Her cries sounded separate from her, as all she could feel was the power of what Josh did to her.

But what was most powerful was that she had allowed herself to feel the full force of their connection.

It wasn't only about the sex, which was the best she'd ever had, or the emotional bond, the deepest she'd experienced. Josh was everything where there had been nothing—a partner, friend, colleague, lover. There weren't enough words to describe what they shared. Except one. Annie wasn't ready to go there yet, mentally, but she knew her heart had already leaped.

"I'm glad you were okay staying here." Josh's husky morning voice vibrated near her nape, as she was curled up spoon fashion with him. It had been a special night together, even though she was wired about the case.

"Some of us are still sleeping." She'd checked her watch only five minutes before and saw that they had a half hour before the wake-up time they'd agreed on.

His chuckle made her aware of his arm, pressed against her breasts, and her nipples hardened. The rest of her body immediately followed, apparently not heeding the slow wake-up request.

"Babe, we are never going to be the kind that sleeps in." He moved his pelvis against her buttocks, and she groaned from the desire his erection stoked in her.

"You're shameless." She turned in his arms to look at him but his eyes were closed, his mouth landing unerringly on her lips. She stared at his long lashes for a heartbeat before closing her eyes, too, and answering the unspoken invitation.

They turned toward one another, and Annie thought there could be no better morning that this one.

An insistent buzz pierced the languid haze of desire she wished she could stay in. "Whose is that?"

"Stay right here." Josh rolled over and looked at his phone, which was on his nightstand. He sat up. "Crap."

She sat up, as well, pulling the covers with her as he made a call.

"This is Joshua Avery."

His back stiffened as he listened, and trepidation made Annie stay still and wait. When a cop was tense, it was real.

"She's okay, though?" More listening. A long sigh. "Thanks for letting me know. I'm on my way."

He stood up from the bed and walked straight to the bathroom, still naked. In what seemed an afterthought, he turned back and looked at her. "It's Becky. She's okay, but a thug tried to nab her from the group she was with this morning at the bus stop."

"Oh my gosh, I'm so sorry. What can I do?"

He shook his head. "Nothing. Be ready to leave by noon. I've got to get over to see Becky, and then meet with Claudia about our case." His eyes were no longer on fire for her, and she didn't fault him for that, as he was obviously concerned about Becky. She'd expect no less.

"Sure, of course. I'll meet you as we've planned, unless you call me sooner."

"Thanks, Annie. And feel free to use the guest bathroom."

He gave her a quick, hard kiss before he disappeared into the master bath and she quickly dressed. Josh was the ultimate man, switching immediately into big-brother mode. His sister, who was in his guardianship, had been assaulted. Yet he remained calm and prepared to take care of it, no matter how upset or crazed he felt.

She was worried about Becky, too, but gave Josh his space. It was a family affair—and Annie wasn't part of it. It bothered her, but she had to push it aside for now. Josh was going to need her to be focused 100 percent on their op, as was Kit.

Chapter 13

Josh couldn't get his car to Becky's apartment fast enough. He mentally went over the routine he knew she was to follow each day. A group of adults from her community walked to their condo association's private bus stop each weekday morning to board the bus just for them. It took them directly to their respective jobs, Becky to the thrift store. Because the stop was inside the apartment complex, which was behind a fence guarded 24/7 at the property's only entry and exit point, it was safer in many ways than having her walk out to the corner in their neighborhood.

But it hadn't been safe enough.

When he drove in, he noticed that the guard gate was broken. He was waved over to an SVPD patrol car, where he recognized both officers who appeared to be comparing notes. He parked his car and got out, hating the delay in meeting Becky but needing the facts. Panic rose in his chest and he reminded himself that Becky was safe and the creep hadn't harmed her.

"Morning, Joshua." Nika greeted him, and her partner, Rachel, nodded. He'd worked with both of them and trusted their abilities.

"Nika. Rachel."

"Becky's okay. While a group of residents waited for their regular ride, a man dressed in a nice suit approached them, on the pretense of being a visitor looking for a friend in the apartments. He asked Becky to follow him to his car, and she refused. Another man showed up, and they both attempted to grab and drag her into their van, which is there." He looked to where she pointed at a late-model standard family van. "One of the group immediately called 9-1-1, and we were dispatched. Since Rachel and I were just around the corner, we got here before the losers could drive away. We apprehended them, and our backup unit has taken them to County for booking."

"How the hell did they get in the complex? And wasn't there an Upward Homes assistant there?" His reasoning left him. Becky could have been kidnapped.

"The security guard had run to the restroom in the main building, and the assistant in charge of the morning routine had forgotten her phone and gone back in to get it. It was as if the perpetrator was waiting for the right opportunity. Usually they don't get any traffic in here in the mornings save for work transport, so both employees thought it'd be fine."

Josh let out a string of his best swear words. "And thus, the difference between civilians and us."

Nika held back a grin as did her partner. They got

it. And they knew him. They knew that nothing was more important to him than Becky's safety.

"You can be proud of what you've taught Becky. She knew not to go with strangers and fought them off. Both men have bruises, and the main instigator is sporting a nice shiner."

"No kidding?" Pride swelled at Becky's evasion, but it wasn't enough to douse the fear that had been roaring inside him since he received the notification. "I've got to go see her. Wait—what were the names of the apprehended?"

Nika's grin turned into a grim line. "Tupolev and Andreyev. We haven't done any further work on their histories yet, but Chief Todd was here for a few minutes, and he said he was certain they both had rap sheets at least a mile long. You already knew about one of them, right?"

"Yeah, I sure did. Thanks." Guilt, frustration and regret churned in his empty stomach. He had no doubt these men were connected to Valensky and ROC. They hadn't scared him off with bullets a few days ago, so they'd gone for his jugular. Becky. While he'd allowed himself to be distracted by a sexy woman, his sister had almost been taken out by mob henchmen. Thank God they were terrible at their jobs.

And he knew it had nothing to do with Annie, that he couldn't blame his time with her. But the guilt over his sister's ordeal wasn't lessened.

He got to the main office and saw Becky talking to the program administrator, Jacqui. Relief rushed through him, so strong his knees felt wobbly. She appeared none the worse for wear. When she saw him she smiled her usual ray of sunshine and jumped up to come hug him.

"Becs." He hugged her tight, needing her to know he had her, she was safe. And he needed to know she was okay, too.

"Why are you here, Josh? It's not the weekend yet." She walked back to where she'd sat with her mentor. Josh smiled at the woman, not wanting to say too much in front of Becky.

"I heard you had an interesting morning, and I needed a hug."

"Becky was just telling me that she's glad the bad guy came for her."

"Is that so?" He struggled to keep his emotions in check. He was so damned relieved Becky was okay.

"Yeah, because I'm the strongest woman in our group."

"Did you know the man, Becky?"

"I never saw him before, but he was a bad man." Becky struck a self-defense pose she'd learned from watching an animated action movie and growled. "I can take down any thief, any day!"

"I'm so proud of you. But if anyone ever tries to lure you like that again, I want you to run away." The realization of how lucky he was that she was okay, all in one piece, made his voice shake.

"I did run away! After I took him out!" Becky's satisfaction at her actions made him smile, something he wouldn't have believed he'd do so soon.

"Can I have a word with you, Josh?" He looked up from Becky's beaming face to see Jacqui. He'd spent hours with her, from the initial inquiries through to the laborious intake process, before deciding to place

Becky. He liked her and admired her professional savvy.

"Sure. I'll be right back, Bec." He gave his sister a kiss on her forehead and followed the woman into her office, where she shut the door behind him.

"Have a seat."

"Why do I feel like I'm about to get chastised?"

Jacqui smiled. It was a warm, compassionate smile. "You are, but not for what you think. What happened at the bus stop this morning is inexcusable, because it was at least partly preventable. The guard would have kept the van out of the complex if he'd been doing his job. He's been fired, by the way." She picked up a pen and turned it over and over, concern stamped on her expression. "But we can't keep all of the dangers out of here. It's a testament to you and Becky that she handled it the way she did. One of the other residents phoned 9-1-1, and it was resolved as quickly as if more able-minded adults had been involved."

"That's a credit to you and Upward Homes, Jacqui. They all knew how to handle it."

"Yes." She put her pen down. "Which brings me to my other point. Crime happens, thefts the most common in our area, but unfortunately our residents aren't any more protected than the average citizen from society's ills. But they're as safe as they can be, and today's actions from Becky and her friends demonstrate that they are adults in more ways than we give them credit for. However, they run a higher risk of suffering longer-lasting effects like PTSD if we reinforce what's happened." She stared at him.

"I'm only here to support Becky and make sure she's okay."

"I know that, and it's the least I'd expect from such a dedicated family member. But Becky's okay. We'll continue to monitor her and the rest of the group for any signs of PTSD symptoms. Many of them have forms of PTSD from dealing with their mental disabilities for so long. And each of them has their own mental health history, as well. We stay on top of it as best we can. I'm sure you know this."

"I do." He'd read everything he could get his hands on, talked to all the experts, since assuming full guardianship of Becky. It was a full-time job, and he was lucky to have Becky in such a solid place. "There's something you're not telling me, though, right?"

Jacqui regarded him. "You're a people expert in your own way, Josh. You have to be, as a police officer. What you might not realize, since your job is law enforcement, is that reinforcing and overreacting to a traumatic event doesn't serve Becky at all. There's no secret that this happened, and we've validated that it was scary and made her angry. She reacted appropriately. We'll continue to validate any expressions of grief that are a fallout from the event. But…" She looked at him expectantly.

"But you need me to back off, not overemphasize it, stop doing the helicopter routine."

She nodded. "Yes. And I'm asking you to trust us that we'll tighten the physical security here and that Becky will be as safe here as she would be at home. Don't take her back home until she asks to go, Josh. She's at a vulnerable place where her self-esteem at living independently is ready to blossom. This morning could make or break her. I for one would like to see it fortify her."

"You realize that there's a chance she was targeted because of my job, right?" Saying it out loud made it all the more real, and frightening to him.

"I do. And as long as you can convince me this will be a one-time incident, I think we'll be okay here."

"I can't promise that, but since we have both parties in custody, I'm confident they won't be back here anytime soon." He mentally counted how much longer he expected the Valensky case to go on.

"You know how you expect the public to trust law enforcement, Josh? I need you to trust that I have a decent idea of what's best for Becky's mental and physical health. It's what I do, day in and day out."

"Got it. And I do. As I'm sure you can imagine, it's devastating to be hit so close to home by what I try to keep the residents of Silver Valley protected from."

"And we need you doing your job, keeping these bad people locked up. All the more reason for you to keep Becky here for the time being. Let all of this play out."

He left her office with the knowledge that Becky was in the best place possible for her needs. But it wasn't the safest place, because nowhere was. His powerlessness against the unpredictability of human behavior was pummeling him.

Chief Todd called him on the hands-free phone as he drove.

"Josh, just want to let you know I'm sorry about what happened to Becky this morning. She okay?"

"Yes, she's fine. Thanks, sir."

"The two men arrested are connected to Valensky—they've worked in his pawnshop for three years, and both have a nice list of petty crimes on their records. They've already admitted they were working for Valensky. Claiming they were only trying to scare Becky, of course."

"Yeah, no one likes a felony charge of attempted kidnapping on their record."

"Right. We'll see you out there, Josh." Colt meant out on the ROC op.

As he drove to the Trail Hiker headquarters to meet Claudia, he reminded himself of what he did have control over. His own actions.

He'd let his relationship with Annie go too far. Emotions and nostalgia were one thing. His sister's life at stake because of his failure to bring in the bad guys soon enough? That was inexcusable.

After she'd showered and dressed, Annie had an entire morning ahead of her, as she'd expected to be on the Appalachian Trail. She used the quiet time to shelve hanks of yarn. And to go over where her head was at with Josh. No matter which angle she came at it from, be it her past history with men and her personal trust issues, or their shared history that would be very sad to lose, her conclusion was the same.

Josh didn't want her to be part of his family. She had no doubt he wanted her in the most primal way, as she did him. He might even want her emotionally, as a friend and confidante. But his actions this morning when Becky had been attacked reminded her that they weren't more than lovers and colleagues at this point. She'd be smart to guard her heart from expecting more than that.

Her phone vibrated in her pocket and she reached for it, absently wondering if she'd need to head out sooner than she'd planned. Her part-time employee was due

to arrive by the time the store opened at eleven, and
she'd be on her way to meet Josh shortly thereafter.

Can we meet in the next hour? I am working on a project I need help with. You can meet me here, at my
place if it's convenient.

Kit. The one person she was assigned to monitor,
and she'd thought of nothing but Josh all morning. Not
her most stellar professional moment. And it felt all too
familiar—the last time she had not kept a client mentally front and center, she'd lost him.

She looked at the time. Kit's house, Valensky's fortress, was in the vicinity of the AT entrance. It was do-
able if she left now.

Be there in twenty.

Annie had found the Valenskys' address without
her GPS—she'd memorized it when going over the
specifics of the property in Colt Todd's office. The entryway was preceded by a long drive lined with birch
trees, which she found a little creepy, even if they were
beautiful. It looked like a slice of Russia in south cen-
tral Pennsylvania.

The house itself wasn't in view even from the gated
front. A concrete wall appeared from the rolling hills,
and a double wrought-iron gate faced her like teeth
bared for a fight. She got out of her car and pressed
the button on the security unit, looking up to smile at
the camera. The birch trees weren't the only Russian
touches around here.

Kit's voice came through the speakers. "Come right in, Annie. And you can park your car at the front steps."

"Okay."

Annie got back in her car and drove through the slowly swinging gates, unable to shake the feeling that they'd reverse and snap shut on her. Being crushed to death wasn't a personal preference.

The house still wasn't visible for another half mile, past a copse of weeping willows across a bridge spanning a crystal clear creek. Valensky had placed his property to take advantage of the nearby Appalachian Trail and all its surrounding beauty, that was certain. She parked in the circular drive and walked up to where Kit waited at the front door.

"Thank you for coming to see me. I'm really struggling with the last pattern I purchased from you." Kit grasped Annie by the shoulders and gave her a very Russian three-cheek kiss, at the same time whispering in Annie's ears. "The entire house is wired. We have to guard our words."

"Good to see you, Kit. Thanks for having me. What a beautiful place!" Annie smiled brightly. She could act the part of overzealous knitting instructor, no problem. If it meant they might gain insight into Vadim Valensky's dealings with the ROC, and more importantly, save a group of young women fighting for their lives, she could stand on her head ad infinitum.

"Come on in. I've made tea, and we can sit out on the back porch. We'll enjoy the view while you help me. My husband is busy at work, so we have the house to ourselves."

Annie followed Kit through the massive oak doors

with inset beveled glass windows, cut and frosted so that an outsider could not see in.

"Wow." She looked around as the foyer widened into a huge great room, imposing artwork on every wall, sculptures in every corner.

"Through here." They walked down a large, wide hall and turned left into a fully modern, contemporary kitchen. Annie tried to appreciate the decor but her nerves were wound too tightly. Valensky wasn't here at the moment but what if he walked in? And if the place was wired, he was as good as here, anyway.

"Do you prefer green, black or herbal tea?" Kit opened one of the massive cabinets above the counter and revealed shelves of tea. Tea tins, boxes and bags Annie recognized from the Silver Valley tea shop, Appalachian Steeps, stocked the generous shelves.

"Whatever you're having."

Kit smiled, genuinely this time. "Lady Grey, then."

Annie took in the full measure of the room as Kit spooned the loose leaves into the large teapot. Water was boiling in the electric kettle plugged into the wall, and it clicked off as the last dried tea leaf hit the bottom of the pot.

"That's the fanciest teakettle I've ever seen."

"My husband settles for nothing but the best. Which is why I want you to help me with the sweater I'm making him."

Kit carried the tray and her knitting out onto the back porch, which overlooked the Appalachian Trail, the mountains making a slow rise past the wall that surrounded every inch of the property.

"I'd never leave home if I had this view." As soon as she spoke, she winced. Here Kit was a virtual prisoner, needing permission to go to and from college and the yarn shop, and Annie so blithely acted as if living here were a choice.

"I have my days." Kit curled up on the cushioned seat next to hers and poured the tea into the two cups, handing one to Annie. "We're safe out here, by the way. It's the one place Vadim can't have monitored. The big bosses told him he had to have a place where they could talk that wasn't being recorded. They even swept it for bugs."

"You're kidding. How do you know all of this?"

Kit shrugged, a very Eastern European gesture. Knowing, weary, smart, enduring. "I live here. And I read up on things on the internet."

"What did you need to tell me, Kit? And you're sure the acoustics from here don't carry?"

"I'm sure. We're okay."

"How are you doing?" Kit looked steady but her eyes were haunted again.

"Since I went to the shelter and came back, he's acting like a new man. Like he really cares." Kit sniffled. "In his own sick way he does, I've no doubt. But of course it's not enough."

"Love and caring are actions, Kit."

"Yes, that's what I've read in the magazines and the self-help books on domestic violence. And they discussed it at the shelter."

"Did you feel safe there?" She had to know why Kit really left.

"No. For a while, yes, but then I knew it was a matter of time before he found me. And if he threatened all the women there, their safety, that wouldn't be good, would it?"

"Your life and safety come first, Kit. It's admirable that you were thinking ahead, but you weren't able to avoid the bruises I saw on your neck."

"No. I'd gotten careless."

"It's not your fault that Vadim abuses you. You deserve to be safe, Kit." Annie wished for the umpteenth time that she could whisk Kit away from all of the abuse she'd suffered. It was a common fantasy that, as a counselor, she could never indulge. The victim had to make the choice to leave. It was the hardest part of her job.

"Vadim's worried about this case, about pleasing his superiors. He's never trusted me with information about his operations, but since I went away, it's been different. I'd worried that he'd become more violent, and I'd have to get out again. But instead he's doing everything to apologize to me, to make it up to me. And he's been sober. All of this isn't like him. I'm afraid he's going to explode from being so unlike himself."

"There's no chance he's decided to stay sober, is there? Do you think he's gone to AA?"

Kit managed a hollow laugh. "No, he'd never go to a place where he had to reveal any of himself. He's sober only because his bosses will kill him if he messes up this job."

"Has he ever hit you while sober?" Kit had already answered this, but Annie wanted to hear it again. To see if Kit comprehended how precarious her situation was.

"No, absolutely not. He's so mortified when he's done something in a blackout. He's twenty-five years older than me, you know. He's been drinking his whole life, and when he cries about hitting me while drunk, I have to wonder if he's not also shedding tears for what he's done in his past."

"Like what?" Annie had a clue from the briefings she'd received from Josh and at Trail Hikers, but maybe Kit knew more. Something that prosecutors could use to charge him with, beyond the domestic charges.

Kit reached over and pulled a ball of yarn and an unfinished sweater from a project bag that had been on the chaise when they'd come out. "Like running some awful illegal deals with the gang he hung around with in Brooklyn."

"Whom he's still in contact with."

Kit nodded. "He came over with his compatriots in the nineties when the economy and his chances to make money from the poor went to zilch. They set up shop here in America, where for them, the streets have been paved with gold. Just look around you." Kit motioned at the house behind them, and Annie got it. This wasn't the kind of money that a specialized professional like a surgeon or highly paid attorney brought in. And it certainly wasn't anything the owner of a pawnshop could afford. Unless he had another source of income.

"Do you think the money he gets comes from bringing the women in, or has he run other businesses?"

"It's the women, and has been the women for at least the time I've known him, so the last six years. Before that? He's bragged about how when he was helping bring in drugs they didn't have the problem they have now with the heroin being cut with lethal stuff like fentanyl."

"Lovely." Annie couldn't help her snide remark as her insides roiled at how casually Valensky spoke of what he'd done, ignoring the countless deaths he was responsible for. She'd read the entire case file on Valensky and his ties to ROC at Trail Hiker head-quarters. Kit didn't know half of the evil Valensky sponsored.

Kit's report was true. She'd been exposed to Va-lensky's ugly dealings since she was a teen, and now as a young woman she'd seen more than a lot of law enforcement ever did. And she'd put up with so much from the physical and mental abuse. Annie wondered how she'd do when it all played out, when Valensky was behind bars for life and Kit was free to live hers. She had the makings of an incredible agent, police of-ficer or psychologist.

The longer Annie remained in Valensky's home, the more anxious she became. This wasn't a safe place for her—it never had been for Kit.

"Take a look at my pattern here—see row one hun-dred on page two?" Kit spoke quietly, and when Annie opened the leaflet pattern, she noticed a huge sticky note atop the printed knitting instructions. It was in Kit's neat writing, and it included what looked like a map of the back of the house.

"Oh, I see the tricky part of the pattern." Annie raised her brow so that Kit would see it.

"Take my notes, you will need them later." Kit spoke fast, urgency in every syllable. Sweat dripped down Annie's back and she had to fight to stop herself from standing up and pacing. Her entire being was telling her to run, get away. Take Kit with her.

"Are you sure we're not being filmed, Kit?"

"We're not being voice-recorded, but I know Vadim plants his microcameras in odd places at times, to 'beat the odds,' as he says, against any intruders. As far as

I know, all he's ever caught out here has been a rabbit who's wandered in through the front gate. There's no other way in or out of here, not with this huge concrete monstrosity." Kit's revulsion was clear.

Annie looked at the paper and committed its contents to memory, noting a couple different buildings behind the house. She folded it with fumbling fingers and looked more closely at the backyard. Only now did she notice the low-profile building that took up two-thirds of the width of the property. If she had to guess, it was almost a quarter mile from the house.

"How big is your yard? I can't even see the back fence."

"You mean wall, right?"

"Yes." It was hard to conceive that the wall was that long, that wide, but she'd seen it herself on the photos from the drones. She didn't remember seeing the extra building, and she knew why now. It was surrounded by trees, whose canopy almost covered the roof.

"Is that the guesthouse over there?"

"It's the pool house, complete with sauna." Kit stood. "Come. Before you help me with the sweater."

The last thing Annie wanted to do was go deeper onto a property that reeked of danger. Escaping the compound wasn't straightforward—it would require running back through the house. She was certain Valensky had purposely built it that way.

They stepped off the deck onto a graveled path that meandered around and in between beautiful perennial gardens. Several had bronze statues that Annie would bet cost more than her condo in Manhattan. "Are you sure this is such a good idea?"

"We're safe now. We can't talk about anything of

importance in the pool house, but I want you to see the interior for reasons you'll understand when you read my note."

"Got it." The leaves crackled under her boots. "Kit, you know I'm a trained counselor, right? I can't help you like…like the others can."

"Their help will be with getting Vadim taken care of. You, you're my friend, no?" Kit angled her head to meet Annie's gaze as they walked, and Annie nodded.

"I'm your friend, Kit, yes, but I'm not going to sugarcoat it. You're in a very dangerous environment, and you need to seriously consider leaving. You know you'll be protected."

"I know. But you know me a little bit by now. You know that I need to be the one to stop Vadim. Because it's not only him, it's the organization he's tied up with." Kit reached for the door to the building. Annie looked over her shoulder, and from here the house was no longer visible. She forced herself to take deep breaths and stay focused on the present. Otherwise her panic at being so far from a safe exit was going to prevent her from doing her job.

"Remember, no talking in here of anything but knitting."

"Okay." Annie noticed the smell of salt water and steam upon entry, as they were immediately ensconced in a tropical environment. Sunlight streamed in thin rays through one large skylight, framed to look like several, the leaves and branches of the trees throwing shadows across them. A junior, Olympic-size pool ran the length of the room, with a large and welcoming seating area beyond. A bar with a refrigerator and, from what she could see, a restaurant's worth of booze lined the far wall. In the corner, surrounded by indoor palms and ferns, a hot tub bubbled.

"This is incredible! I take back what I said about staying on the deck to knit. I think I'd come in here and hit the hot tub in between rows."

"Here, let me show you the sauna, too." Kit led her alongside the hot tub, where a cedar door opened to a large room with tiered wooden benches. It wasn't like the sauna at the gym, though. It was larger and appeared to lack the typical electric heating unit. She noted a large wooden bucket, filled with salt.

"How does it heat up?"

"Here." Kit opened a chute-like door and pointed inside. "It's a wood-fired sauna, just like you'd find in Russia."

"I've never been to Russia. This is very impressive." She smiled at Kit, but she wasn't looking at her. Kit's gaze was frozen on the entrance to the sauna. Chills ran down Annie's spine, but she turned with what she hoped was innocent curiosity.

And for the second time in one week she came face-to-face with Vadim Valensky.

"When you said you were having your knitting friend over, I didn't know it would include a tour of my house." His heavy accent added to her sense that Annie was where she shouldn't be. And while it sparked the fear humming through her into full-blown fright, it also ignited a deep anger. This monster was about to be apprehended, if she had anything to do with it.

First, she had to get her and Kit out of here. Alive.

Chapter 14

"I needed help with a project, and my school schedule is busy. I asked Annie to come over for some tea and to help me." Kit walked past Valensky without batting an eye, clearly not fearing he'd hurt her with an outsider in the house. Annie wasn't so sure.

"With the prices you charge in that shop of yours, you should make house calls." Valensky glared at her, his attempt at casual banter falling flat.

"There are some local knitting instructors who are willing to do individual lessons. Kit doesn't need lessons, just an adjustment here or there." Annie followed Kit, but Valensky's arm snaked out and he grabbed her elbow. She whipped around to face him.

"Be careful, Annie Fiero. My wife is complicated." His beady eyes sparked with venom, and she made a clean move out of his hold. In one swoop he'd let her know he'd done some research and knew her full name, and also told her he was worried Kit had spoken to her. She'd have to ignore her desire to chastise him for his physical boundary issues. Feigned cordiality was best with this beast.

Tilting her head and frowning, she placed her hands on her hips. "Is there something I should know? Is she healthy?"

Kit was already out the door, leaving Annie alone with Valensky in the pool house. It didn't take a lot of imagination to realize how easily a man like him could overpower a woman, drown her, kill her. Annie drew on every single tool in her arsenal to stay focused on the mission and not freak out. She headed for the door and let out a silent breath of relief when Valensky followed.

"Kit's healthy. Just a little, what would you call it, skittish?" He reached out again and she jumped, but this time he grabbed the door handle to open it for her.

"You seem skittish, too, Annie. Has Kit been telling you ghost stories?" His skin was sallow and his nose red. She wasn't a medical doctor but had treated enough alcoholics to see the physical signs. And his passive-aggressive, cat-and-mouse interpersonal skills reeked of abusive behavior.

She had to get Kit out of here; the sooner the better.

"We haven't had a chance to talk about much more than knitting. I'm busy at the shop most of the time, and Kit's said she's got a full load of classes this semester."

"I am proud of her. Don't tell her that, of course. I don't want her to get too full of herself. But she's doing well for who she is."

Annie didn't comment as her incredulity tangoed

with pure feminine rage. She added "complete dirtbag" to her list of descriptors of Valensky.

They walked through the trees, and when the house came back into view, her stomach sank to see the porch empty. Where had Kit gone?

"You have a beautiful property, Mr. Valensky."

"Call me Vadim. It's a nice resting place, don't you think?"

She stared at him, frozen in place. Was he—

"I'm sorry, I meant a nice place to rest. My English is still rough after all my years here." His smile didn't reach his eyes. He meant to frighten her, to tell her he wouldn't hesitate to kill her.

"Sure." She wasn't going to give this man an inch.

His breathing was harsh, and she noted his potbelly, which could be a sign of an enlarged liver or simply overeating. Either way, it was plain to see that her pace was beyond his comfort zone. Good. She mentally rehearsed the process of taking him down if she had to. He waved for her to go up the deck steps first, and she grabbed her bag from the chaise. She was out of here. Her only regret was that she knew Kit wouldn't come with her.

Fortunately Kit was in the living room, waiting for her. "Thank you so much for helping me with the sweater, Annie. I'll be by the shop after my exams."

Annie nodded. "I'll be there. I've got a nice shipment of Shetland merino coming in next week. If you'd like, I'll put some aside for you."

"I'll call or text."

"That'd be great." Always aware of Valensky watching them, she refrained from hugging Kit the way she would if they were alone. Let him think they weren't too close—it was for the best. She looked him in the eye. "Nice meeting you again, Vadim." His name was a bitter poison on her tongue, but couldn't match the sheer hatred reflected in his eyes. Annie ignored him. "Kit, thanks again for the tea and the tour. I'll see you soon."

Annie forced herself to walk slowly to her car, fighting her instinct to bolt. The entire time to the gate, and until she was through the fortress and back on a legitimate Silver Valley highway, Annie's hands gripped her steering wheel. Her calf twinged from tension, prepared to floor the gas pedal if Valensky or some unseen thug gave chase.

She pulled to the shoulder after a mile and quickly texted Josh the basic details. Tossing the phone aside, she shakily pulled back onto the road.

This was why she was a counselor and not an operative in any sense of the word. It was too easy to read into a person's actions and put motives where they didn't belong. With dangerous criminals like Vadim Valensky, it was best to have a trained cop or agent who didn't care about anything but taking the bad guy out. While keeping the innocent safe.

Someone exactly like Josh.

Josh sat with Colt in Claudia's office at Trail Hiker headquarters. They faced one another for the last time before Josh would leave with Annie on the Appalachian Trail stakeout.

"Any idea when Annie's showing up, Josh?" Claudia seemed anxious to get him and Annie out on the trail.

"Yes, within the next twenty minutes." As if Annie had heard him, his phone pinged.

Be there in ten.

He wanted to at once shout and run out of the room to go get Annie, which was stupid as she was on her way here. If she were his law-enforcement partner he'd be proud of her. But pride had nothing to do with what settled in the depths of his soul. Stone-cold fear. Didn't Annie know she could have been killed? That ROC, like other organized crime units, didn't value life—it was all about its own self-preservation?

"The FBI's provided some information for us, but SVPD's to be on standby only. I've told the officers to report anything suspicious immediately to you, Josh. Josh?"

He looked up from Annie's text. "Yes, sir. Annie's on her way in. She's been at the Valensky place."

"What?" Claudia leaned forward in her chair. "Is she okay?"

"Yeah. She went up there to work on a knitting project with Kit Valensky, from what I can make out from her text. It's pretty cryptic—we agreed to keep it that way in case ROC is intercepting our cell phone transmissions."

"Damn it, they're going to be tracking Annie for sure now if they haven't already been." Colt's brows were drawn together, a signal to tread lightly with him. Claudia's expression wasn't quite as annoyed, but she didn't look happy, either.

"Colt, we always assume ROC is tracking everything all the time. Annie didn't cause this to escalate." Claudia put a hand on her husband's forearm, and Josh watched as Colt's anger morphed into concern within two heartbeats. That's what the right life partner did for you.

It was what Annie did for him.

But did she want to do it, be the one for him, for the rest of their lives? He didn't even know if she was going to stay in Silver Valley, and she'd made it clear whether she went or stayed, it wouldn't be the result of their relationship. Or lack thereof.

Before his gut could settle into the hard knot it did whenever he thought about Annie not being a part of his and Becky's lives, the conference-room door flew open and Annie whirled in, her flaming hair floating around her like a tempest.

"I'm sorry to burst in, but I've got something from Kit." Annie shut the door behind her, and her gaze swept the room. When it landed on him, Josh saw the anxiety she had over the case, but there was something deeper, a new light in her eyes that he hoped like hell had to do with him. Annie plopped into an empty chair next to him and pulled out a crumpled sticky note, the kind Becky loved to put on her mirror with her favorite movie quotes.

Annie looked hesitantly at Colt. "Is it okay to discuss all things related to the case in here?"

Josh imagined cartoon steam shooting out of Colt's ears. "It's safe in here, yes." He looked at his wife. "Claudia, do you agree?"

"Yes, we're good." The retired marine in Claudia was visible in her assured manner, no matter the stakes.

"What do you have?" Josh leaned over to see the paper better.

"Kit gave this to me via a knitting pattern. According to this map of the back of Valensky's property, which matches up with the satellite and drone photos we looked at before, there's something new behind the pool house." She pointed at the pool house. "Kit made it look like a knitting pattern in case Valensky intercepted it, but look—this is the pool house, and back here is another, smaller building. You can't see it from above because of the tree canopy and what Kit's drawn as a camouflage netting over the entire structure. So where it looks like the pool house might extend a bit, there's actually an entirely unknown structure."

"A toolshed?" Josh didn't want to burst Annie's bubble, but a lead rarely unfolded this easily. His anger at her had nothing to do with worry that something could have happened to her on Valensky's property.

"Actually, Annie, that might be what our agents have been looking for. Every little piece of evidence or information helps." Claudia interrupted Josh's thoughts and put a cold shower on the anger he was trying to turn his anxiety into. He had to face facts. He was in deep with Annie.

"I wish I could have taken interior photos, but I was very careful about what I did after Kit warned me that most of the property is wired."

"Did she say if it's audio or video?" Colt looked at the sticky note in complete puzzlement and passed it to Claudia.

"There are security cameras everywhere—I noticed them in just about every room. Kit thinks there's audio in the house but not on the outside porch."

"With technology being what it is, the entire property is probably bugged." Josh looked at the mystery building.

"Do you think the women could be in that building?" Her expression was so hopeful he hated to be the one to crush it. But he could be wrong.

"I think you would have heard them, if it's up against the pool house. And what's this here—is she showing some kind of walkway between the two buildings?"

"Yes, I noticed that there is a ladder of sorts that runs up the side of the pool house. You can see it from the inside, on the outside corner. That'd be the one closest to this other building. I thought it was probably there for access to the huge framed skylight. It's quite spectacular, if only it weren't the brainchild of a man like Vadim Valensky." Annie's observations were priceless.

"It's not his idea. There are other Silver Valley homes with similar pool houses, but not as big as what he has." Colt paused. "What do you think, Claudia?"

She frowned at the sticky note. "It's hard to say. It could be a soundproof building that he had constructed specifically for the purpose of bringing in the women, but it'd be awfully risky to have recently trafficked persons on his property. But it syncs with the intel we're getting, that the women are on the AT and disappearing for a bit, right around Valensky's wall, I'd say. He probably has some kind of hidden entrance either in the wall itself or a tunnel under it, from the AT."

"That doesn't play well with how careful ROC is to keep their criminal activity very separate from their family lives," Colt mused aloud.

Annie turned to Josh. "But Valensky runs his pawnshop in town. That's close. Maybe he doesn't care. And he's at the bottom of the ROC food chain in comparison to the superiors who are sending him the women to manage and distribute."

Josh shook his head. "No, it's not the same. The pawnshop is a local small business, that's one thing. And he's kept it clean, legally and on his books, because he's had no choice. He knows he's being watched closely, with his previous record."

"You need to qualify that, Josh," Claudia cut in, looking at Annie. "Trail Hikers is doing the work to monitor Valensky that the FBI can't, and that SVPD isn't in the business of doing."

"Right. Sorry about that. I keep forgetting you're not a full Trail Hiker." And he had; Annie had been doing such a great job as the go-between with Kit and TH that she fit in like any other highly trained agent.

"Trust me, I'm very aware of my lack of tactical training. I do people, not criminal stakeouts. Going on the camping trail to monitor and save these women will be the furthest I've ever gotten involved in any kind of operational activity. I don't even do ride-alongs very often. Most of the officers come in to see me at the department."

"Don't play your abilities down, Annie. Kit trusted you with her life." He was mad at her but hated hearing her put herself down at all.

"She trusted both of us." Annie looked at him, her eyes wide and lit from within. She'd said "us" almost reverently, and they were both fully clothed and in the company of Colt and Claudia.

"You two definitely make a good team, no arguments." Colt coughed. "We've still got a problem to solve. A group totaling thirty women has been flown and shipped out of Azerbaijan and Kazakhstan over the last month. They've been verified as entering the US at the border with forged passports and visas, but then, like so many young women in similar circumstances, they've disappeared. They were given false names and IDs almost immediately to facilitate their incorporation into sex slavery. There is a minimum of ten who are unaccounted for. We believe this is the group Valensky's responsible for dispersing throughout Silver Valley and the greater Harrisburg area." Colt paused as they digested the information.

"Our job is to intercept the ROC shipment of women that we know from our sources is on the Appalachian Trail. Claudia, you know my department is standing by to help wherever you need it, but it looks to me like this is mostly TH territory."

Claudia nodded. "Exactly. We'll need the extra SVPD patrols where Josh's sister was assaulted, and I'd appreciate it if you could send one or two of your officers to question the men you arrested for the crime. I know FBI wants to interrogate them but it'd be best if we could link them to ROC ahead of time."

"How's Becky doing?" Annie turned to face Josh. He quickly filled her in on what had happened. "They have two men in custody." Josh looked over at Colt. "We've not gotten anything out of them, but we think they're thugs working for Valensky. His way of threatening me because he knows I'm working this case."

"I've already had the suspects interviewed, and they're not talking." Colt took the sticky note from Claudia. "I'll make a copy for both our records, and I'll email one to the FBI agent assigned to this."

"Do you still want us to conduct the stakeout at a public camping site?" He looked at his bosses.

"Yes, but I'm wondering if you still want to go, Annie. Josh is correct—you're not a fully affiliated agent and you only have the firearms training that you needed as a basic part of working at NYPD, am I right?" Claudia said.

"Yes." Annie looked at Claudia, her spine straight. Josh couldn't read Annie, and it bothered him. "I trust Josh, and I will not make things more complicated if that's what you're asking. I'd like to be there for the experience and to support the hostages. It's what you hired me for, I thought?"

"It is. I'm shorthanded right now with several global ops. I don't have anyone to spare, which is why Josh is going to take time from SVPD and clock in with TH."

"SVPD is stretched incredibly thin, too. The one psychologist I normally contract for these types of ops is committed to another case clear across the state," Colt said to Annie. "I appreciate your willingness to serve, Annie. The yarn shop's covered?"

She nodded. "It is."

"It's settled, then. You're the team to intercept the women heading for Valensky. Our TH agent is reporting their location hourly. They'll be in the area by tomorrow. You'll both head out like any other hiking couple and pitch your tent less than a quarter of a mile from Valensky's back wall." Claudia pointed on the blown-up version of Kit's sticky note. "You were supposed to set up here, on the outskirts of the main camping area, but actually if you pitch your tent here—" she pointed at a place in the middle of the designated camping site "—you'll be closer to that back wall. And better give the appearance of being normal, run-of-the-mill Appalachian Trail hikers."

Annie looked at him. "Ready when you are."

Josh stared back at the woman he realized was who

had been missing in his life for too long. The woman he should be trying to keep out of a risky position. Her courage was immeasurable.

Josh stood up. "Let's do it."

They left Annie's and Josh's cars at the station and took an old, beat-up Jeep Wrangler that one of the officers brought in for Josh to borrow. Even the officer who owned the Jeep didn't know what they were up to—he thought Josh was really going camping, for fun.

"I'm so sorry about what happened to Becky, Josh." She spoke as he drove, and the brilliant hues of the rolling mountains that rose up and around Silver Valley were reflected by the midday sun. It was going to be hot at the campsite, but they'd have the woods for shade.

"She's fine, really. I'm the one who's most upset. To her it was an adventure, and she took care of it. I'm so damned proud of her." The ferocity of his love and pride in his sister made Annie care about him all the more.

She was beyond caring about Josh, as she realized with a jolt of shock that she loved him. It should be too much, too soon. The counselor in her knew and preached to her clients that real relationships took time. Yet her feelings for Josh were very mature and while they seemed to have appeared overnight, they also had been a part of her for a long, long while.

As if they'd simmered, untended, for the twelve years they'd spent apart.

The wind whipped her hair around the Jeep's front seat. She found a tie in her pocket and fastened a ponytail.

"I like your hair this long." Josh's compliment was his way of changing the subject and no doubt the focus of his concern to the present.

"Thanks."

Josh pulled off onto an area designated for Appalachian hikers, and they hopped out of the Jeep. Annie grabbed her backpack and slipped into it. She was already in hiking boots and clothing, as she'd changed at the station.

"Thanks for pulling your supplies together so quickly." Josh was next to her, fastening the buckles on his pack. She met his gaze and wondered if he could read her heart. Did he know she'd fallen in love with him?

"No problem. All I care about is the tent you brought—I'm not an 'under-the-stars' girl, not with the snakes and bears around here."

Josh laughed. "The snakes aren't going to bother you, for the most part. Only two kinds are poisonous, rattlers and copperheads, and they avoid humans. Black snakes are more the norm. As for bears—if a bear shows up, no thin nylon tent will protect you."

"Thanks. That makes me question my sanity to willingly sleep in the middle of bear country."

"Ah, no worries. Just steer clear of any cubs and mamas."

"That's reassuring. I may stay up all night." They would be awake, she knew, on watch for the women. They were being sent their exact locations by an undercover TH agent who stayed near them. The part of the Appalachian Trail they were on abutted Valensky's compound only a quarter of a mile away. "It doesn't look like rain, so we'll be okay on the ground, right?"

"Not sure. See those silver-gray clouds, over that hill? They might mean rain, especially as this breeze picks up. It's dropping the temp." Josh had his pack on and looked at her with raised brows. "Ready?"

"Lead on."

"I want you to go first, Annie. You won't be able to see around me if I'm in front. We'll follow these white symbols." He pointed at the first one, on a brown marker nailed to a tree.

"Okay." She loved the crunch of leaves and twigs under her thickly treaded soles. And she loved being with Josh in the beautiful setting even more.

"Are you really okay with Becky staying in her apartment?"

"Of course not. I want to be there guarding her every move. But that's not putting my faith in her, is it? And besides, those men turned out to be Valensky's hired thugs. They're still not talking, but each of them work at the pawnshop. It'll come out that he sent them to shake her up. Enough to send me a warning."

"You don't think they were going to take her, do you?"

"No. If I did, you know I wouldn't be here."

"And you're certain they're not related to ROC, right? Whoever Valensky works for there, anyway."

"Yes, I'm sure. Valensky wishes he was a big part of the ROC. He's handling a huge op for them with these women, but it's a one-off. Since his falling-out with them years ago, he's merely a point person for them down here."

She grimaced. "He insisted I call him Vadim at his place. He is so *gross*."

"I hate that you were in his presence again, Annie."

"Hate that you weren't there, or you're worried about me, too?" She stopped in the middle of the path, a stretch that cut through a horse farm. The AT turned into a ladder that straddled the fence, so nothing separated the hikers from the horses. It was just her, Josh and two chestnut mares munching on grass several feet from them. "I missed this. I forgot about how amazing this part of the trail is."

"The trail itself or the horses?" Josh evened up to her and she felt his body heat. They were both working up a good sweat. Something she liked to do with Josh. Too much.

"Both. All of it." She sighed. No more pretending it was sex only, or a casual relationship. And Josh deserved to know how she felt, but no matter how beautiful their surroundings, she wasn't about to share her deepest feelings in the middle of her first undercover op.

She turned to continue the hike, but Josh's hand on her arm stopped her. "Look at me, Annie."

She complied and a thrill shot through her, as it always did when their gazes connected. Their bond was palpable and joy rushed over her, in the midst of all the turmoil of a lethal op.

"Josh."

"You don't have to know what tomorrow will bring for you and me, as a couple, you know. We can take it as it comes." His voice was gravelly as he cupped her face. Annie couldn't help it; she turned her face into his palm and nuzzled it.

"You smell so good."

"It's just the laundry soap I used. I washed all my camping clothes, including these gloves, before I packed.

Annie. Aw, hell." He stepped fully in front of her and lifted her chin. She didn't resist as he lowered his lips to hers.

It was a kiss of connection and a way to communicate, to let one another know they were still in sync, that they were in this together. The scent of his musk was heavy in the air, and she wondered if her sweat smelled as good to him. He tasted of toothpaste and himself, the texture of his teeth smooth and his tongue insistent as he clasped her face in his hands and thoroughly kissed her. Annie reveled in it, the warmth of their breath, the moist sexiness of the contact in such a raw natural setting.

They both moved to deepen the embrace at the same time, but their camping backpacks didn't cooperate and Annie almost ended up on her butt. Josh held her forearms as they both laughed.

"This isn't going to work." She grinned at him, but her hormones were anything but feeling silly. The insistent pounding in her center needed satisfying, and if it weren't for them being so out in the open, in the middle of the field, she'd have no problem showing Josh how she felt in full view of their equine companions.

Josh's expression looked as frustrated as she felt, but a little more apologetic. "Sorry. I meant to save that for later, under the stars."

"I'll be in my tent, thank you very much."

"About two tents—yours won't be necessary unless you insist. My tent is big enough for both of us."

"Aren't we supposed to be working, watching for anything unusual once we get to the campsite? There won't be time for this." She tugged on his arm. "Come on. Let's keep going. I don't want to have to set up camp without full daylight."

Josh's grumbles followed her into a dirt path that wound through a forest and across two creeks. Annie never thought of herself as a camper or even a hiker, but with Josh, it seemed like everything else they'd done together: natural.

Chapter 15

By the time Annie and Josh made it to the campsite and set up the tents, the sun slid into late afternoon. Situated in the middle of at least six other groups of hikers, she took stock of their surroundings.

"Seems we've come across a camping convention." She spoke quietly, not wanting their fellow campers to hear as they heated up soup on the portable butane stove Josh had carried.

"It's the busiest time of year on the AT. Check them all out. If any seem out of place, tell me," Josh replied, as though they were discussing how to cook dinner and not the possibility of rescuing women from the indescribable horror of sex slavery.

"You mean more than me, the city girl?"

She immediately regretted her words. Josh's expression sobered. "You miss it, don't you? New York."

"I miss being able to go out at any hour of the day, or *my* day, at least—I'm a night owl—and get a decent cup of coffee or fresh-baked roll. I miss having regular work, not that it's totally predictable but I do up to four clinic hours per day, so that's pretty routine. I miss some of my colleagues, yet I know if I was there I'd still be knee-deep in my funk over Rick's death. But no, I don't miss the city as much as I thought I would."

"You're not giving yourself enough credit, Annie. You've been feeling your pain on his death all along, if you ask me. Coming here doesn't mean you ran from your grief, or what he meant to you."

"Thank you." She hardly trusted herself to speak without sobbing. "This is a big reason I've been so happy here this time around. You."

"If it wasn't me, it would be someone else." His face was closed, defensive. "Don't you think you'd miss it a lot after the newness of Silver Valley wears off?"

She twisted her mouth into a scowl for his benefit. "You know, Josh, you sound like you want to believe that will happen. Have you forgotten that I grew up here, just like you? And my reasons for staying away weren't all that you might think they were. It wasn't because I didn't still love Silver Valley. My work had taken me elsewhere." She still didn't want to tell him about the job offer with TH. But was it him or herself she was afraid of disappointing if she didn't take it?

"I think I've made a mistake, Annie." His serious tone, completely out of sync with what they'd been sharing, sent a frisson of warning down her spine.

"Oh?"

"I'm sending you mixed messages. Or the completely wrong message. As much as I'm happy when we're together—"

"Oh, no, Joshua Avery. Hold it right there. You are not giving me the 'it isn't you, it's me' speech again." He'd said the same thing right after their first failed attempt at having sex after senior prom. He'd not wanted to try again, he'd been so embarrassed. She'd been just as mortified, thinking she didn't turn him on. "When we were kids was one thing—we didn't have the life experience to handle a sexual relationship. We're adults."

"Will you give me a damn minute, Annie?" Hands on his hips, he stared at her as annoyance marked his face. "What I'm trying to say is that I never, ever want to hurt you. You're all I ever could hope for in a woman, but I'm not the guy that's going to hold you back from your goals. Your dreams." Her stomach sank at his words, spoken as if he needed to let her down gently. It was more like a kick to the teeth.

"That sounds like a nice kiss-off line, Josh."

"It's not meant that way."

"You're still upset about Becky being assaulted. We were having a good time together when she was so vulnerable. It's natural for you to doubt your judgment in spending time with me while she was facing danger. And maybe you've got some guilt over us taking time from the case to make love. But don't put it on me, on what we've shared."

"I never want to have to tell you Becky comes first, Annie."

"Then don't. Put yourself first. You deserve a life, too, you know. What the hell kind of brother are you to her if you only do what works for her? She needs to see that you know how to take care of yourself, too. It's the best way to teach a child. By example."

"Becky's not my child, and she's obviously able to care for herself, enough anyhow." His grim expression made her ache to take him in her arms.

"If she were completely independent, you wouldn't be so worried." Annie shut the burner off as the soup was boiling. "This will need to cool a bit. I have a little something extra to have with it." She turned away, needing the break from the intensity of their interaction as much as her grumbling stomach needed food. A small packet of gourmet cheese and sleeve of water crackers was calling to her. A tiny jar of tapenade and a large apple completed her appetizer selections.

Josh eyed the spread of goodies and frowned. "Did you bring food like this for the next several days? Your pack has to weigh as much as you do."

"No, I figured that if we run out of food we're close enough to hike back to the Jeep and reload." She'd left a cooler chock-full of nonperishables, without the ice.

"We're not done with our conversation, Annie." He took the apple and opened his Swiss army knife to the paring blade. "I can't have loose ends with things, and that includes us."

"Why do there have to be any ties to worry about? I thought we were enjoying this while we can. I'm not going to try to make you commit to something more than you want." Did he think she was going to make him agree to a more permanent arrangement before she decided to move back to Silver Valley? Any regret she had over not telling him she loved him back in the glen dissolved. When was she going to learn to put herself, her heart, first?

"It's not about what I want, Annie. It hasn't been about me since my parents died."

"Have you ever allowed yourself to consider that you'd benefit from having someone to lean on, besides yourself?"

"Sure. But then the complications that can happen with Becky, and my job, outweigh any good I have to offer a life partner."

"Is that what happened with your previous girlfriends?"

"Girlfriend. I've dated enough, but I've only had one long-term girlfriend. And when we broke up, it hurt Becky for a long while." Annie wondered how long he'd hurt but didn't want to pry. Not here. Not now.

He shot a quick grin at her. "You're dying to know, aren't you?"

"What? Your past? None of my business." And she meant it. She loved him for who he was, today. A stubborn mule.

"We dated for two years, lived together for two. Four years of wondering when we'd tie the knot. And then—" He broke off.

"You broke it off because of Becky?"

Josh snapped back to the present. "No. She found another guy, one without any added complications."

"I'm sorry, Josh." She regretted his hurt but rejoiced that they were together now.

"Don't be. It saved me from all kinds of hurt later, is how I look at it. And while it did upset Becky, it would have been a mistake to marry anyone. I'm a man with a tough career, and it's bad enough that Becky has to deal with what could be the consequences of it. She didn't have a choice."

Annie didn't think she had a choice about how she felt about Josh, but wasn't ready to broach it with him now. They were on a stakeout, which she'd quickly forgotten about. She forgot about a lot of things that she'd always thought were so important when she was around Josh.

The sound of footsteps caught her attention, and she looked up from the beef and vegetable soup. A group of five women were huddled together as they cautiously moved to the area farthest from where the other campers were cooking and making conversation. They appeared skittish, not relaxed and enjoying nature like the other campers.

"Josh, do you—"

"Yeah. Didn't you say you had to go to the bathroom?" He didn't have to tell her twice. She put down the small spoon and wiped her hands on her pants.

"Don't burn dinner, dear." She reached up and kissed him on the cheek, in case anyone was watching them. No one would suspect two average-looking hikers of being on the lookout for trafficked women, would they?

He watched Annie head toward the group of women, watched how her hips swayed and forced his focus to remain on their objective. Stop the women from reaching Valensky.

How had it happened that since he and Annie had been teens, quaint Silver Valley had turned into a hub of criminal activity? His mind knew the right answers. Silver Valley was centrally located, making it a center point for legitimate logistics. The same interstates used by manufacturers to send forth their wares also worked for the bad guys, bringing in opportunists from pyramid business schemers to drug traffickers who laundered their money at the big department stores on the Silver Valley main pike. But like his relationship with Annie, he hated to see what he'd thought of as perfect ever change.

He and Annie had an incredible bond, a connection that he knew would still be there in fifty years. He had no explanation for it. But it didn't mean he could take it for granted by asking Annie for more than their time together now. He had nothing to give her but a lot of hours and days apart.

She deserved so much more.

Annie heard the women speaking Russian and from what she understood, conversationally, these women were friends and able to communicate in monosyllables, probably to avoid drawing attention to speaking in a foreign language. There were five women, all of varying heights but all very slim and very young. She'd place them around fifteen, sixteen, but knew with a little makeup they'd look a decade older. The sadness she imagined in their eyes reflected old, abused souls. Their journey here had to have been harrowing once they discovered they weren't going to be nannies or legitimately paid workers.

None of them were dressed for the heat. Their clothing was almost like a uniform: tight blue jeans with some kind of decorative rhinestones, high-heeled black boots, sleeveless tank tops. Most had some kind of thin jacket, which was good, as the nights grew cold. It was as if they'd literally flown in from their native country a day or two ago and found themselves on an American campout.

Annie pulled a small plastic bag of toilet paper from her pocket, slowly and quietly so as not to draw attention to herself. She'd never known the poverty or despair that probably drove these women to make a choice to leave their families and native country for the unknown, but she understood feeling lost. The ferocity of her compassion for their situation was like what she'd experienced when she'd heard that Becky had been approached by Valensky's thugs. An instinctive, protective urge.

The women paid her little notice as she headed for a private place in the woods to take care of business. They were doing the same, using shrubbery or outcroppings for privacy. She noted they were definitely not observing the rules of the Appalachian Trail to take out anything you carried in—they tossed wadded toilet paper and paper towels like popcorn to birds. More confirmation that they had the right group of women. Annie lingered near the rock and bushes and waited, out of sight, to see if she'd hear anything useful. The conversations were mostly unintelligible, as the women spoke so low and in a tone that indicated trouble. Until one of the girls let out a high-pitched squeak, followed by shushes from the others.

A motion caught her eye, and she leaned around the rough boulder to verify the dread that dropped her stomach to her knees. Valensky clomped through the woods not two hundred yards away from her. She'd have expected one of his lackeys, but with three of them in custody he might be shorthanded. Without hesitation she pulled out her phone and snapped several photos, after which she texted Josh and Claudia that she'd seen their person of interest, using the code phrases they'd agreed upon. She couldn't risk texting the photos in case of the ever present risk of interception.

Sometimes modern technology blew.

Soup's on. Come eat.

Josh's immediate text back had a double meaning, she was certain. He didn't want her facing Valensky alone. The man was unpredictable, no matter what Kit said about him being in control when sober. And they'd found the women and wouldn't let them out of their sight.

Need to see end of show. She texted back, referring to why she was lingering. She didn't want to leave her perch too soon. According to Claudia, the assigned TH agent's mission was complete the second she and Josh laid eyes on the women. They had the baton.

She'd never forgive herself if Valensky disappeared with these women on her watch. She wasn't an agent and didn't have any illusions she was. But opportunity presented itself, and Annie dug in her heels.

Soup will be cold. Come now.

Another text came on the heels of Josh's, from Claudia. Using the agreed upon code word, Claudia relayed that they'd confirmed there were women in Valensky's compound. Annie and Josh's job remained the same: stay with the women on the Appalachian Trail.

"Okay, okay." She spoke low and under her breath,

but it was too loud. She heard the snap of twigs, the pad of feet on the hardened dirt. Someone was coming to check out who'd spoken, and it could be Valensky.

Grateful she'd put her hair in a ponytail, she fully tucked it under her a bandanna and pulled up her collar as she shoved her sunglasses on. It was getting late in the day for shades, but she couldn't risk Valensky recognizing her.

She made like she was leaving a bathroom area and walked casually back to the campground. Only a few hundred yards separated the outcroppings from the campsite, but it seemed like miles as she kept her face forward, her stride even, when all she wanted to do was to break into a run and throw herself into Josh's arms.

A heavy hand suddenly covered her mouth as a strong arm hauled her up against a large body. Shock jolted through her as she moved to crush Valensky's instep, but he was wise to self-defense tactics and easily outmaneuvered her. His meaty forearm was across her throat, threatening her airway.

"Fancy meeting you out here, Annie." Valensky's thick accent filled her ears as his cigarette-and-coffee-laden breath hit her nostrils. Panic melded with nausea and she held tight to her focus, refusing to allow revulsion to cost her her objective.

She jerked every which way possible, a keening sound coming out of her throat, but it was muffled by the monster's bulk. Josh would never hear her. She'd never see him again.

No, no, no. She forced her body to be still, gathering her wits.

"Make another noise and I'll slit your throat. Then I'll take out each of the girls. Understand?"

He didn't want to kill her, not yet. He had the women to think about and if she screamed, even if he did murder her, the others would get free—Josh would make sure of it. And there were more, hidden on his property, according to Claudia. She might be the only chance to help free them.

He shook her from behind, his arm cutting off her air. She moved her mouth to bite him but before she could, a massive blow to the side of her head floated stars in front of her vision.

"Start walking, slowly, or I'll kill everyone in the campground. Do you understand?" Menace and nastiness peppered every syllable of his request. She wasn't sure that he had a weapon; she'd seen nothing and didn't feel a barrel in her back. And she knew that men like Valensky, with rap sheets a mile long, were smart enough to not carry a weapon. But she couldn't risk it. And more than anything, she trusted Josh. He'd know something had happened and would come to find her, or call in backup. Plus, weren't these mountains crawling with Trail Hiker agents?

You're okay. You're safe. Stay focused.

"Yes." Her voice matched the grogginess his hit to her temple caused. Nausea made her head swim, and she realized in a far-off way that he'd probably given her a concussion. She had to stay conscious at all costs or she'd be no help to anyone.

"Move." He forced her to walk farther into the woods, away from the campsite, away from the women.

She turned to look at him. "What about the others?"

His face crunched up in a mean scowl. "None of your business. Move or you're dead."

She had no choice but to do as he told. He shoved

and prodded her each time her steps faltered on the slippery, leaf-strewn path. They were heading downhill on a steep grade and her hiking boot caught on a tree root, flinging her forward and down the rocky path on her belly. A sharp pop sounded as hot, searing pain lanced her side.

"Oof." Her cry was quiet, subdued. Not at all expressing the incredible pain she was in. It had to be a broken rib. And the pounding in her head—it was like trying to move and think through a fuzzy skein of mohair yarn.

"Get the freak up." Two rough hands on her shirt, yanking her up by the shoulders. Pain washed over her, and she braced herself for a fall into unconsciousness. Before it came, she found her feet moving again, but this time Valensky was right behind her, the front of his body up against her back. "You're too heavy to carry. If you fall, you die."

His words were punctuated by heavy breathing. A part of her brain wondered if she could make him have a cardiac arrest by turning and running up the mountain, making him catch her again. But she knew she couldn't do it. It was hard enough moving in a straight line downhill.

Her vision blurred, but she made out the wall that surrounded his property. The campsite was only a half mile from the property as the crow flew and as the mountainside allowed, but it would be at least twenty minutes of driving on the twisting highway that the Appalachian Trail crossed. She struggled to stay focused, to pay attention to details she could tell Josh later. So that they'd find this pathway again, find wherever he was taking her. Save the women.

Without warning Valensky yanked on her arm, forcing her sharply to the left. He placed her against an outcropping, and she had a sense of him using something—his phone?—pointing it out in front of him. A hole appeared in front of her where the rock had been. Fear permeated every cell of her being. The instinct to keep moving, save the women, proved stronger. Cold, hard rock scraped her back and she used it as a grounding point. He hadn't killed her yet; hope still existed for the women. He shoved her down metal stairs, keeping her upright via her shirt collar. Her neck chafed and she struggled to fill her lungs, fighting the black spots that clotted her vision. The door that opened in the rock shut behind them, the darkness total. A scream ripped from her throat. It reverberated like a howling specter as lights lit up the space where the stairs ended and a short corridor that led to a large commercial double door.

"Move!" He pushed her through the doors, and she was up against another set of stairs going upward.

"I…I can't." She gasped, the pain with each breath excruciating.

"Move or I'll break your arm." He twisted her arm behind her, the pain joining the sharp shocks of agony in her side. Her knees buckled and slammed onto the concrete floor.

Valensky's string of Russian epithets were the last sound she heard.

Chapter 16

Josh's brief annoyance at Annie for not returning to camp immediately turned to anxiety when he saw the women they'd tracked arrive back and sit around the small tent they appeared to share, followed by Claudia's text confirming more captives were on Valensky's property.

He'd sent a text to Claudia as soon as Annie walked off into the woods, indicating they'd locked eyes on the group. The objective was to watch and see where the women went. TH agents had called in sightings all along the trail from ten miles away. The groups of women came and went and disappeared. Some were taken off the trail sooner than others, and a few had been rescued with the help of TH. They'd ascertained that this group had made it this far and was expected to be under the control of Valensky. But the group TH reported moving this far south had ten women, not five. What had Valensky done with the other five women?

Stay in camp. Have personnel working it.

Claudia's reply via encoded text wasn't enough. He needed to know Annie was okay now, not when some TH agent got back to them.

He couldn't go over to the women, not without scaring them or blowing his cover. Frustration and fear morphed into near panic as a text from Claudia came in.

Annie is down. Repeat. Annie is down. Come out of camp immediately.

Like hell he would.

Josh ran through his mental checklist. He had all the tools he needed, and ducked behind a tree to quickly holster the weapon he'd carried in his backpack. He threw on a beat-up flannel shirt over his T-shirt to hide the SIG Sauer .45 and took off for the area where Annie had disappeared. Images of Valensky's paws on Annie clawed at him. He'd thought he knew what fear and anxiety were when the thugs had assaulted Becky. Wrong. Knowing the love of his life might be suffering, taking her last breath at the hands of Valensky, took his experience to unimagined levels of terror.

Breathing heavily, he scanned the boulder-dense, treed swath, and campers looked at him with wariness. It wasn't usual for a hiker to be so nosy in what was clearly a natural place to take care of bathroom business. Making out a definitive trail through the woods, he started the long trek down the side of the mountain. Only to be brought up short by a firm grip on his arm as a figure darted out from his right side, from behind an especially large outcropping.

He turned to neutralize his attacker. As soon as he looked into their eyes, the fight left him.

"Claudia."

She didn't reply verbally but held her finger to her lips and motioned for him to follow her.

Only because of years of training and dedication to duty did he fight his instinct to go after Annie. After only one hundred yards they were up against what appeared to be a huge, overgrown hedge. They stood in the middle of several rock piles, surrounded by bushes and sapling trees. Josh followed Claudia into what looked like an impossible bunch of scratchy branches, under which he knew a portable command unit operated. The van had had bushes and branches affixed to it by horticultural experts. The most trained AT hiker wouldn't see anything amiss. As he went into the van with Claudia, he broke out in a cold sweat.

"Annie—"

"Hang on, Josh." Claudia's whispered command brooked no argument.

I'm coming, Annie. Wait for me.

Dear God, please let her wait for him.

Bright light shone through Annie's closed lids, causing a pain in the back of her head that made nausea swell. With her eyes still closed and head pounding, she turned her head to the side and threw up.

"Oh my God. You son of a bitch, what did you do to her?"

"Kit?" Was that her voice? It sounded like a cricket.

A cold, damp cloth wiped her face. "It's me, Annie. You're…you're okay." Kit's voice. Annie couldn't open her eyes yet.

"Stay here or you're both dead. There are cameras on you, and my team is under orders to kill either of you if you disobey my orders." Valensky's voice. Annie cracked her lids and saw Kit's knees, in the usual black leggings the woman wore. Kit was still here, which meant she was risking her life, too. Just past her were heavy, muddy shoes. Valensky's.

Rage flared, and Annie tried to sit up.

"Don't, Annie. Rest for a minute." Kit's hand was on her shoulder, keeping her down. Some memory of Kit saying she knew how to handle Valensky spoke to her, and Annie relaxed back onto the floor. She recognized the smell of the water from the pool and hot tub. They were in the pool house. But hadn't Valensky taken her through a tunnel? And wasn't it under the wall?

It hurt too much to think.

"I am going in with the team that takes him down." Josh spoke to Claudia in the Trail Hikers' mobile command unit, fully equipped with the newest generation technology available only to agencies like Trail Hikers. No hiker would think twice of the local flora, and obviously the ROC criminals moving shipments of women had paid it no heed, either.

Josh and Claudia sat in the middle of a bank of seven screens as three other TH agents worked the equipment, keeping comms open with the agents on the AT and near Valensky's compound.

Where Annie was, condition unknown.

"I support that, but know what you're getting into first, Josh. Are you going to be able to remain clear-headed, keep the mission first, with Annie's life at risk?" Claudia's eyes observed him in the way that only a boss who'd been in the same position could do.

"I have to go in there, Claudia."

"Right." Claudia looked past him to the agent watching the video taken by a camera the TH or FBI had placed on a tree overlooking Valensky's compound. He couldn't look at it again, couldn't go through the torture of seeing Annie at the hands of a madman, but he couldn't rip his gaze from it, either. As if by watching it he was shouldering some of her suffering, relieving her of her terror. The feed showed Valensky coming from behind a rock out of nowhere, hiking up the forest path that led to the campsite where he and Annie had been. Valensky forcing the unmistakable shape of Annie, her head bowed, feet shuffling, down the same path. Their images disappeared once around the side of the outcropping. Then Valensky reappeared, ran up the path and returned with the five women, going around the rocks the same way he did with Annie.

"What have you figured out, Candy?" Claudia's question jolted him from his despair.

A petite blonde with her hair showing tints of pink and blue didn't take her eyes off the video feed as she spoke to Claudia.

"There's definitely an entrance to some kind of passageway that goes to Valensky's place, probably the unidentified building. The time between taking the first captive, Annie, into his lair and then retrieving the five remaining women is less than five minutes.

He was in a hurry to get those women in there once he'd trapped Annie."

Josh's gut clenched at the word *captive*, and he turned to Claudia. "Are there any agents there yet?"

"We're waiting for a tip from the FBI. They're the ones who have to go in there, Josh. TH is in the operation to provide intelligence, to take out the head of ROC if needed. Dima Ivanov is long gone, somewhere in the Poconos or closer to New York City. As always, TH has to remain invisible." Claudia's disappointment that they'd lost their chance to capture the head of the East Coast ROC was keen. But all Josh cared about was getting Annie out of there.

He stilled. For the first time in his career, he didn't care about the case, except as a means to an end. A way to save Annie.

He loved her. And his life would have no meaning without her. She was his life.

"Josh, you with us?" Claudia's intuition was downright creepy at times.

"I'm here." He met her gaze head-on. It was a hell of a time to figure out he loved Annie, but so be it. He'd do whatever it took to save her.

"Use your emotions to fuel your focus." Spoken like a true Marine.

"Got it. I don't have to be invisible as an SVPD officer, do I?" A plan had begun to gel, but he had to have Claudia on his side.

"What are you thinking?"

"I can show up at Valensky's place to talk to Kit. As a uniformed officer."

"Go on."

* * *

"What are you doing here?" Annie's mind had cleared enough to wonder why Kit had shown up as Valensky dumped her here in the pool house.

"Vadim caught me right after I found where he's keeping the women. There are women here, Annie, in the building behind us."

"You should have run."

"I know this now. It's too late for me."

"No. It's not. Let's work through this. Where is he?"

"He left but he'll be back. He's getting angrier each time he walks back in here. Like he always does, before he explodes."

"Where are the men he said will kill us?"

Kit rolled her eyes. "There are no men—not on this property. Of this, I'm sure. He wanted to scare us."

"Then let's get out of here, Kit." She could get Kit to leave, then do what she could to get to the women.

"Can you get up? If you can walk, we can try to get to the main house." Kit was next to her on the deck of the pool. The concrete floor was cold under her back, but she felt the heat of the pool, heard the bubbling spa water.

"If we go slow, I can. I think I broke a rib."

"Let's try. Take in a few shallow breaths instead of one big long deep one." Kit spoke like someone who'd had her own share of broken ribs, and Annie decided then and there that pain was the least of her worries. She had to save Kit, save the women who Valensky had corralled.

"Where did he bring me in, do you know?" She spoke through puffs of breath, her body oxygen deprived and aching.

"He came through the back doors with you. I was out here, looking around. Thank God I was, or he might have—" Kit stopped. "I think he had you in that building. Where were you before the pool? Do you know?"

As Annie got to her feet and they slowly made their way to the pool house exit, she told Kit what she knew in as few words as possible.

"How much time do you think we have before he comes back?" She looked at Kit as they stood at the door, preparing to head out on the wooded path to the house.

"I've been so close and not able to help them."

"Worry about that later. Let's get out of here first."

"Call 9-1-1." She spoke through puffs of breath. It was easier to move and breathe while upright, but the pain was still considerable. Her thoughts kept going back to Josh. Was he okay or had Valensky got to him, too?

She was going to do all in her power to save Kit and the women. This would not be a repeat of what she'd lost in New York. And if she made it out of this alive, she'd tell Josh she loved him at the first chance. She'd been so stupid.

Physical pain kept her from losing focus.

"How many women are here?"

"Five, and he just brought more in."

Annie stopped, as much as her body urged her to keep moving before she couldn't take another step.

"I caught Vadim going to the building with cases of water. He shouted at me to go back to the house, so I couldn't follow him in. There has to be a separate entrance there."

"I didn't see tools, but I'm pretty sure I was close to

the women. I passed out right after he brought me in from the trail. Where did you see me first?"

"In the pool house." Kit appeared puzzled. "Which doesn't make sense. Why didn't he just put you with the other women?"

Cold fear gripped Annie. "He wanted to use me as bait."

"For what?"

Annie didn't answer her. With clarity that she'd only ever felt once before, when she knew something was horribly wrong with Rick, she knew what she needed to do.

"We have to go back there. I think Valensky's booby-trapped the pool house. To kill you and me. It'll be a distraction while he gets the women out, and he can escape, too."

Kit's eyes widened. "Then why would we go into it? We're not crazy!"

"We're the only ones who can disarm it. Let's go."

Josh pressed the buzzer at Valensky's front gate. No answer.

"I'm going around to the back." He spoke to Claudia and the team in the trailer, as well as several TH agents, on his headset. He drove expertly around the perimeter of the property, the three-wheeled all-terrain utility vehicle he'd procured moving too slowly for him. Annie. He had to get to Annie.

"It's clear." Claudia's confirmation that an entryway had been blown through Valensky's wall. Josh saw it within thirty seconds of her reply, and drove through the opening. He raced to the front of the house and jumped off the ATV and onto the front porch. The front door stood open, and he entered the building. He cleared space after space, room after empty room, with no sign that Valensky, Kit or Annie was there. Until he made it to the back porch and saw a familiar scrap of material.

Annie's bandanna. She'd had it around her neck in the campground. He picked it up and held it to his face, inhaling her scent. *Where are you, Annie?*

He looked at the ground surrounding the porch area, and saw several sets of footsteps in the graveled path leading to a wooded area in the back of the property, which he had memorized. Josh took off for the pool house.

"Talk to us, Josh. What are you doing?"

He relayed his position and intention.

"No, Josh, do not go in the pool house. It's a setup. Valensky has Annie there. He wants you to show up. There's no way of knowing what he's done."

Josh ignored what Claudia told him. Mostly.

Annie and Kit stood on the deck in between the lap pool and hot tub. "I need you to find the main power switch for this building and turn it off."

Kit looked puzzled. "Why?"

Annie looked around for something metal. "Valensky was explicit that we stay right there." She pointed at the space right next to the pool. "Give me that pool hook."

Kit walked to the wall, grabbed the long-handled hook and brought it to Annie. "Now, don't put it in the water, not while you're touching it. Hold it in the middle and toss it into the water."

Kit did as Annie asked, and they both jumped as

sparks arced over the water and the plastic handle of the hook folded and wrinkled in front of them, sinking in the water.

"Oh my gosh. He wanted to electrocute us." Kit stood frozen, and Annie needed her to move. To shut off the power. Before any agents, before Josh showed up.

Exasperation made Annie's pain spike. "Just. Shut. It. Off."

Kit walked over to a large utility closet, disappeared inside it for a few seconds, during which time the overhead lights shut off, as did the underwater pool lamps. Annie let out a tortured sigh of relief. At least the water was now safe.

She waited for Kit to emerge from the closet but when she did, Annie's breath stuttered in an excruciating gasp.

"Do you want to tell me what you do besides run that crappy little yarn store in town?" Valensky stood with Kit next to him, a gun in his hand.

The windows that ran alongside an entire wall of the pool house were out as far as Josh was concerned. He'd be too visible if he tried to look inside. But the ladder at the corner of the building led to the skylight that Annie had talked about, and within minutes he was atop the building, on his belly, peering into the room where Valensky stood next to Kit. Annie was in front of the pool, and while he couldn't see her eyes, he thought from her stance she looked pained. Yet her steely strength was evident in the way she didn't back up, didn't appear like she was going to run.

"Do not go in until we have the women out." Claudia's voice jarred his focus.

"Damn it, Valensky has her and Kit next to the pool and he has a weapon. SIG Sauer." He wasn't going to be able to wait much longer. Vadim Valensky wasn't a man to corner.

"We've got the first five, and we're waiting on the rest."

Josh kept watching the three figures ten feet below him, preparing to jump before Claudia cleared him. He'd do whatever it took. All at once, Annie started shaking her arms at Valensky, yelling. He couldn't make out the words but saw that Kit had disappeared. Valensky didn't seem to care; his focus was on Annie.

"I've got to go in, Claudia."

"Wait. We've got eyes on Kit. She's coming out of a different doorway we hadn't detected. Four women are with her." He heard Claudia's elation. They'd saved all but one.

"The last one is probably dead, or very sick."

"Our team is going into the space to find the fifth. Stay put, Josh."

As Claudia spoke, he saw Valensky look behind him and realize that Kit was gone, which had to have been Annie's objective all along. Josh watched in horror as Valensky raised his hand with the gun. He didn't wait for Valensky to turn completely back toward Annie, who was lying low to the ground, something clearly wrong.

"We've got the last victim, she's okay."

As Claudia's words sounded in his ear, Josh jumped.

Annie heard the splintering glass a second before a loud groan left Valensky's mouth and his weapon fired aimlessly in the pool house. As she watched from the pool deck, Josh's feet landed squarely on Valensky's shoulders, knocking both men to the floor. The struggle seemed almost effortless for Josh, who sat on Valensky's back. Within seconds, although it felt longer with the pain she fought, Josh forced Valensky facedown on the concrete deck and cuffed him. He'd saved them all. Except her. Annie tried to fight against unconsciousness, pain keeping her from whooping in relief.

Josh's face, his dear face, filled her vision.

"Annie." He spoke with conviction, but she didn't hear what she'd hoped for. His voice was heavy with concern, brusque with his sense of duty. Like any other police officer.

"Kit. She's safe now?" She had to know, fought the dark clouds to find out. "The sick woman?" Had they saved the one who had appendicitis or an ovarian cyst?

"Yes, and so are all the women. You did it, Annie. You saved them." His voice wrapped around her, and she clung to it, knowing it was the last time she'd see him.

She'd done it. She'd been able to do her job this time, not erasing Rick's and his wife's deaths, but doing what they would want her to do. Save others.

She'd also lost the man she loved. Josh was a cop and Becky's brother, unable to open his arms to more. As she slipped into unconsciousness, Annie tried to tell him she loved him, anyway.

Chapter 17

"The X-rays confirm you have a fractured rib, and your symptoms point to several more that are bruised. You're fortunate that the fracture is hairline, so no risk of a punctured lung. Let's see how your shoulders are."

Annie gritted her teeth as the ER doctor assessed her injuries, moving her arms one at a time to their farthest range of motion. She'd really thought she was dying on the pool house floor. She'd regained consciousness on and off on the ambulance ride to the hospital, and the pain from her injuries confirmed that indeed, she lived. And she wanted Josh by her side, but he'd stayed behind at the crime scene.

"My shoulders are fine. It's. The. Rib."

"Bear with me. We're almost done." He pulled out her left arm, lifted it over her head while feeling the shoulder joint with his other hand. "Does that hurt?"

"No, not in the shoulder, anyway."

"Okay." He put her arm down and offered a smile. "You've suffered no other injuries. You'll be sore for quite a while, and it'll take about six weeks for it to heal. I want you in physical therapy in two weeks if the stiffness and pain haven't begun to ease. But mostly you'll be recovering at home."

"How long before I can work again?"

"As a cop?" The civilian doctor had no clue about Trail Hikers.

"I'm a police psychologist, but I'm on a break right now. I'm running the yarn shop downtown."

"Does that involve lifting merchandise?"

"Yes."

"Then you'll need to find someone else to do it for you, until you're better. But feel free to go back to work for as long as you can handle it. I'd suggest an hour or two at a time, at first. Standing and sitting are going to be painful until that rib starts healing."

A commotion exploded outside the examination room and Annie eyed the door. Within a heartbeat, Josh had burst into the room, two SVPD officers behind him, talking to two hospital security guards.

"Hey, this is a private examination." The doctor faced off with Josh.

"It's okay, I know him." But what was he? "He's my colleague."

The doctor looked at Josh one more time, then at Annie. "You're okay with him in here?"

"Yes, of course."

Josh walked to her side. "How are you doing?"

"I'm okay."

The doctor finished with her aftercare instructions,

including prescriptions for physical therapy and anti-inflammatory medications.

"You'll need help getting dressed." He looked at Josh.

"Got it. Thanks, Doc." Josh's dismissal made Annie giggle, which sent her ribs into paroxysms of pain.

"Ow." She held up her hand on the uninjured side. "It's okay. Hurts to laugh."

"I'm afraid that's going to be the way of it for a couple of weeks, six weeks for total healing. If you have any questions, call the number on your discharge paper. Otherwise, you're free to go. Thank you for your service." The doctor left through the swinging door, and Annie saw the SVPD officers congregated in the hallway.

"It looks like all of SVPD is out there."

"They're worried about you. I'm worried. Are you really okay, Annie?"

Josh stood awkwardly in front of her.

"You heard him. I'm fine. Bruised ribs. One's cracked. Hurts like hell but nothing permanent. How's Kit?"

"Good. Now that Valensky's in custody and the shipment of women was prevented, we're all feeling pretty damned good." His words caught her up on the operation but his eyes, they spoke of deeper things.

"How are you doing, Josh? You could have been killed. It's not a dream—you jumped through the glass ceiling, didn't you?"

He nodded. "And I'd do it again, as many times as I have to." His eyes filled with tears. "If I'd lost you, Annie, my life would have no meaning."

His words bolted through her, made her sit up straighter to reach for him.

"Ow."

"Annie." Desperation soaked his words. "I have to kiss you but I don't want to hurt you."

"Do it, Josh. Kiss me."

He leaned in as she sat on the exam table, his legs in between hers, and touched his lips to hers. His arms at his side, she felt the shudders he suppressed at not being able to hold her. Her body, her soul yearned to be up against him but her ribs were party poopers. She opened her mouth to his kiss and expressed her love for him as best a woman with a cracked rib could. With her heart.

Josh pulled back and caressed her cheek, wiping a strand of hair from her face. "Annie, I have to be with you for the rest of my life. I'm in love with you and I was a fool to not recognize it sooner. I'm never going to take it for granted—being able to tell you I love you. I love you."

"And I love you, Josh." They kissed again, sealing their bond. "I've been thinking that Silver Valley is the perfect place for me to relocate, especially if I'm going to take Claudia up on a position with Trail Hikers. And, Josh, I'll be the best sister-in-law to Becky. I'll never come between you two."

Josh shook his head. "Becky's my sister, Annie, but you—you're my life. I love you and need you. For the rest of our lives."

They kissed again, until Annie's ribs complained. "We're going to have to figure out a work-around for making love. Because I can't wait six weeks to be one with you again." Their gazes locked as she spoke and saw that he needed to be with her, too.

Josh kissed her eyelids, her nose, her mouth. "Will you keep working in the yarn shop?"

"No, when Grandma Ezzie comes back, I'll move out. Find a place of my own."

"I happen to have a very large home with a free room for rent."

"Do you?" She grinned at him. "How about helping me get out of this hospital gown and into my clothes? We can talk about our options on the way—"

What should she say? On the way to her grandmother's apartment? Or to Josh's house?

"On the way home, Annie. You're coming home with me. To our new life together."

* * * * *

Don't miss the other thrilling romances in Geri Krotow's Silver Valley P.D. miniseries:

The Fugitive's Secret Child
Secret Agent Under Fire
Her Secret Christmas Agent
Wedding Takedown
Her Christmas Protector

All available now from Harlequin Romantic Suspense.

#2007 COLTON'S TWIN SECRETS
The Coltons of Red Ridge • by Justine Davis
After suddenly becoming guardian to his twin nieces,
K-9 cop Dante Mancuso takes the first nanny he can
get: Gemma Colton. Despite their differences, they find
themselves growing closer, even as the gunman Dante is
investigating circles closer.

#2008 CONARD COUNTY WATCH
Conard County: The Next Generation
by Rachel Lee
Paleontologist Renee Dubois may have the find of a lifetime
in a cleft in the Rocky Mountains. But when someone starts
shooting at the dig site, it's clear that she needs protection—in
the form of Carter Copeland, a reserved college professor and
former marine.

#2009 RANGER'S JUSTICE
Rangers of Big Bend • by Lara Lacombe
As FBI profiler Rebecca Wade and park ranger
Quinn Gallagher work together to find a serial killer, their
attraction grows. But can they overcome the ghosts of their
past and, more important, can they prevent another murder?

#2010 ROCKY MOUNTAIN VALOR
Rocky Mountain Justice • by Jennifer D. Bokal
Ian Wallace has spent years obsessively pursuing an
international crime kingpin, but when his ex Petra Sloane
is framed for a murder the man committed, he realizes that
keeping her safe is his true passion.

Ian heard Petra's scream and his blood turned cold. He leaped from the floor and sprinted out the door.

The walkway was empty. Petra was gone—vanished. The echo of her shriek had already faded.

He turned in a quick circle, his eyes taking in everything at once. He saw them—a set of hands clutching the bottom rung of the railing. Petra. Her knuckles were white.

He dived forward and grasped her wrists. "I've got you," he said. "But don't let go."

Petra stared up at him. Her face was chalky and her skin was damp with perspiration. His hands slid. He clasped tighter, his fingers biting into her arm. One shoe slipped from her foot, silently somersaulting through the air before landing with a thump in the courtyard below.

"Ian," she gasped. Her hands slid until just her fingers were hooked over the metal rung. "I can't hold on much longer."

A sharp crack broke the afternoon quiet. It registered as a gunshot and Ian flattened completely.

Just as quickly, he realized that the noise hadn't come from a firearm, but someplace just as deadly. One of three bolts that held the section of railing in place had cracked.

If one of the other bolts broke, the whole section would topple, sending Petra to the courtyard twenty feet below. Then again, maybe that was the best way to save her life.

"Look at me," Ian said to her. She lifted her wide eyes to his. "I have an idea. It's a long shot, but the only shot I have."

Her face went gray. "Okay," she said. "I trust you."

"I'm going to let go of your arms," he said.

Petra began to shake her head. "No, Ian. Don't. This railing's weak. It could fall at any minute."

He ignored the fear in her voice and the dread in her expression. "That's what I'm counting on. I'm going to kick the other bolts loose."

"You're going to what?"

"You have to hold on to the railing and I'll lower it down. At the end, you'll have to drop, but it'll only be a few feet."

"What if you can't hold on to the railing?"

That was the real question, wasn't it? Ian refused to fail. The alternative would be devastating to Petra—to him. "I won't let you get hurt," he vowed.

Petra bit her bottom lip. Their eyes met. "There's no other way, is there?"

Ian shook his head. "Hold on," he warned, "and don't let go until I tell you."

"Got it," she said.

Ian paused, his hands on her wrists. He wanted to tell her more, say something. But what? The moment was too important to waste on words.

"Don't let go," he said again.

Find out if Petra falls in
Rocky Mountain Valor *by Jennifer D. Bokal,*
available September 2018 wherever
Harlequin® Romantic Suspense books
and ebooks are sold.

www.Harlequin.com

HRSEXP0818

Need an adrenaline rush from nail-biting tales
(and irresistible males)?

Check out **Harlequin® Intrigue®**
and **Harlequin® Romantic Suspense** books!

New books available every month!

CONNECT WITH US AT:

Harlequin.com/Community

 Facebook.com/HarlequinBooks

 Twitter.com/HarlequinBooks

 Instagram.com/HarlequinBooks

 Pinterest.com/HarlequinBooks

ReaderService.com

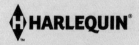

**ROMANCE WHEN
YOU NEED IT**

SGENRE2017

LOVE
Harlequin
romance?

Join our Harlequin community to share your
thoughts and connect with other
romance readers!

Be the first to find out about promotions,
news, and exclusive content!

Sign up for the Harlequin e-newsletter and
download a free book from any series at
www.TryHarlequin.com

CONNECT WITH US AT:

Harlequin.com/Community

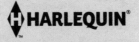 Facebook.com/HarlequinBooks

Twitter.com/HarlequinBooks

Instagram.com/HarlequinBooks

Pinterest.com/HarlequinBooks

ReaderService.com

H HARLEQUIN®

**ROMANCE WHEN
YOU NEED IT**

HSOCIAL2017